A Love To Cherish

by Beverly Clark

A Love To Cherish

Tracey Hamilton has made a wonderful life for herself and her five-year-old twins', helping her father manage their soul food restaurant. Suddenly, her serene existence is shaken to its foundation by the reappearance of Cornell Robertson in her life.

They were both in college together. Since then, Cornell has enjoyed a professional football career. But money and fame have not brought him happiness. The moment the two former lovers see each other, sparks fly and they realize their love was never extinguished. But Tracy and Cornell have secrets — secrets that could jeopardize the new reationship they are trying to build.

Beverly Clark is also the author of *Yesterday Is Gone*. She lives in Lancaster, California.

Visit our Web page for latest
releases and other information.

http://www.colom.com/genesis

Genesis Press, Inc.
315 3rd Avenue North
Columbus, MS 39701

Genesis Press, Inc.
315 3rd Avenue North
Columbus, MS 39701

A LOVE TO CHERISH

ISBN: 1-885478-35-6

Manufactured in the United States of America

First Edition

A Love To Cherish

by Beverly Clark

Chapter 1

Tracey frowned as she glanced up at the clock on the wall. Barbara was late again, leaving her to take over at the register, play hostess and face the dinner crowd. She shifted her gaze to the front door of the restaurant, willing Barbara to walk through it. "The woman would be late to her own funeral," she grumbled, as she stood absently unfolding the newspaper.The headline splashed across the front page immediately captured her attention.

CHICAGO GRIZZLIES MAKE SPRINGFIELD THEIR NEW SUMMER TRAINING CAMP SITE.

Tracey didn't think a quiet town like Springfield would be this supportive of a sports team. Evidently she was wrong. As she lowered her gaze to the picture, a jolt of pain sliced through her temples and a lump rose in her throat. Her hands started to shake.

No, it couldn't be him!

But it was. Of all the teams in the football league why did Cornell Robertson have to get traded to the Grizzlies. And why in God's name did they have to pick Springfield for their summer training camp?

At the sound of the guest arrival bell, Tracey looked up

from the paper expecting to see Barbara come waltzing in, and she was ready to read her the riot act.

ꕥ

"Man, I haven't had any real honest to goodness soul food in I can't remember how long," Cornell Roberstson bantered to his friend Bubba Harris as they walked through the door of the Soul Food Heaven Family Restaurant."

"Me either," Bubba answered, flashing a big wide grin. "The coach says this is the best place in town to eat."

"I'll reserve judgement on that." Cornell laughed.

ꕥ

Tracey stood frozen to the spot staring at the one man she'd never thought to ever see again. Never wanted to see again! How, after all these years, could the sound of his voice still have the power to send tingles of sensation shuddering down her spine? And the sensation didn't stop there, it travelled down her legs into her feet, curling her toes.

Cornell! My God! Tracey's heart started racing and her breathing turned ragged as though her lungs were suddenly starved for air. And for one earth-stopping moment, she felt the urge to run in the opposite direction.

It had been six years since she'd seen this man. Good Lord, what should she do! Barbara wasn't here yet and that meant she Tracey would have to play hostess and show him to a table.

I'm never going to forgive you for this Barbara.

Absorbing the shock, anger and growing resentment at what fate had laid on her, Tracey pasted a smile on her face and grabbing up a pair of menus, stepped into the lobby entryway under the light and said, “Welcome to Soul Food Heaven.”

The smile on Cornell Robertson’s face faded as realization hit. “Tracey!” He choked out.

“May I show you gentlemen to a table?” she coolly asked. “Would by the windows be all right?”

“That’ll be fine, but—”

“If you would please follow me?” she instructed expressionlessly.

“Trace, I—”

Ignoring his entreaty, Tracey guided them to a table by the windows. As they took their seats, she rattled off the day’s menu. “Our special today is Collard greens, smothered pork chops and country fried potatoes.” She placed the menus in front of them. “A waitress will come and take your order in a few minutes. Enjoy your dinner.”

As Tracey moved to walk away, Cornell called out to her. “Tracey, wait, I—” When she kept right on walking, all he could do was gape at her retreating figure.

“Close your mouth, man,” Bubba Harris teased. “I take it you know the lady.”

That was an understatement, Cornell thought. Bubba had no idea how well he knew Tracey Hamilton. When he’d found out the training camp had been switched to Springfield, he knew there was a possibility that he might run into her, but—

“And you want to get to know her better. Right?” Bubba

added, waiting for his friend to speak. When he didn't, Bubba said, "It's the first time in a long while that I've seen you at a loss for words, my man. Is this my friend, the great Cornell Robertson."

"Get off it, Bubba," he finally answered. "Me and that lady go way back."

"How far back?"

"We—"

Bubba's eyes flickered with curious interest. "What?"

"That's none of your damn business." Annoyed, Cornell picked up the menu and then after quickly thumbing through it searched the room and snarled, "Where in the hell is that waitress?"

"Cornell, man, cool it. It's not that serious." Bubba's concern for his friend filtered into his voice. When he saw that no explanation was forthcoming, Bubba backed off. He knew from experience when not to lean on his best friend, and he could see that this was definitely one of those times. The lady must have really meant something to Cornell for him to react this way. He'd give every one of his trophies to know the story behind the tension that crackled between his friend and the pretty hostess Cornell called Tracey.

Just as Tracey made her way back to the register, Barbara Willis swept through the front door of the restaurant, babbling a barrage of excuses for being late—again.

"It's about time you got here," Tracey snapped, grabbing up her account books.

Barbara bent to put her purse in the locker under the counter. "Did I miss something?" When there was no answer, she straightened. "Tracey, I—" Barbara found herself talking to air because her boss had disappeared down the hall into her office.

Tracey didn't hear the last part of what her friend said because her mind was in deep turmoil. Why, after all these years, did she have to see him again? Why? Why? Why?

Once inside her office Tracey collapsed against the door. Cornell was as devastatingly good looking as she remembered. His dark, golden-brown skin with its Native American tinge of bronzed-copper begged a woman to touch it. His near-black eyes above strong high cheekbones sparkled like polished onyx. The sexy fullness of his lips was an inducement any woman would find hard to resist. His black hair, which he wore in a close-to-the-scalp cut, outlined the well-shaped perfection of his head.

Tracey closed her eyes and immediately her mind conjured up the image of his hard muscular body; and oh, God, it was even more magnificent than before. She didn't have to imagine how those strong, slender oh-so-arousing fingers would feel on her skin. Oh, yes, she remembered Cornell Robertson. And how she wished she could forget those memories.

Tracey pushed away from the door, walked over to her desk and tossed the account books on top of it. Then hugging her arms close to her body, she stepped over to the window and looked out. There in the parking lot sat a silver Lexus. The license plate read: 'Chicago's #1.' She didn't have to be a genius to know to whom the car belonged.

Damn you for coming back into my life, Cornell Robertson!

It had taken years for her to get over this man. At least

she had thought she had gotten over him. But just the mere sight of him was enough to pitch her mind and heart into overload. What was the matter with her?

After all he'd done—she wouldn't think about that. She couldn't bear to think about that. When she heard a knock at the door, her heart stopped and her stomach knotted tight with tension. She waited.

"Tracey it's me, Barb."

Relief as well as disappointment washed through her. Why the disappointment? She wondered.

Why wonder, the man's still got a hold on you, girlfriend. The best hold in the world.

She shook her head to clear it. No, she silently cried out, covering her ears.

Tracey quickly gained control of herself. "Come on in, Barb."

Barb peeped around the door. "You sure I don't need to throw in a menu for a test to see if it's safe to come in?"

"No. I'm sorry if I snapped at you out there."

"You sick or something?" Barb said as she walked through the door.

"No, I'm just suffering from shock, that's all."

"Shock!" Barb frowned. "Shock from what?"

"I don't want to talk about it. What's your excuse for being late this time?"

Barb smiled. "Last minute shopping. You know me. Shop-til-you-drop."

"I feel sorry for any man who marries you. He'd better be rich as Midas or own several dozen department stores. Just clothing you will send the man to the poorhouse."

"It won't work, Tracey. Want to tell mama all about it?"

"Not now, Barb. All right?" She eased into her chair.

"You know you can tell me anything and I'll understand. I am a very good listener." Barb flopped down in the chair in front of Tracey's desk.

Tracey smiled weakly. "Yeah, I know you are, but it wouldn't do any good right now."

"All right. Barb's eyes suddenly lit up like a neon sign.

"Do you know who we have eating with us right now: Cornell Robertson and Bubba Harris. They just happen to be *the* super stars of the football world." When Tracey didn't react with any spark of interest whatsoever, Barb frowned. "They wouldn't have anything to do with your being in such a bad mood, would they?"

"Who's minding the register?"

"Deidre. I just had to come back here and see what's up with you." Barb studied her friend for a moment. "I'm right, aren't I! Her eyes widened. "It *is* them. Which one of them is it? I'll bet it's Cornell Robertson. Come on, Tracey, tell me about it. You know, I'm going to bug you to death until you do."

"Barb!"

"All right, I'll wait until closing, but not a minute longer."

"Nothing is wrong, Barb. Now, please—"

"Just go? All right, I get the message."

"Listen, Barb—"

She stood up. "I won't bug you any more. I can see that

whatever it is has your mind messed up." Barb headed for the door then glanced back at Tracey before quietly leaving the room.

Tracey gazed for a long time at the pictures of her children. Then placing her elbows on the desk, she covered her face with her hands.

⁂

"Man, why aren't you eating. These Collard greens and pork chops are jammin'."

"I can tell that you think they are," Cornell half smiled.

"The lady's really gotten under your skin, hasn't she?"

"Bubba!"

"All right, I'll shut my mouth."

"I'm sorry, man. I just seem to have lost my appetite, that's all. We can leave whenever you're ready." He squirmed restlessly in his chair and stared out the window.

Bubba watched his friend closely, continuing to eat his dinner, refusing to take Cornell's hint. It wasn't like him to leave a meal, any meal, untouched, especially not good food like this. The encounter with Tracey must have really done a number on him.

It was times like this that he wished he had attended the same college as his friend. Cornell had always been one to keep personal things personal. Cornell wouldn't admit it, but Bubba knew there had to have been something deep between the two of them. Eventually, he'd worm the information out of him one way or another. Cornell <u>would</u> talk to him.

Barb observed the two super stars, wondering which one

Tracey had been involved with. She smiled suddenly. It was probably Cornell Robertson as she first assumed. He seemed more her speed. Barb had never seen anyone fill out a T-shirt quite the way he did. In her opinion, he was the reason jeans were invented, and he looked fine to the bone in them.

Bubba Harris looked good in his, too. And he was cute. Now he was more her kind of man. He was more heavily muscled than Cornell Robertson, just the way she liked her men. Her eyes widened in dismay when they rose from their chairs and headed toward the register. She wasn't ready to see them leave yet.

"I hope everything tasted all right?" she inquired cheerily.

"Oh, it did, pretty thing," Bubba answered in a husky voice.

"Bubba!" Cornell elbowed him in the side, the inflection in his words punctuating his growing impatience to get out of there.

Ignoring his friend, Bubba asked, "What's your name, sweetheart?"

"Barbara." She smiled. "But my friends call me Barb."

"I definitely want you to consider me as a friend, Barb," Bubba replied smoothly.

Cornell rolled his eyes. "Are you going to pay for the food or what?"

"Chill, man. I was only—all right." Bubba let out an annoyed sigh, and taking out his wallet, turned back to

Barb. "I'll be seeing you around, pretty thing." He handed her a fifty-dollar bill."

Barb moved to make change.

"Keep it."

"B-But your food added up to only fifteen dollars," Barb protested.

"Someone who looks as good as you deserves a generous tip." He winked at her.

Barb flashed him a pleased smile and watched as the pair strode out of the restaurant.

❧

Tracey sat in her office looking out the window, waiting until she saw the silver Lexus leave the parking lot before allowing the tension in her body to drain away. She was glad that he had left because she didn't know how long she could have stood it. Maybe he wouldn't come back.

Dream on, Tracey Hamilton. You, better than anyone, know how tenacious he can be.

She swiveled her chair back around to her desk and reached out to touch her children's pictures. A tear slid down her cheek and she brushed it away.

Oh, God, what am I going to do?.

She didn't know how long she'd sat there without moving when a knock at the door jarred Tracey out of her reverie. Before she could answer, Barb opened the door.

"Tracey, you've been hiding out in here long enough. It's closing time. What are you doing sitting in the dark?" Barb turned on the light, walked over to her friend's desk then sat down in the chair in front.

"I was more or less *trying* to relax."

Barb ignored the gibe. She could not only take barbs she could dish out some of her own. She was nicknamed Barb for a reason. "This is me you're talking to. I know you, remember? When we were kids, it was your way of escaping things you didn't want to face. Seeing Cornell Roberston *is* the reason you're so stressed out, isn't it?" I didn't even know you knew him. Just what does he mean to you, Tracey?"

"What makes you think he means anything to me?"

"You know he does. 'Fess up."

Tracey sighed. "I knew him in college."

"And?" Barb crossed her legs and waited.

"We were—close."

"How close is close? Do I have to drag the answer out of you?"

"Barb, do you have to be so—"

"Relentless?" Barb studied the woman who had been her friend since childhood. "He was probably Saturday's hero and captain of the football team. You fell for him and he broke your heart. The usual. Right?"

"It was not the usual at all, Barb," she said defensively.

"Okay, so give."

"He's London's and Lincoln's father."

"Say what?" Barb sprang forward in her chair. "You never told me their father's name, but I would never in a million years have guessed that he could be the one."

"My parents and now you are the only ones who know."

"You mean you didn't—he, Cornell Robertson doesn't?"

"No! And you've got to promise me that you won't tell

him." Tracey warned.

"But why? He has a right to—"

"No! He doesn't have any rights at all where my children are concerned."

"He's making the big bucks playing football, Tracey. I read somewhere that he just signed a multimillion-dollar contract with the Grizzlies. You should be making him pay child support."

"You don't understand, Barb, and I can't explain it to you. I can take care of my children myself without any help from him."

Barb could see the subject had just been closed and she would get no more information out of her friend and employer. Cornell Robertson must have really hurt her. Barb knew from experience that men could be real bastards about some things, but somehow Cornell Robertson didn't strike her as being that kind of man. But then what did she know?

"When you decide that you want to talk about it, I'll be there for you. It's time I headed for home. Call me if you need me, Tracey."

"I will."

Chapter 2

Tracey ended up taking the account books home with her. There had been no way she could concentrate on the figures after that little encounter with Cornell. As much as she wanted to forget that she'd once had feelings for him, that fact continued to plague her. Her nerves were shot to hell and her brain tortured by ghosts from the past.

It had been her parents' dream to send their only child to college. Back then, their tiny restaurant had barely paid the bills. There had been little or nothing to put aside for their daughter's education. Tracey had gotten a partial scholarship, but it didn't cover all of her expenses. She had to take a part-time job at the campus coffee shop. Her third year her parents had miraculously managed to get a small loan to help Tracey. They had been so proud of her. She could still hear her mother's words, as if it were yesterday.

"Baby, you're a daughter any mother would be proud of."

When it came to showing his inner feelings, her father rarely said much, but the day she'd left for the University of Chicago his eyes were suspiciously moist, shimmering with his emotions. She knew in that moment how much he loved her. Tracey had never wanted to see anything but smiles on her parents' faces when they talked to or about her.

Thanks to Cornell Robertson, their pride in her had been tarnished. She could never forgive him for that. But if she were truly honest, she knew she couldn't put all of the blame on him. She had been a trusting, naive fool when it came to Cornell. When Tracey had fallen in love, she'd fallen hard and completely.

She walked over to the liquor cabinet where her father kept his scotch and took out a glass and poured herself a shot of whiskey. It burned her throat and seemed to explode when it reached her stomach. If it could only burn away the memory of Cornell and obliterate him from her thoughts.

His face floated before her mind's eye. She recalled exactly how it felt to be held in his arms, the feel of his sexy full lips moving over hers, the intoxicating taste of his mouth. The sensations he caused to current through her body were ones no woman could ever forget. Damn him for making such a lasting impression on her.

Tracey was glad her children were spending the summer with her parents, who were vacationing with relatives in Mississippi. She didn't know if she could handle having them all here right now. She had some difficult decisions to make.

Tracey put the empty shot glass down on the coffee table, and after taking off her shoes, eased back on the loveseat and tucked her legs beneath her. She closed her eyes, letting her mind drift back to the day she'd first met Cornell. It was her senior year at the university, several months into the first semester.

Tracey had watched him from a distance for three years. Every girl on campus wanted to belong to him. She never thought she stood a chance of fighting her way through the ranks of the competition, running the gauntlet to gain his attention.

One day they'd literally run into each other.

Tracey had been on her way to the campus coffee shop where she worked part-time and Cornell had been on his way to football practice. The hard contact forced the football shoes he'd been carrying into her stomach, knocking the breath from her, causing her to collapse to the ground. He immediately reached down to help her up.

"I'm sorry. Did I hurt you?"

The concern in his eyes made it even harder for her to catch her breath and she sat on the ground in silence.

"Oh, God! I've hurt you. Let me get you to a doctor."

"No! I'm all right, really." She rose to her feet only to sway helplessly against him.

When his arms went around her, she looked up into his face. Their eyes met and held.

Tracey felt the flutter of excitement in the pit of her stomach. He had the darkest, most beautiful brown eyes she'd ever seen.

"Are you sure you're all right?"

"I'm in better shape than these white pants." She laughed, moving out of the circle of his arms, attempting to slap some of the dirt and grass stains off them. She reached for her purse.

"Hey, what's your name? I've seen you before." He smiled. "And each time I have you've always been in a hurry.

"It's Tracey Hamilton."

"Mine is Cornell Robertson. Look, I'm going to be late for practice if I don't get going. Give me your phone number."

"I don't usually give it out to strange—"

"You have to give me your number." He favored her with a heart-melting smile. "How else can I call and find out if you're really okay?"

"You don't have to worry, I—"

"Never mind, I'll give you mine." He searched his pockets. "I don't seem to have any paper on me." Wait! He pulled out his wallet and took out a dollar bill and wrote his phone number on it. "Here. I'll expect a call. If I don't hear from you by Wednesday, I'll make it my business to track you down and demand an explanation. And that's a promise." He grinned, lifting his hand in a wave. "See you around."

She stood watching as he sprinted across the football field.Tracey couldn't believe her luck. He was the captain of the football team, not to mention being the university's star running back. Vowing to never spend it, she caressed that dollar and virtually floated to the coffee shop.

That night she'd dreamt about Cornell. The dream was so erotic that she'd woken up hot and achy with an urgent need for satiation.

The phone rang, shattering her foray into the past.

"Hello."

"Mama?"

"Lincoln?"

"Yeah, it's us, me and London and Paupau and Nana. Do you miss us?"

"I sure do, baby. How is London?"

"Fine. You wanna speak to her?"

"Mama? I miss you and I wanna come home."

Tracey picked up on the tinge of homesickness in London's voice. She wanted to see her children more than anything, but the last thing she needed right now was for them to come back home. And it was Cornell's fault for making her feel so guilty about that. Damn him.

Tracey thrust aside her angry reaction to that thought, then clearing her throat asked, "Aren't you enjoying your vacation with Paupau and Nana?"

"Yeah, it's okay, but it's not like being home with you."

"I know it isn't, sweetheart. Let me speak to Nana and Paupau."

"How are things going?" Ruby Hamilton came on the line.

"All right, Mama."

"You don't sound like it is. What's wrong, baby?"

"Nothing is wrong, Mama. Are you, daddy and the kids having a good time?"

"Yes, we are. Tracey, what is it? Your voice—"

"I'm just a little tired, Mama."

"You sure that's all it is?"

"Yes, Mama. Let me speak to Daddy."

"I'll put him on."

"Tracey, is everything going all right?"

"Yes, it is, Daddy. When are you and mama planning to head back to Springfield?"

"Your Aunt Mavis wants us to stay an extra week. She and your Uncle George have fallen in love with London and Lincoln and they're spoiling them rotten."

"There's no need for you to rush right back. I've got everything under control."

"In that case we'll stay. If anything were wrong, you would tell us?"

"You know I would, Daddy. Let me say good bye to my babies."

"Mama!" Lincoln exclaimed. "Uncle George wants to give me and London ponies to ride while we're down here. You don't mind if we stay?"

"No, baby, I don't mind. I love you. I don't ever want you to forget that."

"We won't, Mama. London wants to say good bye."

"Mama?"

"Yes, baby?"

"I love you. Lincoln said to tell you he feels the same way."

"I love you both, too. I'm going to hang up now, I'm kind of tired."

"Bye, Mama."

"Bye, baby." Tracey was suddenly all choked up as she put the receiver down. How could she truly hate the man who had given her two such beautiful children?

How would he feel when he found out about London and Lincoln? What would he do? Would he try to get them? He hadn't wanted her or the responsibility of a baby six years ago. How would he feel about it now?

Why did he have to show up and disrupt her life?

After tossing and turning for hours, finally a fitful sleep came to Cornell and he dreamt.

"Daddy, don't go. I don't want you to go!"

"I have to, Cornell."

"Why do you have to? Can I come with you?"

"No, you can't, son. It's something I have to do alone; for myself.

"Can't you wait until Mama gets home?"

"No." His father pulled his suitcase down from the top of the closet and started throwing his clothes into it.

"You can't go, I won't let you."

"There's nothing you or anyone else can do to make me stay. I'm tired and miserable, son. And I just can't take this anymore."

"Take what, Daddy?"

"I wanted to be an architect, but—I don't know how to explain it so you'll understand. Oh, God, this is hard. I have to leave or else I'll go crazy. I want you to promise me that you'll get an education and be somebody. I want you to promise me that you won't let anything or anyone get in the way of achieving your success."

"But, Daddy—"

"Promise me, Cornell."

"I promise, but—"

"I don't want you to end up an angry and bitter man like me. You hear me, son?"

"I hear you, Daddy."

"Never lose sight of your goal. Whatever you do, don't let anyone sidetrack you."

"Daddy, please don't go!"

"Daddy, come back!"

"Please! Please, come back!"

Cornell awoke with a start, jolting to a sitting position on the bed, his heart racing, his body drenched with sweat and tangled in the sheets.

"You all right, man?" Bubba turned on the light. "You were moaning and groaning as though you were in excruciating pain."

"I'm all right, Bubba. I'm sorry I woke you up, go back to sleep. It was just a nightmare. I don't even remember most of it."

Bubba gazed at him, an uncertain look on his face. "Are you sure that's all it was?"

"Yeah."

"All right if you say so." Though reluctant to do so, he turned off the light.

Cornell lay staring at the ceiling, sleep continuing to elude him for what seemed like hours. He hadn't had that particular dream in years: six to be exact. Seeing Tracey again had triggered it. And with it came the same guilt and feeling of shame that permeated his soul back then and tortured him still. The look she shot him at the restaurant, that could have frozen water, had torn at his guts. There had been a time when she'd gazed at him with love in her eyes. He wanted to see it again. He had to see her again, he had to—

What, Robertson? She made it plain that she doesn't want to have anything to do with you.

He couldn't accept that. He wouldn't accept that. But, he wondered if he really had a choice.

"That's the third time you've lost your concentration, Cornell. We've run that play dozens of times and you've never failed once to execute your part in it. What's wrong with you, man?" Bubba asked.

"I don't know, Bubba." He let out a frustrated sigh. "I just can't seem to get it together today, that's all."

"It's not just today; you haven't been able to get it together for the last few days. Is it the hostess at the soul food place?" Bubba demanded.

"Why would you ask me that?" Cornell's tone was defensive.

"You know why. You seem to be hung up on the woman. Why don't you go see her?"

"Because I'm sure she doesn't want to see me."

"How do you know if you never try?"

"There's a lot that you don't understand."

"So make me understand," Bubba insisted. "What happened between you two?"

"It's hard to explain." A haunted look came over his face. "You see, I did something that she'll probably never forgive me for, and I can't really blame her. I'll never forgive myself."

Bubba's eyes widened. "What did you do?"

He looked away evasively. "I can't tell you that."

"It's that bad, huh?"

Cornell glanced toward the playing field, a sigh of relief blew from his lips. The team was getting into formation for the next play. "Bubba, the coach is signaling to us to join the team."

Bubba put a hand on his friend's arm. "Cornell, man,

you're going to have to talk to somebody. You scared the hell out of me the other night when you had that nightmare. This thing, whatever it is, is going to tear you apart if you don't let it out. It's already started to affect your game."

"I know, you're right,' he said dully. "But Bubba, man, I just can't talk about it right now."

In the showers Cornell thought about Tracey. When he told Bubba he couldn't blame her for her attitude, he wasn't lying. He'd been a stupid fool all those years ago. What they had was special and he'd thrown it all away because of his obsession with being a success.

So much had happened to him since then. If he could only go back and change things. He thought ironically; hindsight was 20/20 as the old cliché goes. No matter how much he wanted to, there wasn't anything he could do to change the past.

Cornell wondered if there was anything he could do about the present? If the way Tracey acted at the restaurant was any sign of her feelings where he was concerned, he stood a snowball's chance in hell of changing her mind. He had hurt her—badly. Her voice had sounded so hard and impersonal and so cold that it chilled him to the bone. He wondered if he would ever draw anything from her other than contempt. When he walked into the locker room Bubba was waiting for him.

"Man, do you want to join me and some of the guys. The coach won't let us have a "really good" time so we'll have to settle for some tame entertainment like taking in a movie. In a town like Springfield it's probably the only thing there is anyway. How about it?"

"I think I'll pass."

"You aren't considering eating dinner at a certain soul food restaurant, are you?" Bubba asked.

Anger flashed briefly in Cornell's eyes. "Bubba, why don't you mind your own damned business."

"Because yours is so much more interesting than mine," he cheerfully taunted. "It has so many different facets, deep dark secrets, twists and turns."

"Bubba!" Cornell warned.

Bubba threw up his hand in a mock gesture of fear. "Don't get bent out of shape, man. We're outta here."

Cornell was glad to see his teammates leave the locker room. He wanted to be alone to think about what he was going to do next.

Images of Tracey and the way she'd looked six years ago came to mind. But the way she looked now really blew him away. She was still slender, but her breasts seemed to have grown larger—maybe larger wasn't quite the right word. Voluptuous, that was it. She now wore her shiny black hair up in a bun.

Six years ago she'd worn her hair down. It had hung below her shoulder blades, and was soft and silky and smelled so good. Her skin, the color of milk-chocolate, made a man want to taste it. Her eyes, the darkest shade of brown he'd ever seen, were incredibly seductive. And though her lips were small, the bottom one was fuller than the top one. When she smiled—Cornell sighed. He had to see Tracey and talk to her. That was all there was to it.

Barbara smiled when she saw Cornell walk through the front door of Soul Food Heaven. "The food must have really been good if you decided to come back for more this soon. Where's your friend?"

"He had other plans. Is Tracey Hamilton around?"

"No, she's off today. Maybe I can help you."

"I'm afraid not. Do you know if she'll be working tomorrow?"

"As far as I know, she will. If it's important I can call her at home."

"No, I don't want you to do that."

Barb smiled. "Ah, will your friend be coming with you?"

"Do you want him to?" Cornell's eyes twinkled with amusement when he saw the eager look that suddenly lighted her face.

"Then I'll make sure he comes," he said heading for the door.

Barb felt the urge to call him back and tell him he was a father, but she knew better than to interfere in Tracey's life. It wasn't her place to say anything to him anyway. She wondered if Tracey ever would.

There had to have been more to it than what Tracey had told her to draw such a violent reaction from her. A lot of men didn't want the responsibility of children especially when they were as young and immature as Cornell Robertson must have been back then. Maybe he regretted what he had done, she mused. Well, however it had been between them <u>they</u> would have to work it out.

Chapter 3

"I'm sorry I'm late," Tracey said to Barbara.

Barb laughed. "That's funny coming from you considering all the times I've been late."

Tracey smiled. "I guess it is. My car finally gave up the fight and conked out. I had to wait until the towing company came to pick it up and then I had to wait half an hour for the bus."

"I told you, you needed to get rid of that clunker."

"If Mel can't fix it, you can bet that it'll be my next big purchase. Has it been busy so far today?"

"Not really. By the way Cornell Robertson came in yesterday looking for you."

Tracey swallowed hard. "He specifically asked for me?"

"Yes. He said he'd be back." Barb monitored Tracey's reaction.

Tracey frowned. She had that hunted feeling like she imagined a gazelle had when being stalked by a lion. She couldn't see him again! Maybe it was time she took a few days—no, she couldn't do that with her father away and besides, she wasn't going to let him keep her from going in to work at her own restaurant. Her life was her own. He had no say or any part in it and never would.

"Did he say when he'd be back?"

"No. I think you should tell—"

"Do you know if that order of crab legs came in yet, Barb?"

"Tracey, you can't just pretend that—"

Tracey started in the direction of the kitchen. "I'll check with Curry myself."

Barbara sighed. Tracey Samantha Hamilton could be the most obstinate person she knew. She had a feeling that Cornell Robertson was the same way. Barbara pondered what would happen when these two strong-willed people locked horns. It seemed inevitable that that was what was going to happen.

Tracey kept busy all morning. She avoided Barbara, not wanting to get into a discussion with her about Cornell. She knew her friend wouldn't pass up any opportunity to start in on her again, and right now she couldn't handle that.

She'd just finished putting several sweet potato pies in the refrigerator to chill when she was called to the phone. "This is Tracey."

"I'm glad I caught you in. I want to talk to you, Trace."

"Cornell!" she said in a strangled voice. "I don't see that we have anything to say to each other."

"Trace, I—"

"Don't call me that."

"We need to—"

"We don't need to do anything." She shot back before hanging up the phone, her heart beating a mile a minute and her hands shaking. Damn him! Why did he have to . . . Why couldn't he stay the hell away from her? Hadn't he hurt her enough?

"I'm leaving early to catch the last bus, Barb."

"Tracey, look, I—"

"I don't want to discuss Cornell, all right?"

"If you say so, but I think—"

"I have a good idea what you think. I won't be in until one tomorrow. I have an appointment in the morning."

"Okay, but I—all right. See you then. If you need to..."

"I don't."

Tracey hated being so hard on her friend, but she just couldn't talk to her about Cornell. She headed out the door and walked across the street to the bus stop. No sooner had she sat down on the bench, a silver Lexus drove up.

"Need a ride?"

Tracey tensed at the sound of Cornell's voice. She was going to kill Barb. She was sure she'd told him she would be out here to catch the bus.

"No, thank you," she answered with cold politeness.

"Trace, we—"

"As I said on the phone we don't have anything to talk about. Please just go away and leave me alone."

Cornell got out of the car and came around to the curb and grabbed her wrist. "We're going to talk, Tracey. It can be the easy way or as hard as you want to make it. Take your pick."

Out of all the times to breakdown, her damned car had to pick today.

"Well, are you going to get in?"

With an angry sigh, she jerked her arm away. He opened the car door and waited for her to get inside. She thought about defying him, but knowing Cornell he'd put her in the car bodily. She looked around to see if anyone was watching. She glanced across the street at the restaurant and saw Barb staring out the window at them.

"All right," she gritted out, "you win."

"This isn't a game, Trace." He slammed the car door and walked around to the driver's side. "Buckle your safetybelt," he commanded firmly as he slid behind the wheel. "You'll have to tell me how to get to your place."

"Look, Cornell, I—"

"Which way, Tracey?"

Tracey grudgingly gave him directions as he drove. When they pulled up in front of her parent's house, he turned to her.

"You have every reason to hate me. What I said was unpardonable."

"I don't want to talk about the past," she said stiffly. "Say what you have to say and then go."

"I know it's too late to say that I'm sorry."

"Yes, it is," she answered, her tone icy.

"Since you don't want to talk about the past let's forget it and start over."

"What? You think after what you— No. I don't want to have anything to do with you ever."

When Cornell reached out to cover her hand with his, she jerked it away.

"Don't touch me."

"You used to love for me to touch you."

"That was a long time ago," she said defensively. The quiver in her voice made her angry because it attested to the fact that he still had the power to draw a reaction from her.

"And you're going to tell me you forgot what it was like between us?" He leaned toward her.

"No, I'm not." Tracey undid the safetybelt and moved to get out of the car.

Cornell lowered a restraining arm across her.

"Let me out, Cornell."

"Not just yet." He pulled her across the seat, onto his lap. She struggled against him, but he lowered his lips to hers.

After a few breath-stealing moments, Tracey felt herself weaken and pushed against his chest.

But he not only refused to release her lips, he flicked his tongue across them. When she gasped, he took advantage, thrusting his tongue inside thoroughly ravishing her mouth so that she couldn't prevent the whimpering sound that had arisen in her throat from escaping.

When she heard him groan, some renegade emotion compelled her to respond to the desire she felt pulsing through his body.

"Oh, Trace, have mercy it's still there," he whispered triumphantly.

His words broke the spell he had begun to weave, lending Tracey the strength she needed to fend off his assault on her senses. "Let me go, Cornell."

"You don't mean it." His voice was rough with desire.

"I do mean it. Let me go, please."

She heard him take a deep composure-gathering breath, then his arms dropped away. She scooted off his lap, across the seat and put a hand on the door handle.

"This isn't the end of it, Trace. You still want me. And I still damn sure want you."

"You're wrong. I don't want you." Tracey got out of the car. "Stay away from me. Whatever there was between us is gone. Don't try to resurrect it."

"I don't have to try." He gave her a satisfied smile.

He was right. He didn't have to, damn him. She slammed the door and hurried through the gate, up the walkway to the house. Once inside she locked the door and breathlessly leaned back against it. Shame washed through her as she thought about the way she had reacted to Cornell's kisses. Even after what he'd done to her, she responded like some love-starved animal.

Oh, God, what's wrong with me?

What did the man have to do to her to make her despise his touch? She had to admit that despite everything she was still attracted to him. Her only hope was that he would lose interest once the novelty of seeing her again had worn off.

But what if it didn't. Oh, God, what if he didn't?

The phone rang and when Tracey picked it up, she heard a familiar voice.

"I saw you getting out of a strange car. Is everything all right, Tracey?"

"I'm all right and everything is fine, Brice."

"I worry about you. With Ruby and James out of town somebody has to look out for you."

"I'm not a child, Brice." Irritation crept into her words. "I can take care of myself."

"I know you can, but you need someone who cares about you, Tracey. I care about you and your children. You know

I do. I want to marry you and be a father to London and Lincoln. When are you going to say yes and make me a happy man?"

"Brice, don't push."

"I'm not pushing you. But, darling, being near and yet so far is driving me crazy. I want you so bad."

"Brice, I—"

"You're probably tired so I won't keep you. When you decide to say yes let me know. But don't take too long, all right? Good night, Tracey."

"Brice!" Tracey let out a tired breath and hung up the phone. As if she didn't have enough problems,— Brice had lived next door to her forever. They had grown up together. He had been several years ahead of her in school.

When his parents died leaving him the house, he'd decided to stay and remodel it, transforming it into a showplace.

Brice was reasonably good looking and dependable. The Clark Kent glasses he wore gave him an intelligent almost nerdy appearance. He made good money as vice-president of one of the city's largest banks. And she didn't doubt his feelings for her, but—

Until Cornell had shown up, she thought she could marry Brice and she and her children would have a stable home life. There was no question in her mind that she would have a secure marriage with Brice, but now—

One thing kept nagging at her. Her children deserved to know their real father. But would it be the best thing for them? Cornell had never wanted a child. If he rejected them, she didn't think she could bear it.

The other burning question was how did she explain to herself the lingering feelings she had for him? His kiss had aroused the long dormant passion only he could stir to wildfire proportions.

She had two weeks to decide what to do before her children got back. Her decision would affect all their lives so she had to be very sure she made the right one.

❧

Cornell drove around for a while after dropping Tracey off at her house. He had to get himself together before he went back to the hotel.

He ruminated over how he'd ever let Tracey get away from him. No woman had ever affected him the way she had back then or since. He'd convinced himself that he could just forget about her and not feel any regrets. He'd lied to himself, he realized, because he knew he would always have regrets about what he'd done for as long as he lived.

Cornell headed out to the Sangamon River. He parked his car, walked out to the edge, and looking out over the water, watched as the waves lazily lapped against the bank, but he could draw no comfort from any of it.

According to society's standards he was a success. He had made a lot of money, would continue to make more, but all the money in the world wouldn't give him peace of mind, a clear conscience or guarantee him love. When he'd made his decisions about his career, he'd had tunnel vision. Being a football star had been the light that he had aimed for. But now—

Now he wanted Tracey Hamilton back in his life, even though she denied emphatically wanting him back in hers. He was sure she was attracted to him even if she wouldn't admit it to herself. He knew when a woman wanted him. He'd had enough women telling him that over the years. But none of them could compare to Tracey. He wasn't about to give up on her now that he'd found her again. He would make her his goal.

His mind made up, Cornell got in his car and headed back to the hotel.

"Man, where have you been?" Bubba asked when Cornell walked into their hotel room, headed over to his own bed and flopped down.

"Thinking," he said, pulling his T-shirt over his head.

"Did you do some visiting while you were doing all this thinking?"

"You want to know if I saw Tracey, don't you? Yes, I saw her." He unlaced his Nikes and took off his socks then got out of his jeans.

"Is that all you're going to tell me?"

"Look, Bubba, I'm tired and I'm not in the mood for 'true confession,' okay? I'm going to shower and go to bed."

Bubba watched his friend as he headed into the bathroom and eased his upper body back against his bank of pillows. Something was weighing heavily on Cornell's mind. He'd seen the pain his friend had tried to hide behind a smile, or tried to bury in his game.

They hadn't been back to the restaurant, and he for one wanted to see that cute little Barb again. He felt sure that

Cornell wanted to see Tracey. The thing was getting him to agree to go back. He'd think of a way.

As he showered, Cornell thought about Tracey. He wondered how he was going to reach her. She would probably go out of her way to avoid him from now on. He would just have to show her that he was serious about his feelings for her.

His feelings for her.

Just how did he feel? He knew he wanted her. He couldn't think past that right now. If he could only break down the barriers she'd built against him maybe he could reach her, but he wouldn't count on anything where she was concerned. It would be hard going all the way.

He knew how determined he could be when there was something he wanted. He wanted Tracey, but he wanted her willing. He'd have to work on that. The coach always said he had more determination than he'd ever seen in a football player. He would just have to put it into practice.

Cornell smiled. He'd have to let Tracey see and come to really know that side of his personality. If she thought he'd give up on her without a fight, she was dead wrong. He'd made a mistake and maybe she would never forgive him for it, but he was sure she still had feelings for him and he was going to make her face them.

Bubba would be pleased when he suggested that they go back to 'Soul Food Heaven' since he had eyes for Barb, he thought with a grin. And as for Tracey he wasn't going to let her go again.

Chapter 4

Brice Carter was waiting for Tracey when she reached the sidewalk in front of her house the next morning. "You going to the summer fair?" he asked.

"I don't think I'll be going this year. The only reason I go any more is because of London and Lincoln. Since they won't be here . . ."

A pleased smile spread across his face. "In that case we can spend some time alone together."

Tracey saw the anticipation in his eyes, but she just couldn't give him the answer he wanted to hear so she remained silent. She felt guilty when she saw the look of disappointment erase the smile from his lips.

Brice cleared his throat. "I haven't seen very much of you in the last week. Things been that busy at the restaurant?"

"With Mama and Daddy away I have a lot to do."

"Even when they're here you do more than your share of the work," he said, his voice half resentful, half scolding.

"Don't nag, Brice. Mama and Daddy aren't getting any younger, you know. After all they've done for me and my children, I think I owe it to them to make their life easier."

"I'm not saying that you—" Brice took off his glasses

and pinched the bridge of his nose and let out a weary sigh, then put his glasses back on. “Tracey, look, if you married me we could hire someone to manage the restaurant and you could dedicate yourself to making a home for me and the children.”

“I like managing the restaurant. It’s going to be mine one day. Who knows, I may even decide to open up another soul food restaurant like the Heaven, or a chain of them. The main reason I went away to college, Brice, was to learn all I could about the restaurant business.” The word college conjured up images of Cornell and her attention strayed.

Brice put his hand on her shoulder. “What’s wrong, Tracey? You look funny.” A thoughful expression came into his eyes. “As a matter of fact you’ve been acting different lately, too.”

“Different? Different how?” She demanded.

“I can’t explain it, but you have.”

Brice was too close to the truth. She knew she hadn’t been her usually cheerful self, but she couldn’t help it. It was all because of Cornell. He hadn’t called her or come into the restaurant as she had expected and that had added to her distress. This waiting around for him to pop up like a jack-in-the-box was nerve-wracking. Maybe he’d given up. She could only hope.

“Let me give you a ride to the restaurant.”

“It’s out of your way, Brice. I can catch the bus.”

“It’s not out of mine, Trace.”

Tracey jumped. She hadn’t heard Cornell’s car drive up.

“I go right by the Heaven on the way to training camp. Get in,” he urged.

"Who is this, Tracey?" Brice demanded, pushing his glasses up on his nose. "Isn't this the same car I saw you getting out of a few days ago?"

Tracey frowned at his accusing look and the way he emphasized her name, revealing his dislike of Cornell's intimate nickname. She glared at Cornell's look of amusement because she knew he was enjoying the effect his words were having on Brice.

Tracey cleared her throat, resigned to the fact that there was no way she could get out of introducing them to each other. "Brice Carter, Cornell Robertson."

"You're not Cornell Robertson, the football star?"

Cornell smiled. "The very same."

Glancing suspiciously from Tracey to Cornell, he asked, "Where did you meet Tracey?"

"We attended Chicago U together."

Brice looked confusedly at Tracey. "Together? You never mentioned it."

"Well it wasn't exactly together." She fumed at the construction Cornell put on his words. "We just went to the university at the same time. There's a difference."

"Well, get in, Trace. I'll drop you off. It was nice meeting you, Carter."

"Same here, Robertson."

When Tracey saw the looks that passed between the two men, she knew that battle lines were forming. On the surface everything was civilized, but she perceived the savagery seething underneath, waiting to erupt. And knowing Cornell he was gearing up for an all-out war. But why? When she meant nothing to him and never really had.

"Don't forget that we have a date tonight, Tracey," Brice said, purposely for Cornell's benefit.

"I haven't forgotten," she ground out, annoyed that he would resort to reminding her like this. "I'll be ready at seven-thirty."

Cornell opened the car door and Tracey climbed in beside him. After driving off, he glanced at her. "He your lover?"

Her chin lifted. "If he is, it doesn't concern you."

"Oh, I wouldn't say that," he said silkily.

"What do you mean?" She sputtered. "There's nothing between you and me any more and never will be again."

"Maybe not at the moment, but things could change." A devilish smile played at the corners of his mouth. "I'd never say never if I were you."

Tracey folded her arms and looked straight ahead. "You're not me, so don't get your hopes up." She heard him smirk and swung her head around. "I'm warning you, Cornell, stay away from me. Stay the hell out of my life. I mean it."

"You protest too much, Trace. Brice Carter's not the man for you," he said smuggly.

"I suppose you think you are?"

"I'm more the kind of man you need than he is. You and I share a history, Trace. I remember what you like and how you like it," he said lowering his voice to a caressingly soft level.

"That's in the past. You must have an ego like granite."

He grinned wickedly. "As I remember, you mastered the art of turning a certain part of my anatomy that hard."

She said through clenched teeth. “If you’re going to—”

“All right, Trace, I’ll cool it for now.”

They rode the rest of the way to the restaurant in silence. Not even saying anything when Cornell let her out.

“Not a word, Barb, I know you saw me getting out of Cornell’s car,” Tracey said as she walked through the door of the restaurant. “What are you doing here so early? You weren’t supposed to come in to work until twelve today.”

“Diedre called in sick and Curry phoned and asked me if I wanted to come in. I said yes, so here I am. But what I want to know is how you happened to be riding in his car. Have you two—”

“No, we haven’t,” she snapped. “Look, I don’t want to get into this right now. Okay?”

“You never want to get into anything lately.” Barb grumbled.

“Barb, Cornell Roberston is a part of my past. Past being the operative word.”

“How can you say that, Tracey? He’s the father of your kids.”

“Barb!”

“All right, have it your way, you will anyway. The breakfast crowd will be tromping in here any minute. I’d better gear myself up for that.”

When Cornell got tackled for the fifth time in as many plays, the coach called time out.

“If you’re not feeling well you shouldn’t have come out to practice, Robertson,” the coached remarked with an irritated grimace.

“I’m feeling all right, coach, just a little distracted this morning."

"When the time out is over, I want to see you play like you mean it."

"You will."

Bubba waited until the coach had walked away then said, "You shouldn't make promises you can't keep."

"Bubba, don't start."

"Don't start what? Telling you the truth?"

"You know what I mean."

"We both know I'm telling it like it is. You haven't been the same since you saw Tracey Hamilton."

"Lay off, Bubba, I'm warning you to stay the hell out of my personal life."

"Then you're admitting that there is something going on between you and the lady in question." Bubba barely managed to dodge his friend's attempt to take a swing at him. "Cornell, man, you're crazy. That's the first time I've ever seen you go off like that about a woman. Not even over Keysha."

Cornell stood gritting his teeth, reaching for every ounce of control he could gather. Bubba was right. What was the matter with him?

Once the time out was over and practice had resumed, Cornell found that he still couldn't keep his mind on the plays.

"I think you'd better take the rest of the morning off," the coach called out to Cornell after he'd picked himself up off the ground for the fifth time.

Cornell removed his helmet and walked off the football field. As he showered, he thought about his performance or the lack of it. He couldn't understand it. He'd never played so badly in his life. The only thing he could think about was how he was going to reach Tracey. How he was going to convince her to give him another chance.

As he drove away from the practice field, he thought about the way Tracey had acted that morning. She couldn't possibly be serious about Brice Carter, could she? Visions of her kissing Carter, making love with him, tied his guts into knots. What could he do, he asked himself, to prove to her that the man was all wrong for her?

And you're right for her? You have to face the fact that you blew your chance years ago, Robertson.

So he'd blown it. He had learned from his mistake, but how was he going to get that to work for him in getting Tracey back?

There was something about the way she reacted to him that didn't ring true somehow. It was as though she—he didn't know. But He'd find out the truth. He'd be patient and woo her slowly.

Yeah, right, Robertson. You're not known for your patience.

Maybe not, but he had the rest of the summer to change her opinion of him.

He felt better after his little talk with himself. Now, all he had to do was get the point across to his lady.

His lady.

She wasn't that right now, but she was going to be if he had anything to say about it, Brice Carter or no Brice Carter. The thought of her going out with that nerd irritated like hell. He'd have to put a stop to that quick, fast and in a hurry.

Tracey had ruined two pans of gravy that afternoon, gravy for God's sake; something she could make in her sleep practically, and she had ruined it. That said a lot about the effect Cornell's presence in town had on her. She'd tried not to think about him, but it was no use.

"What kind of gravy are you trying for, girlfriend? Mississippi mud? The real mud," Barb teased.

"Very funny. I'm just having a bad hair day."

"Your hair looks fine, it's this kitchen that's the mess."

Tracey had to laugh. "You know how to make me feel better."

"I've had nearly a lifetime of practice. You remember when we were seven and you got it into your head to dye your hair?"

"I remember."

"You'd heard that peroxide would turn your hair red. You were so determined to get your hair the same color as Pippi Longstocking's. When I brought you a mirror and showed you the results and how ridiculous you looked, you laughed it off. It took close to two years for your hair to get back to its original color."

Tracey laughed. "Poor Mama tried so many different ways of fixing my hair so the dye wouldn't show when it was growing out."

"Let me make you feel better about Cornell Robertson."

Tracey's smile faded. "Sorry. Not unless you're into performing magic. Like making Cornell disappear. Frankly, my dear, you don't look a thing like Harry Houdini."

"I hate seeing you like this. You're not yourself, Tracey."

"I know, but I can't help it. I'll return to being myself when Cornell is completely out of my life for good."

Barb shook her head. Didn't Tracey know that was impossible considering that she'd given birth to the man's children. Giving her friend a contemplative glance, she asked, "Have you ever seen Cornell play football?"

"Not since college. Why?"

"The man can find holes in the other team's defenses a groundhog would have a hard time spotting, and then run a path right through to the end zone."

"What are you trying to tell me?"

"That if he's made up his mind you're his goal, nothing short of paralysis will keep him from going after you."

"I'm not a football, Barb."

"You know what I'm trying to say. Cornell Robertson doesn't strike me as a man who'll give up anything he's set his sights on. Don't say you haven't been warned. I guess I'll get back to *my* game of playing hostess."

Tracey made another pan of gravy, this time it was as smooth as the others should have been. She smiled until she tasted it and realized that she had forgotten to season it. This distraction and inattention to her cooking was all Cornell's fault, she grumbled, wishing she could erase him from her thoughts.

Tracey left the restaurant early because she wanted to get home in time to prepare for her date with Brice. As she walked out the door and headed for the bus stop, Cornell's silver Lexus pulled into the bus zone. He'd probably been watching and waiting for her to come out of the restaurant. Damn him for his persistence in pursuing her like this.

"I thought you might like a ride home so you can dress up for your, ah—date." His lips quivered with amusement.

She shot him a curious sidelong glance. "Why should you care how I look when I go out with another man?"

"You're so suspicious. I was just trying to be a gentleman by offering a lady a ride."

"Yeah, right, and I'm Marilyn Monroe. What are you doing here?"

"I told you."

"Why can't you just leave me alone, damn you?"

Cornell smiled. "If you were really honest, you'd admit that you don't really want me to." He patted the empty seat next to him. "Now, get in."

"Cornell!"

"Get in the car, Tracey."

He said it softly, but she wasn't fooled. "You're nothing but a bully."

"Just get in the car, Trace."

She crossed her arms over her chest. "I'd rather wait for the bus."

Cornell started to insist, but decided against antagonizing her any further. "Have it your way, this time. There'll be others."

"I get my car out of the shop tomorrow," she said triumphantly.

"You think I'll let that stop me? Later, Trace." And he pulled away from the curb.

The bus was an hour late, so Tracey had to rush to get ready for her date.

You could have gotten home in plenty of time, If you . . .

No, damn it, she admonished herself. “Don’t even go there.”

Chapter 5

Do you think Beauty Shop II was as good as the first one?" Brice asked Tracey as they came out of the Springfield Playhouse.

"I guess." She shrugged.

"Are you even listening to me, Tracey?"

"Of course I am," she answered, absently twirling the strap of her purse around her fingers.

"I bet you don't even know what happened. A couple of times I caught you staring into space as if your thoughts were focused a million miles away."

"I'm sorry, Brice. It's just that I have a lot on my mind."

"Like Cornell Robertson?" he said sourly. "You got the hots for the guy or something?"

Tracey's face heated up at the insinuation. "Brice!"

"Don't look so shocked. I saw the way you were eyeing him this morning."

Throwing a glance at him, she said, "And just how was I looking at him?"

"Look, Tracey, I don't want to argue with you."

"How was I looking, Brice?" she persisted.

"Like—like you wanted to go to bed with him."

"Brice!" Her voice rose. "Where do you get off saying something like that?"

"Because it was there in your eyes, Tracey. If it's not true then why are you going off about it, huh?" He said, his voice as affronted as hers. " He'll be gone in a few weeks. If you get involved with him, where will that leave you?"

"What is that supposed to mean?"

"That he'll be gone and I'll still be here," he said matter-of-factly. "I may want you, Tracey, but I refuse to be second choice to the woman I love."

"Brice, you promised not to push me."

"I know I said I'd give you time, but I meant it when I said I won't be second choice. You'd better make up your mind about which one of us you really want. I was going to take you to Sophie's for a drink, but I think I'd better take you home."

Her lips tightened. "So do I."

Tracey looked up from the newspaper she was reading when she heard Barb greet Cornell and Bubba. She got up from the table, ready to make an escape into her office.

"Trace, why don't you join us."

"I've got some work to do."

"Come on, Tracey," Barb pleaded. "The books can wait. It's not everyday Cornell and Bubba come in to eat with us."

Tracey wasn't in any mood to deal with Cornell, not after her evening with Brice. On the way home, the temperature in his car had lowered to twenty degrees below zero and he had barely said a civil good night to her. She knew he was angry, but she couldn't help the way she felt. And she had

Cornell to thank for creating the situation.

"You wouldn't have gotten that much work done anyway. It's almost closing time."

"I—all right, but only for a little while." Tracey rose from her chair. "I'm going to turn the sign around and begin locking up."

Cornell rose too. "I'll help you."

Tracey didn't understand how half an hour later she found herself agreeing to come along with Cornell to even the numbers, making up a foursome with Bubba and Barb.

Tracey reasoned there'd be safety in numbers once they got to Sophie's. But minutes later Bubba and Barb slipped away into a corner booth to talk privately, leaving her alone with Cornell.

"That leaves you and me, Trace." Cornell grinned. "By the way how did your evening with Clark Kent go?"

"Don't call Brice that."

"Listen, I'd prefer not to talk about the guy at all."

"Maybe we'd better call the evening off."

"You wouldn't want to disappoint Bubba and Barb," he said glancing in their direction. "They seem to be hitting it off."

"<u>They</u> are."

Cornell's brows arched, challenging her. "Is that to say you and I aren't or couldn't?"

Tracey sighed. "Cornell, look, I don't—"

"Relax, Trace, I'm not going to throw you down on the table and have my way with you."

"I wouldn't put anything past you."

"You wound me to the quick, woman."

Not as much as you wounded my heart six years, Tracey silently cried.

"That's what I call a good movie!" Barb exclaimed as they came out of the movie theater.

"I agree with the hero." Bubba put his arm around her.

"About what?" Barb asked, snuggling closer.

"Hugging your woman whenever the opportunity presents itself." He demonstrated by tightening his hold with enthusiasm.

"I'm your woman now, am I?"

Tracey smiled at them, but gave Cornell a look warning him not to try what his friend had.

Cornell, sensing that she might make a big deal out of it, decided to heed her warning.

Tracey felt strangely disappointed. Her hormones must definitely be out of whack. She knew that the best medicine was to stay away from Cornell, but how was she supposed to do that when he made it his business to be wherever she went?

"Don't look like that," Cornell said softly.

"Like what?" Tracey's eyes narrowed.

"Like a frustrated mouse, who can't find a convenient hole to escape into."

"I don't look like that," she said, incensed by his analogy of her emotional state.

Cornell reached out and lifted her chin with his bent forefinger and brushed his lips across hers.

"Come on you guys, let's go. I'd like to spend a little private time with Barb. We have practice tomorrow morning, don't forget," Bubba reminded Cornell.

Cornell grinned. "We'd better get you two over to Barb's place as soon as possible then, hadn't we? I'll be back to pick you up later."

"Make it as close to two hours later as you can, okay?" Bubba said with a pleading inflection in his voice.

When Barb and Bubba got out at Barb's apartment and headed up the walk arm in arm Tracey tensed.

"I think you should drop me off at the restaurant so I can drive my car home."

"You're not afraid of being alone with me, are you, Trace?"

"Of course not," she bristled.

"That's good because I don't want you to feel that way."

"Just how do you want me to feel? You want me to fall all over you the way I used too?"

"I made a mistake, Tracey." A muscle in Cornell's jaw twitched at the reminder. "Haven't you ever made any?"

"Lots of them." She glared at him.

"I guess you consider me your number one mistake."

"You said it, I didn't."

"Yes, I know. Look, Tracey,—"

"Just drive me back to my car. Please."

He eased his car away from the curb and instead of making a left to go back to the Heaven, he made a right.

"Cornell!"

"We're going to talk first, Tracey."

Tracey remained quiet until they reached a secluded spot near the river. She could feel the warm night air whispering around them. And the moon silvering down on the river reflected serenely on the water. She was curious to know why he'd really brought her to this particular spot.

He stopped the car and cut the engine, then turned to Tracey.

"Are you serious about Brice Carter?"

"Cornell, I—"

"Well, are you?"

"If I am, you have nothing to say about it. I wouldn't think you would want to have anything to say about it." Tracey got out of the car and started swiftly walking down the well-worn path paralleling the river.

Cornell followed and as soon as he caught up with her, fell into step beside her.

"You're judging me by the past, Trace. I've changed," he said softly. "I've grown up and I know what's important now."

"The past is all I have to go by. You can say you've changed, but I, more than anyone else, have reason to doubt it. Being a success was all that was important to you, Cornell. It became your mistress." Anguish filled her heart at the truth of her own words. "I couldn't compete with her then and I don't want to now."

"Trace, look, I—I admit that I let my ambition come between us," he conceded, " but I never cheated on you with another woman. I cared for you, girl."

"I think you did to some degree. But it wasn't enough then any more than it would be enough now." She threw her hands up in frustration. "Can't you see that?"

"Trace, we could try," he pleaded. "You aren't giving it a chance, damn it."

"Tell me, what can you offer me besides money? Can

you offer me a normal family life?"

Cornell thrust his hands in his pockets and whirled away from her. "We'd have each other, Trace."

"We had that and more, but you threw it all away."

He spun around to face her. "Don't you think I know that, Trace? Over the years I've come to regret that decision more than you'll ever know."

"I can't believe you regret getting to where you are today."

"No, I can't regret that."

"There was no room for me in your life then or now. I think we'd better leave."

Cornell reached for Tracey, pulled her roughly, almost violently, against him, and lowering his head, he claimed her mouth, delving his tongue past the soft fullness of her lips, probing deeply, tasting the heady sweetness within.

He eased his head back. "I've missed you so damned much, Trace." He groaned. "Give me another chance, give us another chance," he said, easing his lips over hers once more.

Tracey moaned as shock waves of pleasure inundated her body. She could feel the urgent demand in his kiss, and her body responded. She felt her knees weaken and her legs tremble, threatening to collapse like a folding chair. As though sensing her predicament, Cornell wrapped his arm around her waist, lending her support as he guided her over to a concealing stand of trees then swung her into his arms.

Cornell moved his hard, athletic body against her soft feminine one. As he rubbed his chest against her breasts, she felt the sensitive nipples tighten and swell against the thin material of her blouse and she whimpered. And when she felt him stroke the swollen tip with his fingers, an involuntary gasp escaped her control. She knew he could feel the fast beating of her heart and hear the ragged quickening of her breathing, but she was helpless to stop the response he aroused within her.

As Cornell started unbuttoning her blouse, she didn't resist nor did she protest when he undid her bra and freed her breast. And while his mouth worked its magic on hers, his clever fingers teased the tips of her breasts.

As his body moved against her hips and thighs, her entire body came alive with need and she shivered. He pressed still closer so that his aroused sex melded into the cradle of her pelvis.

"Oh, Cornell. Please don't—" She moaned.

"I want you, Tracey. I want you so bad." He moved his lips to the sensitive area behind her ear, that he knew gave her pleasure and then let his lips travel down her throat to the hollow of her collarbone, and lower still to the swollen tips of her breasts.

"This is wrong, Cornell." Tracey gasped. "We can't go back. Everything is different now." She tried to pull away, but he swiftly pulled her body back against his.

"Except that we still want each other."

He snaked his arms around her waist, his fingers seeking the button that would undo the waistband of her skirt.

As his words sank in, her mind began to clear from the spell he had spun around her senses. How could she let him do this to her? After everything that had passed between them, that wanting should no longer exist. But it did. Why did she still want this man, she asked herself desperately.

Tracey broke free from his embrace and refastened her bra and started doing up the buttons of her blouse as she headed back to the car. How could she have let this happen? She knew one thing, she couldn't let it happen again.

Cornell caught up with her and swung her around to face him.

"You were with me all the way back there, Trace. What happened? Why are you fighting me? Why are you fighting yourself?" He demanded "And why, for Christ's sake, are you torturing us both like this?"

"You know damn well why. We can't have a relationship. It's impossible." Her voice rose. "Please, just take me back to my car."

He'd thought that he could—Cornell swore silently. He'd been close, so damned close. But then she had responded to him. He smiled. That was a start at least.

Still there was something about her response that puzzled him. Why was it so impossible? If she truly hated him the way she said, then how could she respond to him like that? There was something more to her reaction, something she was hiding from him. If he didn't know better he would say it was fear, but that was crazy. What did she have to fear from him? He frowned. If it wasn't fear then what else could it be?

"All right, Trace." He walked around the car and slid behind the driver's seat and waited for her to get in.

They drove back to the restaurant in silence and neither one spoke as Tracey got out.

Cornell trailed her all the way to her house, not leaving

until Tracey had let herself inside. He never wanted anything more than he wanted to make love to Tracey Hamilton. But the way he felt about her went beyond physical gratification, he realized. He wanted more, much more. He wanted that special closeness they'd shared six years ago.

Yeah, and people in hell want ice water.

How did he begin to rebuild their relationship? Was there a spark of love for him hidden somewhere inside her? If there was he'd find it and nurture it until it blossomed into a love they could both cherish. He wanted to move slowly in his campaign to win her heart, but he wasn't a patient man and he knew that would work against him. He'd just have to learn patience, that was all there was to it.

The phone rang just as Tracey locked the front door.

"Tracey, this is Brice. Was that Robertson's car I saw driving away?" he demanded, anger making his words sound like an accusation. "Did you know he was following you?"

"Yes, I did. Brice, if you call yourself spying on me, I want you to know that I don't appreciate it worth a damn."

"Don't get mad at me, Tracey. I care about you, woman! Everytime I see you near that guy, I go ballistic, and I feel like killing somebody, preferably Robertson."

"Brice, you—"

"I know what you're going to say, but I can't help the way I feel."

"Maybe we had better call things off."

"No!" Anxiety sharpened his voice. "Tracey, I love you and want to marry you, make a home for you, help you raise those two beautiful children."

"I know that, Brice, but I won't be dictated to or spied upon. Do you hear me?"

"I hear you all right," he grumbled. "Everything was fine until Cornell Robertson came to town. I'll be glad when he's gone. Then maybe things will get back to normal and we can get on with plans for our future. I'm sorry if I've upset you. Good night."

"Brice—" She heard the hum of the dial tone in her ear.

After what had happened with Cornell that conversation with Brice was the last thing she needed. Tracey slammed the phone down. Most women were only blessed with one man at a time to deal with. But, oh no, not Tracey Hamilton. She had two male headaches to contend with. It was worse than dealing with the twins when they were being cranky. Why did men have to make a woman's life hell? What in the world was she going to do? All of a sudden her peaceful life was like a spacecraft spinning out of control, headed straight for an alien universe.

Brice was acting as though he owned her, and Cornell was acting as though what had happened between them six years ago could be easily disregarded. He just wanted to pick things up where they'd left off. Well, she had news for him. What happened between them was very real, but it had ended there. She'd somehow make him believe it. One thing she could definitely not do and that was to let him find out about London and Lincoln yet.

If only she could make Cornell believe that she and Brice

were on the verge of getting married. Yes. That might just work.

As Tracey got ready for bed, she realized that her body still tingled from Cornell's arousing caresses. The memory of how her body had betrayed her when he started to make love to her shamed her. It mocked everything she had believed about herself. It forced her to admit just how attracted she still was to Cornell. If he continued to pursue her she didn't know how she was going to resist him. That determination she remembered so well, that surrounded him like a force field, seemed to be gathering strength with each passing day.

And what about Brice? She'd always liked him. But like wasn't love. She could depend on him. He could give her security. But all that wasn't love, at least not the kind of wild passionate love she'd shared with Cornell.

Until Cornell had come to town, she'd been able to talk to Brice about anything. Now that had all changed. And Brice was changing into a man she doubted she could even like. They were practically engaged and he had every right to question her feelings, to know where he stood, but—

Her life was turning into a nightmare and she had no idea what was she going to do about it.

"I thought I told you two hours, man," Bubba grumbled as he got into the Lexus. "It's only been a little over an hour since you left."

"That was the plan, but unfortunately—"

"You and Tracey got into it. Right?"

"Something like that. How did it go with Barb?"

"She's really something, Cornell." Bubba smiled. "I

could grow to like her a lot."

"Are you thinking about marriage?" Cornell asked.

"It's too soon for that, but I feel good when I'm with her."

Cornell grimaced. "At least one of us is happy."

"You will be too once you and Tracey smooth things out."

"I'm beginning to think that it'll never happen."

"You sound down. You aren't giving up on the lady!"

"No, but, there's so much—never mind. I need some sleep. I feel as though I've been run over by a semi-trailer truck."

"Yeah." Bubba laughed. "A semi-trailer truck named Tracey Hamilton. The great Cornell Robertson is experiencing sexual frustration. I love it. Seems that the lady is just as stubborn as you are. It's going to be interesting to see who wins." He laughed again. "My money's on you, buddy."

Cornell grinned. "Thanks for the vote of confidence, Bubba."

"That's what friends are for. If you need to talk—"

"I know I can count on you to listen, Bubba." Cornell squeezed his friend's shoulder. "I always did."

Chapter 6

Cornell figured he was tired enough to fall asleep right away, but that didn't happen. Instead he found himself lying awake the rest of the night, thinking about his relationship with Tracey.

Six years ago, when she'd told him she was pregnant, he'd had the audacity to suggest that she get rid of the baby. She'd evidently done it and regretted it so that now she didn't want to have anything to do with him. That had to be the reason for her attitude, he decided.

He had to admit that if she felt that way, she had pretty strong reasons for not wanting to have anything more to do with him. He still couldn't believe he'd actually told her to abort the baby they'd made together. She would never know how much he regretted it. He'd tried to find her and stop her, but didn't see her until a week later and by then it was too late.

There was nothing he could do to change the past. But damn it, he wasn't the same person he was back then. If he had known how much he'd have to suffer for being such a macho bastard, he'd never have suggested it.

He had been so strung out on having a pro career that he

didn't want anything or anyone to get in his way. Not even his own child.

Cornell closed his eyes. What a damn fool he'd been. He could have had a son or daughter right now. He had the career he prized so highly, but it was cold comfort at times. He'd tried to find that special closeness with another woman, but no one was like Tracey. He had to somehow convince her to forgive him or else—

Or else what, Robertson?

He didn't know the answer to that question. All he knew was that he had to.

"Man, didn't you get any sleep at all?" Bubba yawned sleepily when the alarm went off.

"No."

"You're not going to be worth a quarter at this morning's practice."

"I know. I was thinking about skipping it and going to the afternoon one."

"You'd better get yourself together soon. The coach isn't going to like it one bit."

"You think I don't know that?" he snapped. "Just when I thought that me and Tracey could— There's something I have to know. We haven't talked about the past because she refuses to discuss it with me. I don't know how to break down the wall she's built around herself." He slammed his fist into his palm. "I have to find that one brick that will make that wall crumble. Right now, I haven't got a clue. I thought I—never mind what I thought." He gritted his teeth in frustration.

Bubba laughed. "She's got you tied up in knots, hasn't

she?"

"Maybe I deserve the treatment I'm getting."

"You still haven't told me why you feel that way." Bubba leaned forward.

"And I'm not going to, Bubba. It's between Tracey and me. We have to sort out our own problems. Thanks for offering, though."

The phone ringing woke Tracey and she sleepily grabbed the receiver.

"Mama?"

"London?"

"Mama, me and Lincoln couldn't wait to tell you that Paupau and Nana are bringing us home on Friday," she chirped. "You happy?"

"Yes, baby, that's wonderful." She gulped. "Let me speak to Paupau." She dragged her fingers through her hair as she waited.

"Tracey."

"Daddy, I thought you were all going to stay a while longer."

"We were, but London and Lincoln got homesick and wanted to come home. Besides, they didn't want to miss going to the fair with their mother." There was a pause. "Is there a particular reason why the idea of us coming home right now should bother you?"

"No, Daddy, I just thought—haven't they been enjoying themselves?"

"They have, but they miss their mother. We should be back in Springfield Friday afternoon, God willing."

"I'll see you all then."

"Are you certain everything is all right, daughter?"

"Everything is fine, Daddy."

After hanging up, Tracey lay in bed staring into space as specters from the past crowded into her thoughts and her mind played back the day that changed her life forever.

"I got your message, Trace. Is anything wrong?"

She'd been waiting for an hour for Cornell to meet her in the park. "It depends on what you consider wrong," she said sitting down on a park bench beneath the spreading branches of a an old Oak tree.

"I don't understand." He frowned as he sat down beside her.

"You remember when I had that bad cold and the doctor prescribed antibiotics?"

"Yeah, I remember. What's this all about?"

"I was on the pill. Evidently that particular antibiotic renders the pill useless. And since you didn't use a condom—"

He jerked his head around. "Are you saying you're pregnant!"

"That's exactly what I'm saying."

"Are you sure!"

"I took a pregnancy test yesterday." She looked him in the eyes. "It was positive."

Cornell stood up then sat back down quickly.

"What are we going to do?" She watched carefully for his reaction. And when it came she shivered at the hard look that settled on his face.

"I've got some money to pay for an abortion."

"What!" Her breath caught in her throat.

"We can't have a baby now."

"*We* won't be having it, I will. Cornell, I—"

"I hope to get drafted to Green Bay. But I don't know for sure. Once I get established and making some money, then we can think about starting a family."

She stared at him in stunned disbelief. "You really want me to have an abortion!"

"Trace, we can—"

"*We* can't do anything."

"Trace, be reasonable. We can have all the babies you want, but later. I can borrow the rest of the money for the..."

Biting her lips, she said in a low, pained voice. "I thought I knew you. You said you loved me, but it was a lie. Have I been just another body to you?"

"You know you weren't—aren't. I do care for you, Trace, but I'm not ready to play daddy or get married right now."

Tears streaked down her face. "All right, Cornell."

"All right what? Are you—"

She stood up and then wiping her tears away with the heels of her hands, said, "Good bye, Cornell."

He clamped a hand on her arm. "What do you mean good bye? Tracey—"

She pulled away from him. Her voice cold with anger and hurt, she said, "I don't ever want to see you again."

He shook his head. "You don't mean that."

"Yes, I do." Tracey glared icily at him. "Don't call me or try to see me." She slashed her hands in the air. "It's over."

"But I love you, Trace."

"Evidently not enough," she said coldly and walked away.

"Just because I won't let you tie me down—"

She turned to look at him. "Good bye, Cornell."

Walking away from Cornell had been the hardest thing she'd ever had to do. He had wounded a vital part of her, ripping her romantic school girl dreams to shreds. She had left the campus that day and didn't come back until a week later. When she returned to work, Cornell was at the coffee shop waiting for her. "What do you want!" she'd demanded coldly.

"Trace, did you—did you do it?"

"You don't have to worry any more, Cornell."

A stricken expression spread over his face. "Oh, God, Trace."

She hadn't cared how he looked. As far as she was concerned their relationship was dead.

Tracey shook off her painful reverie. Delving into the past wasn't doing her any good. It was just that— past. There was nothing she could do to change any of it. She'd done what her conscience dictated and had London and Lincoln.

She had thought to have more time to make a decision, but now it had suddenly run out. Her babies would be home in a few days. What was she going to do about Cornell then? She had her children to think about.

Over the years she'd felt guilty about not telling them who their father was. But because Tracey lived with her father and mother they hadn't questioned why their father was never around. But now her children were at the age when having a father would become more important. She knew she would have to tackle that particular problem very soon. Maybe sooner than she wanted to.The twins would be starting regular school in September. The other kids would be talking about their fathers. And quite naturally they'd want to know about their own.

London and Lincoln deserved a good father, but was Cornell the kind of father they needed? He'd once urged her to abort them. If she had insisted back then that he take responsibility for his child, would he have married her? She would never know the answer to those questions because she had been the one to do the walking. But given his attitude, she was sure he would have resented her and the baby if she had insisted that he do the right thing.

She couldn't help being curious as to how he felt about children now. Six years ago he certainly hadn't wanted the responsibility. He said he'd changed. Had he really changed in the ways that count? Could she believe him? She had more at stake to lose if she found out later that she was wrong about trusting Cornell. London and Lincoln were too important to her to risk making that kind of mistake.

And there was steady, dependable Brice. He got along well with the children. He would be a good father. But what would happen if she told him Cornell was their father? How would he react? It was plain that he resented Cornell on sight. How would knowing that he was raising that man's children affect his relationship with London and Lincoln, or with her for that matter?

All these problems had kept her tossing and turning for most of the night. And no sooner had she fallen asleep than the phone rang.

Her children were coming home. Despite her worries she

was looking forward to seeing them. She missed them so much.

The fair they loved going to would officially start on Sunday, but Brice would expect to take them to the parade on Saturday. But what if they should run into Cornell? She didn't want to think about it. She knew she had to find a solution before then. She pressed her hands against her eyes. But how on earth was she going to do it?

The restaurant had always been her haven, she reflected as she dressed for work, but now she wished she could avoid going there.

From her place at the window, Tracey watched and waited until she saw Brice's car leave before going out to her own. She knew she was being a wimp by not facing him, but she just couldn't handle him this morning. She had to think about what her next step should be before she tackled that.

"You seem to be on cloud nine this afternoon, Barb," Tracey commented when her friend virtually floated through the door of the restaurant.

"I am. Bubba is something special, Tracey." Her smile faded when she saw the distressed look on her friend's face. "If I have my head in the clouds yours must be under the ground. What happened between you and Cornell?"

"I really don't have time to talk about it right now. The lunch crowd will descend any minute."

"That bad, huh?"

"That bad. But at least someone salvaged something from the evening." She tried to inject a bright note into her voice. "Is it serious between you and Bubba?"

Barb smiled. “It could get that way with a little encouragement.”

“You’re something else, Barb.”

“Bubba thinks so too.”

At four o’clock the object of Barb’s affection came into the restaurant, but he was alone. Tracey wondered why Cornell hadn’t come with his friend? She knew she should be glad, but for some reason she wasn’t. She didn’t know how she felt. Cornell was really messing with her head and he didn’t have to be there in the flesh for that to happen.

When Barb’s break came, Tracey watched Barb leave for a drive with Bubba who had apparently rented a car. Tracey wondered if it meant that he and Cornell would no longer be coming in together. Could that also mean that he had decided not to pursue her anymore? No, that was too much like right. She couldn’t see Cornell giving up on her that easily, not after what happened between them last night. Maybe he needed time to regroup. Probably the only thing to change would be the tactics he would implore.

When Barb got back, Tracey took a break and went into her office. As she sat behind her desk, she stared at the pictures of her children. She could see that Lincoln was beginning to take on some of Cornell’s features. She wondered if anyone else would notice.

She recalled the times over the last few months when she’d looked at her son and all the old feelings for his father would emerge, grabbing hold of her emotions like a swamp thing grabs its helpless victim pulling it under the water.

And like that victim she felt as though she was drowning, only not in a literal river, but in a river of emotions. Life shouldn't be that complicated, but then it wouldn't be life if it weren't. She could tell herself she could straighten it out, but could she really do it?

As she gazed into her son's smiling face, Tracey wondered if he would one day play football like his father. Already the playground director at the Play School Center had remarked on Lincoln's growing athletic abilities. For a five-year old he had amazing agility as well as plenty of rough and tumble stamina.

Tracey gazed at her children. Both London and Lincoln had their father's coarse black hair which had a tendency to wave up. And they had inherited his golden brown skin coloring. For the first time she truly realized just how many things that they had inherited from their father that could give away their parentage.

Brice was another story. Did her future lie with him? Was he the father her children needed?

"Tracey, can I come in and talk to you?" Barb knocked then peeked around the door.

"Sure, come on in."

She flicked the light on. "I see you're in one of your escapist moods."

"Barb!"

"Calm down, I didn't come in here to rake you over the coals about your problems. I want to know what you really think about Bubba."

"He seems like a nice guy. He certainly is a hunk."

She grinned. "You definitely won't get an arguement out of me about that. He says that he wants to see more of me."

"He does? How much more?" Tracey giggled. "You

wear pretty provocative clothes as it is."

"Cute." Barb laughed. "You know what I meant."

"It doesn't look like you need my input. Go with your instincts, girlfriend."

"Can't that advice apply to you?"

"Barb, I don't think it's quite the same thing."

"Isn't it? I like Brice, he's a great guy, but he's not the right kind of man for you."

"And you think Cornell is?"

"He was once." She glanced at the pictures of London and Lincoln on the desk. "The two of you created these two gorgeous kids."

"Despite their father's attempt to prevent it from happening."

"He did?" A surprised look came over her face. "I can see that you're still bitter about that."

"Don't you think I have every right to be, Barb?"

"They're here now and they're his children, too. You have to think about their needs."

"You don't think I'm doing that?" Tracey demanded.

Barb sat down and crossed legs. "I'd have to say you're letting your feelings get in the way of rational thinking. Any kid that I know of would be prouder than punch to call Cornell Robertson their father." She gave her friend a sidelong glance. "How do you think they'll feel later when they find out that you kept it from them. Kept him from them."

"Just because they're his children doesn't mean that he'll make a good father."

"You don't know how he'll react when he finds out

they're his children. As far as I know he doesn't have any others. I read somewhere that he was married at one time to Keysha Barrette—you know, the high fashion model."

Tracey had forgotten that. "If he wanted children, why didn't he have any with her?"

Barb shrugged. "The only way you'll find out is to go to the source and I don't mean the magazine."

"Are you ready to get down off your soap box now?"

"I was just trying to be a friend."

"And I appreciate it."

"But you want me to butt out?" Barb rose from her chair. "You got it. I have to get back to work anyway. Just think about what I've said, Tracey. Please?"

"All right."

After Barb had left, Tracey prowled around her office. She knew her friend was right. She had to find out if Cornell really wanted a family. How did he feel about children? And most importantly if he had really changed. She knew that growth and change were an inevitable part of living. Everyone changes in one way or another. If he had changed, was it for the better? If she found that he really didn't want children, she knew she would have to consider telling Cornell that she was serious enough about Brice to consider marrying him.

There was only one way to find out what she wanted to know and all it took was one phone call. But could she bring herself to make it? Just as she reached for the phone, it buzzed and she jumped. The button that read manager's office lit up.

"Tracey? It's Cornell. You there?"

"I'm here."

"I want to see you." He paused. "Please."

Tracey hesitated.

"Trace, look, I—"

Deciding to bite the bullet, she answered, "When?"

"Tonight, at say seven?"

She heard the surprise in his voice and smiled. Evidently he wasn't as sure of himself as he would have her believe.

"Seven, here at the restaurant?"

"Maybe you should go home and change. I want to take you somewhere special." His voice lowered. "How would you feel about going to the Embers?"

"I don't know how my father would feel about me going to another restaurant." She laughed.

"Believe me, he doesn't have a thing to worry about. The food they serve there isn't in the same league as Soul Food Heaven's. You can't touch that."

"Thanks, I'm sure he would be tickled to hear your comment. All right, you can pick me up at my house at eight."

Cornell couldn't believe his luck. Tracey had actually agreed to go out with him. Far be it from him to complain about this unexpected blessing, but he had to wonder what had changed her mind. He suddenly felt nervous, but he knew that he had to get a grip on his emotions.

He had wanted this from the first time he'd seen her again. Now that it was really going to happen he didn't know how to react.

"Whatever happened to change you, Robertson, I hope it continues," the coach said to Cornell after afternoon practice had ended. "You were as sharp as I've ever seen you. You're looking good."

"Thanks, coach."

Bubba walked up as the coach strode away. He threw up his arms. "I'm scared of you, man. I haven't seen you play like that since we got here. What's up?"

"Tracey agreed to go out with me this evening." Cornell grinned.

"Things are looking up for you, I guess?" Bubba laughed.

"I wouldn't go that far. It's a start, though."

"You look happy, my man."

"That's because it's the way I feel right now." He smiled thinking about it.

"It's about time, but I hope she doesn't burst your bubble."

His smile faded. "What do you mean?"

"Nothing." Bubba fondly slapped his friend's shoulder. "I hope it goes the way you want it to."

"It will if I have anything to say about it."

Bubba recognized that look in Cornell's eyes. He knew all hell would break loose if it didn't.

"We'd better head for the showers. The last one there is a warty bull frog."

Bubba shoved him back and ran. Cornell tackled him.

"Now were're going to start again, at the same time—this time." He laughed.

Bubba joined him. Laughing and out of breath, they

made it to the showers at the same time.

Chapter 7

As Tracey pulled into the drive, she saw Brice sitting on her front porch steps. She let out a weary sigh. He was just what she needed before going out with Cornell.

Brice stood up and dusted off his pants as Tracey walked across the lawn to the front porch. "We need to talk, Tracey."

Why did everyone have to pick today to want to talk? Did she look like Dear Abby? "I really haven't got time this evening, Brice."

He frowned suspiciously. "You're going out with Robertson, aren't you?"

"That's it, isn't it?" he demanded when she didn't answer immediately. Then he grabbed her and kissed her so hard that it took her breath away.

"Brice, stop it!"

His lips came down on hers again, harder this time, then he wrenched his mouth away. "You belong to me, Tracey. Do you know how much I want you, woman?" He gave her a shake. "Do you? You haven't let me come near you since Cornell Robertson came to town."

"You don't own me, Brice." Tracey pulled back. "I'm

my own woman and don't you forget it."

"I'm not likely to. I know exactly what kind of woman you are. You trying to prove your point by sleeping with Robertson."

Tracey slapped him. "Go home, Brice, before I say something I'll be sorry for."

"I guess I deserved that." He moved his fingers to his cheek. "Can't you see what you're doing to me? Make up your mind, Tracey, and do it soon." He turned and strode down the walk.

Tracey watched him go with a feeling of despair. She didn't want to hurt Brice, but right now she didn't know how to keep herself from doing it. But he wasn't the only one confused and feeling pain. Cornell's arrival in town had thrown her for a loop, arousing her passion and resurrecting her pain.

Yes, he had certainly done that all right. A wound she had thought healed was once again open and very painful. The passion hadn't died either. It still raged behind the walls she'd erected against it.

Would being alone with Cornell breach her defenses? She couldn't forget that he had almost demolished them the last time they were alone together. She'd be prepared this time. All the same, she had to wonder if she would ever be prepared for the way he could make her feel.

She had to find out. She was afraid, but it was something she had to do. She sighed deeply. Tonight should tell the story, but would the ending be the right one for her?

Tracey bathed and chose a simple red and white sundress.Red had always been her color and the dress fit as though it had been made just for her.

She decided to wear her hair down, something she hadn't done much over the years. For some reason she felt like the old Tracey Hamilton tonight. Even some of her old insecurities were back although for a different reason entirely. It felt like a first date even though she'd borne this man's children.

Tracey reached for *Mystic*, a new cologne she'd bought. It had a quality about it that really did something to her senses, making her feel more feminine. She likened it to a potion that revived every female instinct on how to attract a man.

After she'd sprayed it on, she wished she hadn't. What was the matter with her? What difference did her choice of perfume have to do with it? The purpose of the evening was to find out where Cornell stood where children were concerned. The point was to work things out for her children's sake, not to attract the man.

Cornell wanted her, he'd already demonstrated that. Her face heated at the recollection of just how he had gone about it. She couldn't deny that she'd wanted him as much as he'd wanted her.

She reminded herself that this evening was about deciding whether to tell him about London and Lincoln. Or making him believe she was involved with Brice.

The twins would be home in a few more days. It disturbed her that thoughts of Cornell could so easily confuse her sense of purpose. What did it really mean?

It could mean that you want him as much as you ever did.

She'd just smoothed on her lipstick on when she heard

the doorbell. It was too late to change her mind. Cornell was here!

Bubba must have thought he was crazy, Cornell smiled, recalling their conversation as he drove up in front of Tracey's house.

"You've changed clothes three times already," Bubba had said when Cornell had brought out still another suit.

"I have to choose the right one. How about this one. What do you think?"

Bubba laughed. "The navy blue one looks good."

"You really think so?" He put the gray one back in the closet and brought out the navy blue suit.

"Man, calm down. They all look good. Just pick one." Bubba shook his head. "I've never seen you act like this."

"You don't understand how important this evening is to me, Bubba."

"Just how important is it?"

He let out a nervous sigh. "It's my chance to convince Tracey that I've changed, and I really care for her."

"And do you really care?"

Cornell laid the navy blue suit across the bed and flopped down in a chair. "All these years since we've been apart have been miserable for me. I've tried to bury myself in my career, but it just hasn't worked.

"I hadn't realized how much that was true until I saw Tracey again." Leaning forward he bent his head and studied his hands "I was a jerk all those years ago." His expression brightened. "It's like I've been given another opportunity to get it right and, man, I don't want to blow it."

"You really love this woman, don't you?"

"I never really stopped, I know that now. I put her through hell, Bubba. I just hope I can get her to forgive me."

Cornell got out of the car and headed up the walk.

At the sound of the doorbell, Tracey started for the door, but stopped short when she saw the pictures of her children. She wasn't ready for Cornell to know about London and Lincoln just yet, so she took the pictures off the top of the television and shoved them into an end table drawer.

"You look beautiful, Trace," Cornell said, eyeing her up and down with appreciation as he walked through the door. He suddenly felt like a lovesick puppy. "Are you ready to leave?"

"In a minute, just let me get my purse."

When she returned, Tracey lowered the beam on the end table lamp. She had another sudden attack of nerves and nearly knocked it over.

"I—I'm ready."

Cornell opened the door and waited for her to precede him outside.

Tracey noticed Cornell's uneasiness as he drove when he put on brakes much harder than he needed to. It seemed that his nerves were in as bad a shape as hers. Knowing that made her relax. He appeared as vulnerable as she felt.

When they entered the The Embers, Tracey wondered if it had been a mistake to come here. The atmosphere was intimate and cozy—too intimate and cozy. The lights were low and the moonlight shone through the glassed-in terrace, illuminating several couples in loving embraces.

The piped in music was always romantic, Tracey thought, as they waited to be seated. She noticed that the place was filled with couples. It made her think of the few times she and Brice had come here and she suddenly felt uncomfortable.

Cornell watched the play of emotions on Tracey's face. Was she experiencing that same sense of intimacy as he? He hoped so. He knew that he couldn't have picked a better setting for them to talk and get to know each other again.

As the hostess showed them to a table, he noticed that there were a few couples out on the tiny dance floor, swaying to the beat of a slow sensuous jazz song by Brenda Russell. After they were seated and had given the waiter their order, Cornell turned to Tracey.

"You want to dance?"

Tracey didn't know if she should when she heard the beginning of the next song, "Until You Come Back To Me" by Luther Vandross

Cornell grinned. "I promise not to maul you."

"In that case—"

He held out his hand and they walked out onto the dance floor.

As Cornell drew her into his arms, the scent of her perfume drew him under her spell. He bent his head and nuzzled his chin against her shoulder, pleased when he felt her shiver.

"You look beautiful, Trace."

"You already said that."

"Did I? I don't remember." But he did. It didn't matter what she wore. She was always beautiful to him. "Does a woman ever get tired of hearing it?"

Tracey didn't answer because she knew she liked hearing

him say it. She also couldn't pretend that being held in his arms like this didn't have an effect on her. The citrusy aftershave he wore was mesmerizing and mingled with the clean scent of male—those oh so wicked pheromones were working overtime tonight.

Tracey was relieved when the song ended. Coupled with the atmosphere such close proximity to Cornell was most certainly a dangerous combination.

Cornell felt frustrated as the song ended and he led Tracey back to the table. He had wanted to keep her in his arms as long as he could. He was tempted to do as the other couples around them were doing and move his chair closer to hers.

The braised lamb they'd ordered arrived. Cornell was sure it was delicious. But if someone were to have asked him how it had tasted, he would have found it impossible to answer them. After dinner when they ordered drinks, he had to make his ginger ale. Although he would have liked for it to have been wine, he didn't want to break one of the coach's cardinal training rules.

As they sat sipping their drinks, Tracey wondered how she could lead into the subject of their past.

"Trace—"

"Cornell—"

They blurted out at the same time.

She smiled shyly. "You go first, Cornell."

"Trace, I don't know how to begin this—I've always regretted what happened between us that last time—before you—I mean about suggesting that you have—I was a fool to let you walk out of my life. I was even more of a fool for giving you a reason to do it. When I think about what we could have had, I—"

"That's water under the bridge, Cornell, we're not the same people and—"

"I know what you're going to say—that I had my career. But it wasn't enough."

"But you eventually got married."

"Yes."

Tracey saw his jaw clench. Was it pain? Regret about his marriage? She wondered if he still loved his ex wife?

"It was both our fault the reason that the marriage didn't work. I married Keysha on the rebound. I foolishly thought that we could have what you and I had shared. I was wrong to expect that it could ever be anything like that with anyone but you."

"Luckily there were no children." Tracey monitored his reaction carefully, looking for some sign of how he felt about fatherhood.

"Luckily," he repeated in a strained voice. He reached across the table and covered her hand with his and gazed into her eyes. "I never really got over you, Trace. I don't think I ever will."

"Cornell, I—"

"I know you don't believe me, but it's true."

"It's easier to say that now."

"No, it isn't. If anything it's harder. I could have saved myself and Keysha a lot of heartache if I'd faced that fact before I married her." He rubbed his thumb across the back of her hand. "You and I could still have that life together."

"Cornell, we can't go back." She tried to take her hand

away, but he wouldn't let it go without a struggle.

"I know that and I don't want to. It's the present that we should be concentrating on now." He paused. "Can you forgive me?"

"I-I don't know."

"I'll have to earn your trust, I know that. I let you down."

"It's not only that."

"Is it Carter?"

"He has something to do with it. Yes. When I graduated and came back home Brice was there for me."

He lowered his gaze. "I see."

"I don't think you do. It wasn't easy to pick up my life and go on after what happened between us."

Cornell sighed. "Are you saying it's hopeless, then?"

"No. I don't know what to say. I admit that I still have feelings for you. How deep they run, I just don't know."

"Trace, give us a chance. Give me a chance."

"Cornell, there is something that I have to—"

He raised her hand to his lips and gazed soulfully into her eyes, effectively stopping the flow of her words. The contact and the look in his eyes made Tracey gasp out his name.

Sensing that she was weakening, Cornell let her hand go, and moved his chair closer to hers. He saw her tremble. For a moment he thought that she was afraid of him, but then he relaxed and smiled when he realized it wasn't that kind of fear she was experiencing, but a woman's awareness of and vulnerability to a man. Though they weren't strangers it almost felt as if it was their first date. It was like starting from the beginning with Tracey, as if they had never been intimate. He knew he had to do some breaking through. He had to find a way to get to the real Tracey.

He smiled. Strangely enough her reaction made him think about football and how at the beginning of a game, he assessed the other team's key player, if he'd never played against him before. But this was no ordinary game. He was playing for much higher stakes than money or career kudos. Tracey's love was the prize. He had to be careful and go slow, checking out all the give-away warning signals so he wouldn't move too fast.

He put his arm around Tracey's shoulder, drawing her closer. It was as though the night at the river had never happened and it was their first intimate contact.

"Cornell?"

"Are you ready to go?"

Tracey hesitated.

He tilted her face and tenderly kissed her lips before he released her. If the kiss had been of a more aggressive nature, she would have given him a different answer. Instead, she found herself whispering yes.

Chapter 8

Tracey studied Cornell through the fringe of her lashes as he drove, wondering what she had let herself in for?

You know what, girlfriend. If you don't put a stop to this now you know what will happen.

"Cornell, maybe—"

"It'll be all right, Trace. I promise." He shot her a smoldering glance, one filled with need and red-hot with desire.

That wasn't what she wanted him to say. But what did she want him to say? What did she want him to do?

Cornell helped Tracey out of the car, and with his arm around her shoulders, they headed up the walk. The contact was like a high voltage shock of a sensual nature. It wrapped them in an aura of sexual energy. It didn't matter that they hadn't been intimate in six years. It was as though the time that had separated them had never existed.

When they reached the house, Cornell took Tracey's keys from her fingers to unlock the front door. Then, pushing it open, he stepped aside for her to precede him.

He closed the door behind them, then pulled Tracey into his arms. He caressed her face with his eyes then lowered his mouth to hers. He traced his tongue over the sweet fullness of her bottom lip and when she opened to let him inside, he explored the moist, luscious inner cavern. His kiss was slow and deliberately provocative.

When he ended the kiss, a moan of disappointment escaped Tracey's lips.

"Trace, you don't know how I've dreamed about having you back in my arms," Cornell whispered. "Since that night by the river, I haven't been able to concentrate on anything. All I could think about was you. How it felt to kiss you, touch you. How much I wanted to make love to you. Tell me you've felt the same way."

"You already know the answer to that." Tracey was so aroused, she couldn't hide her feelings.

"That may be true, but I want to hear you say that you want me as much as I want you." He moved his long, lean fingers across her shoulders and slipped the straps of her dress down so that he could caress her bare back. He felt a shudder ripple through her body.

"Say it, Trace." He kissed her naked shoulder. "Say it."

"Oh, Cornell!" She moaned.

His fingers slipped down to her breast and fondled her nipples.

Oh, God, how I want you," she cried out. Her legs turned the consistency of jelly, threatening to send her shimmying to the floor. "Cornell, please."

"I want to please you more than anything in this world, Trace. Will you let me?"

"Yes," she whispered in a voice husky with need.

He lifted her in his arms. "Where is your bedroom,

baby?"

If she was going to change her mind, now was the time. But she knew she wouldn't. She couldn't. The sensations he had surging through her body were persuasive, so persuasive, that any thought to not giving herself to him fled her mind. She pointed him in the direction of her bedroom.

He recaptured her lips with ravishing speed, sending her mind swirling in a whirlwind of ecstasy. Any thought of escape slipped out of her head.

Tracey hadn't noticed that they had made it to her room until Cornell turned on the light and lowered her feet to the floor. Even in doing so, he didn't break the contact. He continued to love her, not giving her a chance to think. As if she could think at a time like this.

He left her for a moment and walked over to the window to pull the curtain closed, then came back and started kissing her all over again.

"God, Trace! Woman, you're driving me crazy," he murmured.

His lips descended and once more she became lost in his lovemaking. Before she realized it, he had removed her dress and underwear and she stood as naked as the day she was born.

He groaned. "Your body is—I can't think of the words to do it justice."

His words made her feel hot and achy with need. Craving to see him as bare as she, Tracey helped him out of his jacket. So eager to feel his naked skin, she jerked his shirt out of his pants, ran her fingers up his torso and tangled her fingers in his chest hair.

She heard the hiss of raw animal pleasure when she caressed his nipples. He literally tore the shirt from his body in his hurry to get out of it, and then quickly shed the rest of his clothes.

Tracey froze at the sight of his magnificent nakedness. She remembered how impatient she'd once been for him to make love to her. She still was, and yet—

"Trace, you're not afraid of me, are you?"

"No, I just—" Her voiced trailed away.

"I swear, I won't hurt you."

His imploring look that she allow him to prove it was her undoing. She'd already decided that she wanted him to make love to her. She wouldn't wimp out now. She gave him an encouraging smile.

Suddenly they were entwining their arms about each other, like Spanish moss around an oak tree. Their mouths meshed. His chest hair sensuously abraded her breasts, as hip thrust against hip, leaving only the ultimate joining as the final step to intimacy.

Cornell wasn't ready for the foreplay to end so soon. He wanted what they were sharing to last as long as he could make it, although forever with this woman would never be long enough.

Tracey's body was on fire, a fire only he could put out. She had been afraid this would happen, yet she had wanted it to ever since Cornell had come back into her life. Only he could ignite her passion to such a dangerous degree. Only he could burn to ashes the memory of any other man, blowing them out of existence.

Cornell hungrily devoured her mouth, feasting on her

passion, inviting her to feast on his, coaxing her to once more experience the heaven only they could find together.

He wanted to touch her everywhere, feel her body's reaction in the most elemental way. He began trailing kisses down her face, her throat and lower to the swell of her breasts.

With each caress Tracey could feel desire pulsating through her body, building, thickening hot and heavy like lava, spreading to the very core of her being. Cornell had awakened the sleeping volcano of her sexuality.

He was the only man she had ever loved completely, and no matter what happened later, she would always treasure these precious moments shared with him. She knew Cornell Robertson had laid claim to her heart for all time.

He noticed a change in Tracey's response to him. "Oh, Trace," he whispered in her ear, "Surrender to me, baby."

His words should have renewed her will to resist, but nothing could douse the sensuous flames which totally engulfed her.

"Cornell, there's something I have to—"

He covered her mouth with his, arresting the flow of her words. "We can talk later, Trace. Right now, all I want to do is make love to you." He moved his lips over hers again and again, until he could hear the moans of ecstasy vibrate in her throat and tremble on her tongue.

Tracey massaged the hard muscular tendons of his neck, coasting her fingers over his shoulder blades and on further down the network of rippling muscles to the curve of his hard, lean buttocks.

When he felt her clever fingers slowly inch around his

hip to his groin and find his manhood, he nearly exploded.

"Baby, don't—"

Tracey stopped his words with a kiss.

Cornell felt himself harden and swell beneath her touch even more than before. When he skimmed the firm mounds of her breasts, rubbing his palms across the nipples, a cry of delight left her lips.

Sensations rushed through her belly, pooling in the crevices between her thighs.

When his fingers found the wet, slick pearl of her femininity, they quickly delved inside the sheath beyond. Tracey felt herself melt over them. Quivers of pleasure undulated through her, reaching deep in the heart of her, making her beg for satiation.

"Oh, Cornell," she gasped. "Please!"

"Soon, Trace, soon." He continued to caress her body with his hands and mouth. When he was sure that she had reached the brink of euphoria, Cornell lifted Tracey in his arms and carried her to the bed.

He eased in beside her and slid a hair-roughened thigh between hers. The shock of this intimacy made Tracey arch her hips and squirm her femininity against his turgid male organ. She heard him groan before he covered her nipple with his mouth and then circled it with his tongue over and over.

She moaned as he explored the center of her passion again with his fingers, working the ultra-sensitive nub, his expert touch sending her to even higher degrees of rapture until desire pounded uncontrollably through her blood. "I can't stand any more, Cornell!" she cried. "Now! Please!"

He didn't answer her with words, but he eased his body over hers and as he thrust his tongue inside her mouth, he parted her thighs and thrust his sex into her to the hilt in one fluid movement.

Tracey's body convulsed and she clasped her legs around his hips, letting her climax catapult her to the heights of glorious bliss.

As the spasms pulsed through her body, Cornell stared in tender disbelief. Tracey had literally gone up in flames around him. He didn't move until the fire within her had burned to smoldering embers.

Breathless, she gasped. "I'm sorry, Cornell, I didn't mean to run off and leave you like that."

"Ssh." He placed a finger across her lips. "I'm not sorry. Don't ever apologize for the way you respond to me. No woman will ever be as hot for me as you, Trace. God, how I've missed this."

"But you didn't reach fulfillment."

He kissed her long and slow. "I will."

He began to play a familiar refrain, sensuously strumming his fingers across her senses like those creating rapturous music upon a harp. The refrain began to build and swell, forming into a soaring masterpiece. Glorious rapture visited her again, making her body throb and ache. The aching gave way to undescribable pleasure as her breath came in ragged jerky gasps.

Cornell thrust in and out, in and out, again and again, with each rhythmic movement delving even further into her wet passage. Tracey rose to meet his thrusts, yearning for a closer union each time. Suddenly the tempo changed and he couldn't seem to move fast enough, deep enough, hard enough.

"Oh, Cornell, oh, baby." She gasped and panted. "Yes! Yes!"

"Trace! Oh, yes." He picked up the chant, grasping her buttocks, moving his hips in circular motions against hers, working her faster, going deeper, seeking that elusive goal. He could feel Tracey's climax spasm around him. He was with her this time, caught up in her wildfire passion. Their desire blazed high like a bonfire and in one hot burst, they shot off like fireworks on the fourth of July.

They rode out every last spark, their bodies glazed with sweat, their skin scented with their lovemaking.

Cornell eased off her body and lay beside her. "Baby, you were fantastic," he murmured in a voice ragged from his exertions.

"So were you." Tracey caressed his cheek then kissed his lips. "It's a good thing I'm on the pill."

Cornell's body stiffened. "Because I didn't use protection this time? Is that what you were going to say next?"

"Well—" She pulled the sheet up over her breasts.

"We did get carried away."

"Cornell, I—"

He raised himself to a sitting position on the bed and gazed at the picture on the wall. His insides tightened with pain at her words. Evidently Tracey was terrified that he would get her pregnant again—little did she know that she had nothing worry about on that score. Back then he'd figured that since he was young, he had plenty of time to think about having a family. Little did he know that fate had other plans for him.

He thought back to the last time he'd seen his father and the nightmares that followed. His father's obsession with being somebody had become his son's. Cornell had been so bent on having everything his own way that in doing so he'd ended up destroying the love he and Tracey had shared. What a stupid fool he'd been back then. And he was still paying for it. The woman he loved wanted him, but couldn't trust him and didn't love him.

Tracey had started to tell Cornell, when she saw the distressed look that came into his face after she'd mentioned the pill, that the reason she was on it wasn't because she was sexually active, but because of a hormonal imbalance. But before she could, that look changed into a faraway unreadable expression. Then when he didn't say anything for long moments, she began to wonder what he was thinking. Before she could say anything, he turned to her and said, "I'm sorry about what happened when you told me you were pregnant. At the time I saw your condition as an end to my hopes and dreams."

"It need not have turned out that way, Cornell. We were both going to graduate in a matter of months."

He frowned. "You don't understand."

"You're damn right I don't understand," she threw the words at him like stones. "Why don't you explain it to me now!"

"Tracey, we—"

"The baby was a product of our love, I couldn't believe you would suggest—that you actually did suggest that I—"

"If you had kept the baby, it would have complicated our lives. Can't you see that!" he exclaimed vehemently"

"Oh, I see, all right."

"I don't think you do." He put a hand on her arm. "You wanted to tell me something earlier, but I stopped you. What was it?"

She turned her face away from him. "Not now, Cornell."

"Don't tune me out, Trace. I want to know."

"It's always been what you wanted that counted. I think you're still a selfish, immature excuse for a man, Cornell Robertson."

"Tracey, you're wrong. Look, I don't want to argue with you." He tried to take her in his arms, but she moved away from him.

"You wanted to talk. Now we are. I don't think we can have a future together. There are just too many problems."

"We could try to solve them." Could they, considering that—"I don't know if that's possible. We're just too different, Cornell."

His jaw clenched tight with tension. "You want me to leave?"

"Maybe it would be better."

"Better for whom?" He got up and gathered his clothes from the floor. She had called him an excuse for a man. She didn't know how close to the mark she was.

"We've complicated things by making love."

"I don't regret it, Trace, and you shouldn't either."

Tracey observed him as he got dressed. He did have a beautiful body. Cornell Robertson was fine. And despite the angry words that had passed between them, desire for him ebbed and flowed inside her still.

"I'll come by the restaurant tomorrow," he said, buttoning his shirt. "What we shared tonight was special, Trace, and I don't mean just the sex."

Tears filled her eyes as she watched him leave. What was she going to do now? She had to admit that she still loved him. But did he really care for her the same way? She hadn't found out how he felt about children. And that was to have been the point of this whole evening.

Yeah right, you know you wanted to make love with him.

Yes, she had, and look what happened.

Chapter 9

Even though Tracey showered after Cornell left, her body refused to calm down. The cool water did nothing to soothe the excited nerve endings still pulsing in her body clamoring for more.

When she closed her eyes, her mind conjured up Cornell standing gloriously naked before her. It was as though she could see him walk over to her, move his body over hers and thrust deep inside. She quivered in reaction to that memory.

She had to stop doing this to herself, stop thinking about him like this. There could never be another time.

Tracey finally dozed off just before the sun came up. She had intended to go to the restaurant early, but it was almost nine o'clock when she woke up. She hurriedly dressed and just as she came out on the porch, Brice opened the front gate.

She started down the walk. "I'm in a hurry, Brice. Whatever it is will have to wait."

"I always have to wait." He glared at her, frowning, accentuating his annoyance. "Tracey, when I came home last night from a meeting, I saw Robertson's car parked in front of this house. How long was he here with you?" he demanded.

"Brice, that's none of your business."

"The hell it isn't. I've asked you to be my wife, woman. I deserve to know where I stand. Did you and he—"

"Brice, I'll talk with you tonight when I get home. Okay?"

He stood gritting his teeth for a few moments. "All right, I'll wait until later, but I won't be put off or lied to. Do you understand?" he said harshly.

"I understand, Brice. I'll see you when I get home from the restaurant."

She had hoped for more time, but she knew that more time wouldn't make her problems any easier to deal with. Nothing could make her life any easier right now. Only going to another planet would do that.

The rest of the morning flew by. And it wasn't until Barb came in to work that Tracey realized it.

"Did you have a good time last night? I know, you don't want to talk about it. Right?"

"Barb. I—"

Before she could say anything more, Cornell strode into the restaurant. He headed toward them, and whatever Tracey was going to say left her mind. He looked so good in his jeans and T-shirt. She couldn't help her reaction to him. He always made her heartbeat speed up.

"We need to talk, Tracey," he said, his tone serious, his jaw clenching and unclenching.

Tracey swallowed her apprehension and then smiled at Barb. "You don't mind taking over for me, do you?"

"No, of course not." A curious expression came into her eyes, and she looked from one to the other.

"I won't be long."

Tracey followed Cornell out to his car.

"Cornell—"

"Don't say anything yet, just get in the car."

She hesitated.

"Please."

Tracey got in the car. When he turned right at the next block, she knew where he was headed.

A few minutes later they stopped at a secluded spot near the river. Today the sun shone brightly above them. The magical quality the moon and a dark night had conjured was no longer in evidence as it had been the last time they'd come here.

Cornell turned to Tracey. "I want to understand what last night was all about. You were with me the whole time, so don't say that you didn't enjoy that beautiful experience we shared."

"I wasn't going to say that. I'd be a liar if I said I didn't."

"Afterward, I felt as though you had been testing me. If there's something you want to know, ask me and I'll try to be as honest and truthful about it as I can."

"I wasn't testing you exactly."

"What were you doing, then? Were you trying to find out something about me?."

"In a way. You mentioned that we could have a future together. I wanted to know what part children might play in it."

He flinched. "You still think of me as that selfish, macho

jerk who cared for no one but himself and his future because I didn't use protection?"

"Well, what are your feelings on the subject?"

He stared straight ahead and sighed. "I didn't expect things to happen quite the way they did."

"In other words you're usually prepared." He wasn't irresponsible about that then. "You didn't have any children with your wife, I just wondered—"

"If I liked them, wanted any of my own? He turned to face her. "Trace, I know what you're trying not to say."

"Trying not to say?"

"I told you to get an abortion all those years ago. You want to know if my views on that have changed. And if the same thing happened again would I want the child." He took her hands in his and raised tortured eyes to meet hers. "Trace, you don't know how ashamed I feel about what I said back then and how much I've regretted having told you to . . . I could have a son or daughter right now."

When she saw the raw emotion glistening in his eyes, a frisson of guilt crept up her spine.

Oh, Cornell, we did have a son and a daughter together.

"As for my ex-wife. It just didn't happen between me and Keysha. Kids are my number one fans. I've done some football camps for boys and have thoroughly enjoyed it. I realized what I've missed. My guilt about our. . ." He let her hand go and looked straight ahead again.

Oh, don't say it, Cornell. I feel guilty enough about not telling you the truth.

She believed that he really did regret what he'd said. What should she do now? How should she handle things with her children? With Brice? And most of all what should she do about about Cornell?

"Have you found out what you wanted to know, Trace?"

"Yes." She looked away.

"Does it make any difference?"

"I don't know. I need time to think."

"Take all the time you need, Tracey. I've hurt you and I can see that you're unsure of me. I was a fool to think that things could be so easily fixed between us. I can try to be patient and wait, but, Trace, I'm not a very patient man. In the meantime, don't stop seeing me. Please."

"Cornell, I-I don't know what to tell you."

"As I said, take your time." He flashed her a crooked grin. "Just don't take too long, okay?"

He started the engine and headed back to the Heaven. Tracey wanted to say something, but nothing came to mind. What else could she say?

For the rest of the afternoon, Tracey was caught up in her own thoughts about Cornell. Not even Barb's comments penetrated her concentration.

Her children would be back in two days. And there was Brice to face when she got home. What did she tell him? She felt sure that he suspected what had happened between her and Cornell.

When Tracey drove up, she saw Brice sitting on the front porch steps waiting for her.

"Are you ready to talk now, Tracey?" he asked as she came up the steps.

She unlocked the front door. "Yes. Come on in." She now understood what it felt like to face the wrath of Khan.

"Sit down. Can I get you anything, a drink or a cup of coffee?"

"You think I'm going to need fortification?" He asked pointedly.

"Brice, look, I've had a busy day and I'm not in the mood for an inquisition. Okay?"

His frown softened. "I don't mean to make you feel that way. You know how I feel about you."

"Yes, I do, but I still haven't accepted your proposal."

"But you know how much I want to marry you. Since Robertson came to town you seem to have forgotten that."

"I haven't forgotten, Brice." She walked over to the fireplace and absently ran her finger over a figurine. "There's so much you don't understand."

"I understand that you and Cornell Robertson were intimate once and maybe still are." He gazed suspiciously at her. "Do you want to pick up where you left off?"

"We had a relationship once." She couldn't look at him. "I don't know how I feel about him."

"Or me either." He came up behind her and put his hands on her shoulders. "About last night—"

She eased from under his hands. "There was something that I needed to find out."

"And did you?"

"Yes, but I need time to sort it out."

Brice sighed. "I can see that you don't feel you can tell me the truth. You're tense and distracted. I won't ask what you did with Robertson. I don't think I want to know."

She swung around. "Brice—I—never mind. London and Lincoln will be home day after tomorrow."

"Maybe their being back will help you make up your mind. Those beautiful children need and deserve a father. I don't think Robertson is father material. I guess you'll be going to the fair after all. I'll be by to take you and the twins to the parade on Saturday."

She wanted to tell him no, but she just couldn't. She was so confused right now. She'd found out something important, but all the pieces to the puzzle just didn't fit. There were parts missing.

"I'll be going now, Tracey. I hope you make the right decision."

As she watched him leave, she hoped the same thing. There was so much to consider. What Cornell had said complicated things instead of clearing them up.

She was making excuses, trying to avoid the decision she knew she had to make. Cornell had hurt her badly, but he seemed to have changed. Did she dare trust him? She trusted Brice, but—

How could she tell Cornell about London and Lincoln? "Oh, by the way, I didn't have that abortion. You have a son and a daughter that I kept you from knowing about all these years, whether you deserved to know or not."

And Brice. "I had Cornell Robertson's children. If you marry me you'll be the stepfather to the children of the man you can't stand."

What about her children? "Your father is in town. He happens to be Cornell Robertson, the football superstar. I never told you about him because he never wanted you in the first place."

She'd considered everyone else's side of it. What about

her own?

She had a choice. A life with Brice or one with Cornell. She trusted one, but didn't love him passionately. She passionately loved the other, but didn't trust him. Both wanted answers yesterday.

She didn't know what she wanted.

Don't you, girlfriend? You're afraid, admit it.

Her head felt as though it would burst. She had offered Brice fortification when she needed it herself. She knew she wouldn't find it in drink. Only within herself.

Brice was safe.

Cornell was dangerous.

Both were strong men. Would she choose the safety and stability of the rock or take a chance with a tiger and risk being ripped to shreds? Who would make the better father?

The next morning at the restaurant Tracey was distracted and such a disaster in the kitchen that Curry ran her out. She was so preoccupied that she rang several people's checks up wrong and Barb had to take over the register.

"You should go home, Tracey."

"The way I'm feeling now, I'll probably run over somebody on the way there."

Barb shot her a sympathetic look. "What is it, men trouble?"

"You guessed it."

"You know which males get my vote."

Tracey smiled. "Yes, I do. I'm sure Cornell and Bubba would be flattered. Is it really serious between you two?"

"I think so. He's so sweet."

Tracey laughed. "Over two hundred pounds of steely

hard muscle and you call him sweet? Sounds like love to me."

"He's so gentle with me, Tracey. When I'm with him, I feel cherished and protected," she said dreamily. "Isn't that how you feel about Cornell? You two practically burn the atmosphere up on sight. The air crackles with energy."

"There's more to life than chemistry, Barb."

"I know, but it sure can be boring without it."

Tracey smiled and shook her head. "My babies will be back tomorrow."

"What are you going to do about them?"

"I don't know."

Chapter 10

Tracey stayed home from the restaurant to clean the house. She saved the twins' room for last. One side of the room was so totally London and the other so totally Lincoln.

She would have to think about giving them separate rooms very soon. Right now they were so close she couldn't bear to part them. They hadn't reached the stage where they wanted their privacy, but she felt it was coming very soon. They were after all only five.

She'd enjoyed them from the moment they were born. When Cornell found out he had a son and a daughter, would he feel cheated? She knew she would, but the circumstances hadn't been conducive to telling him.

What about now, Tracey? Doesn't he deserve to know now?

She wasn't sure. He'd sounded sincere when he mentioned the pleasure he had experienced working with the kids at one of the football camps he gave.

She wondered what had made him react that way to her pregnancy six years ago? There was something so puzzling about that time. What could have driven him to suggest such a drastic step? Whatever it had been back then, he seemed to have changed his mind about it somewhere down the line.

Tracey left the twins' room and went out to the kitchen. The kids and her parents would probably be hungry. Her father hated traveling at night so they would be home before dark.

Tracey heard the car turn into the driveway and rushed out on the front porch.

"Mama," the children shouted in unison, throwing the gate open and running into their mother's waiting arms.

"You glad to see us, Mama?" London asked.

"I sure am," Tracey answered, closing her eyes and hugging both of her children tight.

"We made pretty good time," James Hamilton said as he helped his wife out of the car.

Tracey's brows steepled in concern. "Is mama all right?"

"I'm fine, Tracey, but very tired. It's a good thing vacations only happen once a year."

"Maybe you should have flown instead of driving."

The corners of James's mouth kicked up. "You know we like to watch the scenery."

"We saw so many things, mama," said Lincoln excitedly.

"Aunt Mavis let us help her gather eggs and pick vegetables from her garden," chirped London.

"We got to ride our own ponies, too," Lincoln added.

"I'm glad you enjoyed yourselves."

"Hi, kids," Brice called out from his yard.

"Hi, Uncle Brice," answered London. "You gonna take us to see the parade?"

"I sure am."

"Does that mean we get to ride on your shoulders?" Lincoln inquired.

"If you want to. Pretty soon we're going to have to work something else out. You two are growing so big." He shifted his gaze to James and Ruby. "Will you be coming with us?"

"I don't think so." James smiled tiredly. "Ruby and I need to recuperate from traveling. We aren't as young and don't heal as quickly as we used to."

"You go on and enjoy yourselves," Ruby encouraged. "Maybe we'll feel up to going to the fair by Sunday."

"We'd better all go inside. I made a salad and cooked a pot of spaghetti."

"Ooh, spaghetti!" Lincoln shouted. "Yes!"

"Would you like to join us, Brice?" Ruby invited. "My daughter always cooks enough food for an army."

Brice glanced at Tracey. "It's your first night together, maybe another time. I'll be by to get you and the twins in the morning at about eight-thirty."

"All right, we'll be ready." Tracey could tell that he wanted to stay and talk, but she just couldn't handle that right now.

After London and Lincoln were fed and put to bed, Tracey found her father waiting for her in the kitchen.

"What's wrong, Tracey?"

"Nothing, Daddy."

"I think there is. I know you, daughter. Ever since you were a little girl you've never been able to hide anything from me, so don't start now."

Tracey smiled and sat down in the chair opposite him. "You know me so well."

"I should. Now tell me what's wrong? You're as nervous as cat cornered by a dog."

"Cornell's in town."

"I see." His brows wrinkled in concern. "Has he been bothering you?"

"Not exactly."

"Then what exactly?"

"He's in town for the summer training camp for the Grizzlies football team."

"Does he know about London and Lincoln?"

"No."

"When are you going to tell him?"

"I—uh— He seems like a different person."

"I've always thought that you should have told the man he was a father. A man deserves to know something as important as that."

"But, he—" She bit her lip.

"I know all that, but right is right," he said sternly. "If he would have rejected them after knowing, the fault would be his, but you never gave him a chance." James put his hand over his daughter's. "I know he hurt you, Tracey, and I'd like to break his neck for doing what he did to you, but London and Lincoln are his children and they deserve the right to get to know their father. If it doesn't work out at least they'll know the truth."

"If only—"

"You still love the man despite what happened, don't you?"

"I'm not sure it's enough, Daddy. Brice wants to marry me and be a father to the twins."

"Brice is a good man, but, Tracey, you don't love him the way a woman is supposed to love the man she is thinking about marrying."

She frowned."

"You have some serious decisions to make, girl. I'm not trying to run your life, just offer advice."

"I know that, Daddy."

"Well, I'd better go to bed before your mother comes looking for me."

Concern darkened her eyes. "Is she really all right?"

"Yes, I think so. She's never been a good traveller. I tried to convince her to fly, but she wouldn't hear of it. You women are a stubborn lot."

Tracey laughed. "No more so than men."

He patted her hand. "Good night, Tracey. I know you'll make the right decision."

"Good night, Daddy."

Tracey went to bed, but she didn't fall asleep right away. Instead she lay awake thinking about Cornell. Would he be at the fair? She glanced at the clock on her night stand. It was too late to call him. She'd better do that after the parade. As to their relationship—well—that would have to wait. She had to put her children's happiness above her own feelings.

"You ready to march in the summer fair parade tomorrow, Cornell?" Bubba asked.

"I guess."

"The kids'll enjoy it and as the coach said it would be good PR, since the Chamber of Commerce was gracious enough to offer their city to the Grizzlies as a training camp this year."

"You're right."

"You've been acting funny since you went out with Tracey the other night. Before you left you seemed so up."

"I was— I've just had a lot on my mind."

"You said the two of you were going to try and sort things out. Well, did you?"

"Somewhat."

"What does that mean?"

"It means that we didn't solve all our problems."

Bubba grinned. "I'm glad me and Barb don't have any."

Cornell glanced at the happy look on his friend's face and smiled. He wished his life was as uncomplicated as Bubba and Barb's. After leaving Tracey's house he drove out to the river. It was like visiting an old friend. He had wanted to stay and make love to Tracey again, but she hadn't wanted him to.

And the next day when they had talked he had come away with a strange feeling. He wondered if she had told him everything that was in her mind? He knew she had been probing for something. He could only assume that it was for the reasons she'd given him. But knowing how she felt about family and children, he realized how much he had hurt her. He could never give her back the baby lost because of his obsession.

"You're awfully quiet, my man."

"Go to sleep, Bubba."

"In other words mind my own business and stay out of yours."

"Listen, Bubba, you're my best friend and I value your friendship, but . . ."

"I understand. When you're ready to talk—"

"I know. Now let's get some sleep."

❧

"Brice, you really don't have to take us to the parade."

"I want to, Tracey. The children expect me to and I don't want to disappoint them."

Tracey had forgotten what a nice man Brice could be. Since Cornell had come to town she'd put a lot of things to the back of her mind. She called out to the children to hurry.

"You don't look as though you're happy that I'll be accompanying you."

"Brice, please, not now."

"Mama, I can't get the knot out of my tennis shoes," London grumbled, close to tears as she handed one of them to her mother.

"Give it to me." Brice urged, holding out his hand.

Tracey placed the shoe in it, thinking what a good father he would make.

"There you are, London," he said with a smile, then handed her the shoe.

London flashed him a grateful smile. "Thank you Uncle Brice."

In a matter of minutes they were on their way. Brice parked the car several blocks away from the parade route which was to begin on Springfield Avenue. The streets were already crowded so they had to walk down a block further.

"Here comes the band, Mama!" Lincoln exclaimed excitedly, jumping up and down in front of Brice, after having decided minutes before that he didn't want to ride on his shoulder.

Her son was growing up. He could act so independent at times, Tracey marveled. And he was so like his father.

"Oh, Mama, the football team's marching right behind the Grand Marshal!" he trilled in his high-pitched child's voice.

For Tracey, seeing them was a shock. It never occurred to her that the team would be in the parade. When she chanced to look at Brice, she knew he was monitoring her reaction. Just what did he expect her to do or say?

Cornell and Bubba were in the front of the marching line. Tracey saw the stunned look that came into Cornell's eyes when his gaze settled on London then Lincoln. Had he realized the children were his? When the football team had marched past, Tracey let out a nervous sigh. Brice was still looking at her when she glanced up at him.

"Are you all right, Tracey?"

Was it concern or was he suspicious? Tracey suddenly felt like a criminal. What would happen now? "I'm fine, Brice."

After the parade they went to McDonalds. The twins were drooping sleepily by the time they got them home.

"It's nap time," Tracey said once they were inside.

Lincoln yawned. "Do we have to?"

"Yes." Tracey laughed. "If you want to be rested when

we go to Chuck E. Cheese later."

"We really going?" London asked.

"If you both take your naps without giving your mother an argument," Brice said firmly.

Tracey ushered the twins out of the living room and down the hall to their bedroom. Minutes later she came back.

"You have a great pair of kids, Tracey." Brice shook his head. "I can't understand how any man wouldn't want them."

"You must be tired."

He shot her a sidelong glance. "Is that a hint to leave? Why is it you always change the subject when I mention the twins' father?"

"Because it's not a subject I want to talk about."

"He hurt you pretty badly, didn't he?"

She turned away from him. "I really don't want to discuss him, all right?"

"Surely you don't still have feelings for the bastard!" he said, his voice incredulous.

"Brice, please!"

"All right, Tracey." He glanced at his watch. "I have a few things to do, I'll see you later."

Tracey flopped down on the couch after Brice left. She couldn't strike the picture of Cornell's stunned expression from her mind. Had she waited too late to tell him the truth?

"What's wrong, girl?"

"Oh, Daddy. I'm not sure. I need to—"

"To what?" her father asked. "You haven't changed your mind about telling Robertson the truth, have you?"

"No, but I think I may have waited too long. He was in the parade along with the rest of the team this morning and saw me and the children."

"He may not have guessed that they're his. Since Brice was with you he may think the children belong to him."

"I'd better call him."

"This is really hard for you, isn't it? It's the reason you didn't want us to come home early?"

"Yes, to both questions. I wanted more time."

"Time won't change anything, girl. It certainly won't make it any easier."

"I hope I'm as wise as you one day."

Her father smiled and patted her shoulder. "Wisdom is a growing process that most of us eventually experience in varying degrees."

She threw her arms around him. "I love you."

"And I love you, daughter. Well, if you're going to call that young man you'd better hop to it."

Tracey watched her father leave the room. She'd been lucky when fathers had been issued. She glanced at the phone, wondering if Cornell was back at his hotel. The only way to find out was to call.

"May I have Cornell Robertson's room please?"

"I'm sorry there's no answer," the clerk said.

"Thank you, I'll try again later." Now that she'd finally gotten up the nerve to call, he wasn't even there.

"Will there be anything else for you?" the waitress asked.

"Two Sprites and add some crazy bread. That'll be all."

Bubba turned to Cornell. "Unless you want something else?
"No," he replied absently.
Bubba waited until the waitress had walked away before asking, "What's bugging you, Cornell? You've been acting like a zombie ever since this morning."
"Huh? I'm sorry, Bubba, what did you say?"
Bubba studied his friend. "The word is pole-axed. You look pole-axed. What is it?"
"When we were marching in the parade, I saw Tracey and . . ."
"And what?"
"She was with Brice Carter and they had two kids with them: a boy and a girl."
"So?"
"The little girl was the spitting image of Tracey. She never told me she had any children."
"Barb never mentioned it to me either. I wonder why?"
"So do I—unless . . . Unless they're hers by Carter. It would explain why the bastard was so protective and possessive of Tracey.
"How old did they appear to be?"
"Five or six, maybe?
"That would mean that she had them not long after you guys graduated. Are you sure—"
"They're not mine. Believe me, I have grounds for knowing that, Bubba." Cornell got up from his chair and walked out of the pizza place.
Bubba gazed after him with a thoughtful frown. He wondered what grounds his friend was referring to. He had the pizza and the crazy bread boxed up and then headed out

the door. When Bubba got back to the car, Cornell was staring into space.

"Are you all right, man?"

"Yeah," he answered dully.

Bubba wasn't so sure about that. He would be seeing Barb later after she got off from work, and he intended to have a talk with her about Tracey Hamilton. She was sure to have the answers to his questions.

Tracey watched her children bounce around on the colorful air mattresses in the jumping room at Chuck E. Cheese.

"They seem to be having fun," Brice commented.

"Yes, they do, don't they?" She sighed.

"What's the matter, Tracey? You've been acting strange ever since the parade. Was it seeing Robertson that upset you?"

"I'm not upset," she snapped.

"Mama! Can I have a quarter for the video machine?"

Tracey handed her son a quarter and he skipped away in the direction of the video machines. She found Brice studying her and wondered what he was thinking.

"You were close to accepting my proposal this afternoon. I could tell. I sense that you've changed your mind."

Tracey made a helpless gesture.

"I think it's because of Robertson, but I can't for the hell of it figure out why. You knew him in college and you dated. Right?"

"That was a long time ago."

"Just how close were you two?"

"I'm thirsty, Mama." London walked up. "Can I have a

soda?"

"Are you hungry too?"

"Kind of. You want me to go get Lincoln?"

"Go ahead. It's getting late. I don't want you eating too late. You both always have nightmares when you do that."

"All right, Mama."

"She's a sweet little girl. She reminds me of you at that age, Tracey."

She smiled nostalgically. "It seems like that was eons ago."

"London and Lincoln need a father, Tracey."

"You don't have to tell me what they need, Brice."

"I think I do if you're considering Robertson—"

"Brice, whatever I do—"

"Can we have extra pepperoni, Mama?" Lincoln interrupted.

"I want pineapples on it," London chimed in.

"All right." She ushered her children over to a table then went over to the counter to order the pizzas, relieved that the twins had come when they had.

As they ate the pizza Tracey felt Brice watching her. She couldn't help wishing the evening would end. She wanted to call Cornell. She was anxious to know what his thoughts had been when he'd seen her with London and Lincoln.

The twins fell asleep in the car on the way home and Tracey and Brice carried them into the house. She undressed them and put them to bed. Her mother and father were in the kitchen having coffee and Brice had joined them.

"What time are you going to the fair tomorrow, James?"

Brice asked.

"It'll probably be late. I want to go to the restaurant and check on things."

"I'm sure Tracey took good care of the place while we were gone, James," Ruby told her husband.

"I'm sure she has, but—"

"You want to see for yourself. Right, Daddy?"

"I've been away for almost a month, Tracey. Are you going in tomorrow?"

"I doubt it. I'm sure the twins have plans for my entire day after we leave church."

"You used to be the same way, Tracey," her mother reminded her.

"I guess most kids are like that. A little more discipline wouldn't hurt where the twins are concerned, Tracey," Brice said. "I'm a little tired. I'll see you tomorrow. Good night, James, Ruby."

"Good night, Brice. I'll walk you to the door." Tracey preceded him out of the kitchen.

"You seem in a hurry for me to go. Why is that, Tracey?"

"We've all had a pretty full day."

"It's not the reason you want me to go and we both know it. You must be meeting Robertson later?"

"If I am, for the record, it's my business, Brice."

"I know it is. I'm sorry, Tracey. It's just that I—I'll see you at church in the morning. Good night, sleep well." He bent and gently kissed her lips.

Tracey watched him close the gate and then walked over to the phone.

"Cornell Robertson's room."

"I'm sorry no one is answering the phone."

Tracey hung up the phone hard and then glanced at the clock on the mantle. It was almost ten. Where could Cornell be?

Cornell had just come out of the shower when he heard the phone ring. By the time he reached it, it was too late: it had already stopped ringing.

He assumed it was Bubba calling since he hadn't come back from seeing Barb. Good thing it was a weekend night. The coach took a dim view of late hours during the practice week. Just as he lay down, Bubba walked in.

"Did Barb tell you anything?" he demanded immediately.

"A little. Those were Tracey's children. They're twins by the way. And Brice Carter is not their father. I'm sure Barb knows who the father is, but she wouldn't tell me. She said it was none of my business and she was right."

"If Carter isn't the father then . . ."

"What difference does it make who the father is?"

"None, I guess."

"I can see that it does make a difference to you."

"Me and that lady were close our last year at Chicago U. She's not the type to go from one man to another overnight like that."

"Since I don't know the particulars I won't offer any comments. Are you going to the fair tomorrow?"

"I don't know."

"If you decide to go, you can join me and Barb.

Tomorrow is her day off."

After Bubba had gone to sleep, Cornell lay awake staring at the light filtering onto the ceiling. Why should the fact that Tracey had children bother him so much? It was obvious she had them in mind the night they'd made love. Did she think he wouldn't accept another man's children or that he didn't like children at all?

She'd probably be taking her children to the fair. Where did Carter fit into this if he wasn't the children's father? He'd have to get the answer from Tracey. Knowing that she had been with another man so soon after they'd broken up made him wonder if what had happened between them had meant anything to her. He intended to find out.

Chapter 11

Tracey tensed when she saw Cornell, Barb and Bubba head in her direction. She and the twins were watching the raised animal exhibit. It was their favorite part of the fair aside from the food stands. Brice had stepped away to find the men's room a few minutes earlier.

Barb glanced from Cornell to Tracey. "Bubba says that he hasn't been to a fair since he was a little boy."

Tracey flashed him a genial smile. "How have you been, Bubba? I've missed seeing you at the restaurant."

"Oh, I've been there." He grinned. "But don't worry, Barb has taken me under her wing."

"I'll bet she has." Tracey smiled knowingly. "She's always been good at playing mother hen."

"Now wait just a minute, I don't know if I should consider that a compliment or not." She smiled down at the twins. "It's good to see you, London and Lincoln."

"We missed you, Aunt Barb," London said.

Lincoln stood gaping at the men beside her. "You're Cornell Robertson and you're Bubba Harris, aren't you?"

"The very same." Cornell said with a smile.

"I saw you guys in the parade. I wanna be a football star

just like you when I grow up."

Cornell grinned. "It's a lot of hard work, my man."

"Will you show me how to—"

"Lincoln!" Tracey warned.

"It's all right, Trace." Cornell hunkered down to eye level with Lincoln. "I'd be glad to give you a few pointers, ah—ah?"

"Lincoln Hamilton," he answered excitedly.

"It'll be my pleasure, Linc." Cornell looked up at Tracey. "It is all right, isn't it, Trace?"

"Robertson."

Cornell straightened, shifting his gaze to the approaching figure. "Carter."

"Do you know Cornell Robertson, Uncle Brice?"

"You might say that, Lincoln." Brice smiled tightly. "You and London ready to take that pony ride?"

"I am, Uncle Brice," London answered, eagerly taking his left hand.

"Me, too," Lincoln put in, taking Brice's other hand.

As he walked away with the twins, Tracey made to follow, but Cornell put a restraining hand on her arm.

Bubba and Barb murmured an excuse and left them alone.

"Why didn't you tell me?"

"I was going to, Cornell."

"When? Where have they been all this time?"

"On vacation with my parents. I really intended to tell you."

"It's obvious they're the reason you wanted to know how I felt about children."

Tracey lowered her eyes. "Not every man wants children."

"Not just any man. You meant me because of what happened when you told me you were pregnant and I—" He saw a shaded area and urged her in that direction. "You must have met their father right after you had the—after you walked away from me."

Confusion blanked Tracey's expression. He hadn't guessed that she hadn't gone through with the abortion! Of course he hadn't guessed the truth. He thought— Her father's words urging her to tell him the truth echoed in her head.

"I never had the abortion, Cornell. London and Lincoln are yours."

"What?" He stared at her, frozen to the spot in complete shock.

Tears swam in her eyes. "I-I couldn't do what you wanted me to."

"But you left school for a week." He shook his head in stunned disbelief. "I thought—" He closed his eyes. "God, how you must have hated me not to have told me the truth."

"I'm sorry, Cornell." Her mouth went dry and her voice cracked. "After our—after graduation I came back to Springfield." She looked away and sniffed. "You have to understand the condition I was in when I got here. Then right after that I found out I was carrying twins." She turned back to face him. "I-I know it isn't any excuse, but—"

"You've had the full responsibility of raising my children all this time." Shock wedged the words in his throat. Finally he was able to speak. "No wonder you were so hostile toward me when you saw me."

Tracey could see the anguish in his eyes.

"I have a son and a daughter," he said, the shock of discovery hitting him with the force of a slap in the face. He swallowed around the lump in his throat. "London looks a lot like you, Trace. And now that I think about it, Lincoln looks like my younger brother Malcolm at that age." His expression turned solemn. "How do you feel about me, Tracey?"

"Cornell, I—I can't . . ."

"Does Carter know I'm their father?"

"No, but I think he's close to figuring it out."

"How do you really feel about him? The man hates my guts. Do you really think he'll want to raise my kids?"

"Brice is kind and generous. He's known the twins all their lives. He'd never blame them for something they couldn't help."

"Maybe not consciously. If you care about him so much why haven't you married the guy?"

"I'm confused about my feelings for you both. Look, Cornell, I think we should leave things alone for now." She started to move away.

"No. We've just scratched the surface, Trace." He held her back. "There's so much I want to know about my children, about you, your life."

"Six years ago you didn't want to be tied to me, Cornell. You wanted a pro career and heaven help anyone or anything that happened to get in your way, your own flesh and blood included. I don't mean to be cruel—" She shook her head. "Maybe I do just a little because you hurt me to the core of my soul."

Cornell looked away trying to regain his composure. Was it too late for them? Had his past attitude ruined any chance for a future they might have now?

"Here comes Carter with the twins, Trace. We have to talk some place where we won't be interrupted. I'll pick you up later at your house."

"What time?"

"About eight."

"I'll get my mother to put the twins to bed."

Cornell eyed Brice with a frown, but when he shifted his gaze to the twins, there was a smile and a look of longing before he turned and walked away.

Brice didn't miss that look and asked, "Tracey, why did Robertson look at London and Lincoln that way? What's going on?"

"I—I'll explain later, Brice."

For the rest of the day Tracey and Brice were polite and cheerful for the twins' sake. She didn't see Cornell again. Her children wanted to get on all the rides, but of course there were only so many that children their age and size were allowed on. Tracey saw Barb and Bubba briefly, but Cornell was not with them. She couldn't help wondering how he was taking everything. He had looked completely devastated. She'd give anything to know how he truly felt.

Cornell left the fair and walked back to the hotel. He needed to be alone so he could sort out his feelings. He had a son and a daughter! And he felt totally blown away by the revelation.

The fact that Tracey hadn't told him about the twins

didn't banish his guilt. He hadn't wanted the responsibility. Tracey had taken it on all alone.

Was it any wonder that she was less than eager to have anything to do with him? Less than eager would be putting it mildly.

There was no way he could avoid the realization that he loved Tracey Hamilton. The fact that she'd borne his children despite what he'd done to her made him love her even more.

He'd pursued his career with a vengeance after he and Tracey had broken up. Then one day he realized how empty his life was. Not long after that he met and married Keysha Barrette. He thought he'd found what he needed to make his life full and rich, but he was wrong. Now he had it all and no right to claim it.

When he saw Tracey again, he knew he still loved her and had never stopped. The demons inside him had driven him to push her away in the past. If she chose not to give him another chance, he had only himself to blame.

Cornell reached the hotel, but couldn't remember how he got there. He felt disoriented by what he'd learned. All he knew was that he wanted a life with the woman he loved and his children. He would somehow convince Tracey that she could trust him. But he couldn't figure out how at the moment.

When Tracey walked back into the living room to talk to Brice, he was seated on the couch with the photographs of London and Lincoln in his hands, studying their faces intently. As soon as he realized she was standing there, he looked up.

Anger glittered in his eyes. “Robertson is the twins’ father, isn’t he, Tracey?”

“Yes,” she said quietly.

“You never told me what happened between you.” His voice tinged with hurt.

“I know I didn’t and I’m sorry,” she whispered in a low apologetic voice. “It was just too painful.”

His voice gentled. “What did he do, Tracey? Deny that he was their father?”

“It wasn’t like that, Brice.” It hurt her to see what the situation was doing him. “Cornell never knew about London and Lincoln until today.”

“I don’t understand.” He frowned, a net of confusion dropping down over his features.

She walked over to her children’s pictures and picked them up. “It’s a long story.”

“And you don’t want to get into it, right?”

“Oh, Brice.”

At the anguished sound in her voice, his anger drained away. “I want you to know that it doesn’t make any difference. I still want to marry you, Tracey.”

She put the pictures down. “Will you want to if Cornell decides to take his responsibilities seriously and play an active role in his children’s lives?”

He seemed to consider it for a moment. “I can handle that.” he answered.

Tracey shot him a skeptical look.

“I can.” His voice firmed and he sent her a probing look. “What I want to know is how you feel about Robertson the man? Do <u>you</u> want to be part of his life?”

"I don't know, Brice." She clamped her hands together.

He walked over to her and gently swung her face around and gazed affectionately into her eyes. "I remember what you were like when you came back to Springfield after you graduated from the university, don't forget." His voice softened. "The sadness and pain in your face was heartbreaking to watch.

"When I found out you were pregnant, I wanted you to marry me right away, but you refused. You know that I've always loved you, Tracey. I've been there for you when you needed someone. Can Robertson make the same claim? Do you truthfully believe he cares for you like that?" He eased her face close to his. "Can you really say that you trust him?" He kissed her gently on the lips.

She allowed the kiss. "No, I can't. I'll admit there are things that we need to talk about and work out."

"You're going to see him again, then?" He said in a-resigned-to-the-inevitable voice.

"Yes, I am, Brice. It's unavoidable under the circumstances."

"I don't know what to say." His voice shook with emotion. "I think he's all wrong for you. He may be the twins' father, but you don't owe the man a damned thing after the way he hurt you."

"I don't think we should talk about this any more."

"No. You know my feelings where you're concerned. The decision is up to you. Only you know how you feel. If you feel you can have a life with Robertson, you have to examine your feelings, Tracey." Brice cleared his throat. "I'd better be going." He headed for the door. "I'll be there if you—good night."

"Good night, Brice," she said softly.

She glanced at the clock on the mantle. Cornell would be here to pick her up in half an hour. She walked out on the porch and sat on the couch. The screen door opened minutes later and her father came out and sat down beside her.

"You told Robertson the truth, I take it?"

"Yes."

"And what was his reaction?"

"He was surprised or maybe shocked is a better word." She got up and walked to the edge of the porch. "I'm not sure how he took the news. I saw something in his eyes. I think it was regret, but—" Her voice trailed away.

"You're not sure?" he said thoughtfully, "You have to give the man a chance to absorb everything you've told him."

"I know that he likes kids and that he's never had any others." She conceded. "I don't know what his plans are concerning London and Lincoln, whether he intends to be a father to them or—he could just as easily walk away."

"I doubt if he'll do that. If he's any kind of man, he'll want to get to know his own children and care for them. If you fell in love with him," her father smiled, "he can't be all bad."

Tracey walked over to him and kissed his cheek. "Thank you for saying that."

"It's only the truth, Tracey."

"I've made mistakes, Daddy. I don't want to make another one. London and Lincoln are too important."

"You love this man, which makes any decision you make

risky. To love is to take a chance. There are no guarantees, Tracey. He sliced a sidelong glance in her direction. "You talked to Brice?"

"Yes." She wrapped her arms around herself. "I feel so guilty about him. He loves me and I can't seem to—"

"Make up your mind who you want to be with?"

She sighed. "That's about the size of it."

"You want a safety net waiting to catch you. It's not fair to use Brice that way. You love him, but if you're not in love with him it's best to let him go."

"I know you're right, Daddy. It's just that I feel so comfortable with him."

"Is that what you really want—to be safe and comfortable, a life empty of passion and challenge?"

"I—"

Tracey saw the silver Lexus drive up. "It's Cornell, Daddy." She and her father waited for him to get out of the car. Tracey felt nervous about the meeting between the two men.

"Cornell this is my father, James Hamilton. Daddy, I'd like you to meet Cornell Robertson, London's and Lincoln's father."

He gave him a perfunctory nodd. "Robertson." James' voice rose. "After what my daughter has gone through because of you, I feel like beating you to within an inch of your life," he said forcefully. "If you hurt her again, young man, you'll have to answer to me."

"I understand, sir," Cornell said quietly.

"Just make sure that you don't forget what I said."

"I won't." Cornell glanced at Tracey. "Are you ready,

Trace?"

"Yes."

"Your father doesn't pull his punches, does he?" Cornell asked Tracey as they walked to the car.

"No. He never has."

"I can see how much he loves you. You're lucky to have a father who cares about you like that."

"I think so, too," she answered proudly.

Cornell parked his car near the river again. There was no moon out this time and the spot he chose was near an artificial light stand.

"I want to be a father to my children, Tracey," he said as he turned to her. Because of my—I've missed so much. I keep thinking about how it could have been so different if I'd only—"

"You weren't ready to be a father back then, Cornell. The question is are you really ready now?"

"I feel that I am. I know you probably don't believe that."

"Only time will tell. What I'm concerned about is London and Lincoln. They have a right to know their father."

"Oh, God, Trace," anguish twisted through his words. "I've denied myself and my children so much." A tear coursed down his cheek.

Tracey reached out and caught it on her finger. She felt his pain. She had been right, sincere remorse was what she'd seen in his eyes earlier. What else was he feeling? She wondered.

"When are you going to tell them I'm their father?" he asked.

"I don't know, I haven't thought that far ahead. I just made up my mind to tell you the night my parents and the twins came home. Before that I—"

"You weren't sure you wanted to. Where do we go from here, Trace? I want to be there if my children need me. But most of all, I want to be there for you."

Tracey looked away. She believed that he wanted to be a father, but did she dare risk believing that he loved her? She didn't know what to believe. She remembered her father's words about love meaning taking chances.

Cornell hadn't mentioned anything about love as far as she was concerned. He wanted her, that was all she knew. What did he mean when he said he wanted to be there for her too? Did she dare hope that he cared for her beyond the fact that she was the mother of his children?

"We can be a family, Tracey."

"Can we?" She chose her word carefully. "You don't have to take me because you want to be a father to your children. We aren't a package deal. I'm willing to let you be a part of their lives without me being in it."

"I want you in it, Trace." He took her hand in his. "Don't you believe me?"

Tracey wasn't convinced. As she had told Cornell, only time would tell how he really felt about her and the twins. She knew she needed to give him that time.

"We'll have to wait and see what happens. We all need time to get to know each other."

"I agree," he said looking out over the river. "It's so peaceful here. Where I grew up was nothing like Springfield. In Chicago—well you know what living in

Chicago was like. There is the view of Lake Michigan, but it's different from this."

"Yes, I remember. When I was going to Chicago U, I missed being home for that very reason."

"I have practice tomorrow morning. What does your schedule look like for the rest of the week?"

"Now that my father is back, I'll be able to take more time off from the restaurant, but I don't want him overdoing his first few days back. Thursday may be a good time to take off. We could take London and Lincoln somewhere for the day if you don't have to go to practice."

"We have morning practice, but the afternoon is free. I can pick you up at one-thirty."

"We'll plan on an outing for Thursday, then."

"Tracey, I—"

"Maybe we had better—" She drew away from him.

Cornell pulled her into his arms. "I want you, Trace."

She didn't resist his embrace. The feel of his hands on her body caused her heart rate to speed up. That unique masculine scent of his made her head spin, making it next to impossible to think.

His kisses sent spirals of ecstasy coiling around her senses, swirling through her body. She trembled in response as her body began to throb in arousal.

"Oh, Trace, what you do to me, girl."

The gentle brush of his lips at the hollow of her throat made her pulse speed up, tapping out a heady code of excitement throughout her body. What was he doing to her? Why was it that she always responded to him this way? He didn't even have to touch her for that to happen. It was always there. It was because of the love she still felt for him. But what did he really feel for her aside from the attraction, the wanting? Or was he just reacting to what he had learned today? Or did he really—

"Come back, Tracey."

"What?"

"Where were you? Is it so hard for you to deal with the present?"

"The past affects the present," she said sagely.

"I certainly know that." He let her go. "It's time I took you back home. I have early practice tomorrow. Will you be working in the evening?"

"Yes."

"I'll see you at the restaurant, then."

Bubba got back to the hotel half an hour after Cornell and found his friend sitting in a chair in front of the window staring out into the night. "Where did you disappear to? Are you okay?"

"I'm—I don't know how I am right now."

Bubba walked toward him. "What happened with Tracey?"

"She answered the question of who fathered the twins."

Bubba didn't say anything.

Cornell turned to face his friend. "You know or you guessed?"

"Lincoln does look a lot like you, man. I saw the question in your eyes. Barb saw it too, that's why we left you two alone. Tracey told you they were yours, didn't she?"

"Yes, she sure did. You could have knocked me down with afeather. When you asked me after the parade whether they could be mine—I was so sure that—You see I'd suggested that Tracey get an abortion when she told me she was pregnant." He lifted his hand before his friend could speak. "Don't say it!"

"Say what?"

"That you think I was a bastard for—"

"It's not for me to judge you."

Cornell sighed. "I wouldn't blame you if you did. It's the truth and your repulsion would be no more than I'd deserve."

"What are you going to do now?"

"I want to be a father to my children."

"What about you and Tracey?"

"I don't know what's going to happen about that. She doesn't trust me. Can you blame her?" He shot to his feet almost toppling his chair. "Man, I have to prove to her that I'm no longer that selfish bastard who hurt her all those years ago."

"Barb believes that you and Tracey will work it out. Like me, she's putting her money on you."

"I just hope Tracey does, too."

"Let's hope you don't blow it this time." Bubba put his hand on his shoulder.

"You and me both. We'd better get some sleep. We have early practice."

"The poor little things were so tired they almost fell asleep in the tub," Ruby Hamilton remarked to Tracey when she got home.

"The fair has a way of doing that to you."

"So what happened between you and their father?"

"I think he plans to be a father to his children."

"What about you, Tracey?"

"I don't know, Mama."

"You love him, don't you?"

"Yes, but—"

"But you're afraid to trust him?"

"Can you blame me, Mama? He put his ambition ahead of me, our feelings for each other and our unborn child."

"A lot of men do that. I'd say there had to be a deeper underlying reason why he was willing to risk losing you. Have you asked him about it?"

"In a way. I'm not so sure that he really knows. His determination to succeed scares me. If he were to—".

"Now that he has this superstar football career, do you believe that he would chose it over you? Obviously you do."

Tracey gazed imploringly at her mother. "What do I do about it, Mama?"

Ruby smiled at her only child. "It's past the time when mama and daddy can make everything all better, Tracey. You're a grown woman and you'll have to make your own decisions. Take it slow and easy. Get to know him, let him come to know you and his children. Eventually you'll find out what you need to know to make up your mind about him."

"In the meantime, there's Brice."

"You can't keep him floating in limbo, Tracey."

"I know. But he's always been there for me."

"Yes, he has. If you're not willing to give yourself to him without reservation, it would be kinder to break it off. I've known Brice Carter all his life and he's not the kind of person to accept being second best. There are things he's willing to overlook, but when it comes to you—"

"He wants my exclusive devotion. He's said as much. I know what I should do about him, but—"

"But you're reluctant to give up what he represents—safety, security."

"You and Daddy certainly know me well. He said pretty much the same thing."

"Of course, we know you." Ruby hugged her daughter. "We love you, Tracey. Well, I'd better go to bed. Your father wants to go in to the restaurant for a while tomorrow. Since it's a day London and Lincoln don't go to play school, I promised I'd take them to the park."

Tracey laughed. "Don't let them run you ragged."

"I won't." A twinkle lit her eyes. "If we could just bottle the energy those two have, we'd be the wealthiest people on earth." Ruby laughed. "Everyone would want to own a bottle."

"Good night, Mama."

Tracey glanced at the pictures of London and Lincoln. She'd had them all to herself all these years. Now she would have to share them with Cornell. Was it crazy to think that they could be a real family? She touched her lips, remembering his kiss. She closed her eyes wishing that things had been different.

Chapter 12

"I won't be in to the restaurant until one-thirty, Daddy," Tracey said to her father over morning coffee.

"You don't have to come in at all today," he said sipping his coffee.

"I want to."

"Robertson meeting you there later?"

She nodded, smiling when he flashed her one of his sage looks on his way out the door.

As she turned to fix breakfast for the twins, she thought about how she would tell them who their father was. How would she explain why he'd never been a part of their lives all this time?

"Mama, can we have pancakes?" Lincoln asked as he flopped down in a chair at the table.

"Somehow I knew that was what you'd want this morning." She smiled fondly at her son. "Yes, we're having pancakes."

"All right!"

"Where's your sister?"

"Looking for her shoes."

"You haven't hidden them from her again, have you,

young man?"

He lowered his head guiltily.

"Lincoln, what am I going to do with you?" He could be so incorrigible at times. He needed the firm guiding hand of a father. Was Cornell capable of being the father Lincoln needed?

Her mother and London walked into the kitchen. London glared at her brother. Tracey shifted her gaze back to Lincoln and shook her head, wondering if Cornell had been anything like his son at that age.

Tracey watched her children from the kitchen window as they played in the backyard. She didn't know how long the truce between them would last knowing Lincoln's predilection for mischief. London was the patient one—up to a point. And quite often Lincoln pushed his luck.

"No fireworks yet?" her mother asked.

"Not yet, but give them time. I'm glad they have each other. I missed that when I was their age. There was Brice, but he was several years older."

"That's the one thing James and I always regretted—that we couldn't have any more children after you and your twin were born. I so wanted to give your father a son to replace the one he'd lost." She shook off her momentary sadness. "What are you going to do today?"

"I thought about looking for a place of my own."

Startled, Ruby said, "You don't have to move, Tracey. We've enjoyed having you and the twins live with us."

"I know, Mama." Affection shone in Tracey's eyes. "It's just that I think it's time we moved into a place of our own."

"Does this decision have anything to do with Cornell?"

"No." Tracey looked away evasively. "Why would you think that?"

"If you decide to break it off with Brice things could get awkward if Cornell started coming around to see the children," Ruby pointed out.

Tracey's shoulders slumped. "It's a way of avoiding possible problems, I guess."

"They won't go away. You're going to have to face things."

"I know." Tracey sighed. "I just wish I had time to—"

"Time to do what? I'd say you've already made up your mind about some pretty basic things."

"Not about—Mama I want a life with Cornell, but—"

"He hasn't asked you."

"In a way, but I have to ask myself what his true motive might be. Does he want me because I'm the mother of his children? Or does he want me because he cares about me?"

"You need to get the answers to those questions from him."

"I know. I'll be seeing him later so I'll probably be late getting home tonight."

"Your father and I'll take care of the children, you know that. That's one of the perks of living with us, you have built-in babysitters."

Tracey smiled. "You're something special, Mama."

"Your father has always thought so." She laughed.

Barb was busy doing her job as hostess when Tracey got to the restaurant so she quietly slipped past her.

Her father glanced at his watch when he saw her. "You're early."

"I had to come and make sure you weren't overdoing."

"I'm not over the hill yet."

"Now, did I say you were?"

"Don't you sass me, young lady." He grinned.

"You're priceless, Daddy. So what's the verdict, Daddy? You satisfied that me and Curry held down the fort while you were gone?"

"I never doubted it for a minute. I wanted to check with Curry and make sure you hadn't done what you accused me of while I was gone." Her father frowned. "He told me you've been distracted lately. He listed all the food you burned."

"I've had a lot on my mind."

"I'd say Cornell Robertson would be a lot on any woman's mind, especially when that woman loves him."

"Now, Daddy."

"I'm sure he's made noises about wanting you back."

"Well, sort of."

"If he's what you want, encourage him to reveal how much."

"I thought you were reserving judgment."

"The jury is still out on what I think of him for the moment. He's going to have to prove himself to me before I'll believe he deserves you."

"According to what you told me when I was sixteen, no man will ever be worthy of that honor."

"Like I said, he'll have to prove himself. I'd better be getting out of here, I promised your mother I'd come with her when she takes the twins to the park. That son of yours can be a handful."

Tracey smiled. "Like his father."

"At least you didn't heap the blame on all us males."

"Daddy!"

He kissed her on the cheek and then headed out the back door to his car.

"You come to work or what?" Barb slipped up behind her. "Thought you could slip by without facing the great inquistion, did you?"

"No, I didn't."

"Yeah, right. Are you seeing Cornell when you get off?"

"He's coming to the restaurant later. It's time that we talked, really talked."

"My money's on the brown eyed, handsome man." Barb grinned. "You and he belong together."

"Still playing matchmaker huh, Barb?"

"I haven't done too badly for myself."

"So you thought you'd help out a friend."

Barb's expression turned serious. "How did Cornell react when you told him he was a father?"

"He was shocked of course."

"What did you expect?" Barb put her hands on her hips.

"I don't know, Barb." Tracey's smiled faded. "I can't talk about it right now."

"In others words, mind my own business."

"In essence, yes."

"I read that magazine all the time."

"Very funny, Barb."

"I thought so. You need to lighten up."

"You weren't all there today, were you?" Bubba asked Cornell as they headed off the football field for the showers.

"I've had a lot to think about for the last twenty-four hours."

"How do you feel about being a father?"

"I don't know yet. When I looked at London and Lincoln, I felt the way I imagine God must have when he made Adam—awed and proud of what he had created. I figured I'd just have to settle for playing uncle to my brother's and sister's kids. To know that a part of you—"

"You're going to do all right as a dad. I can tell."

"How can you know that?"

"Just call it male intuition." Bubba grinned. "You know, seeing London and Lincoln has made me think seriously about getting married."

"Barb?"

"Man, she really turns me on. She's funny, she's beautiful and her kisses drive me out of my mind."

"I'd say you were hooked, then."

"About as hooked as you are."

"You back to playing locker room shrink?"

"I don't have to be a shrink. I've got eyes."

"I'm not trying to fool myself, Bubba. I do love the woman, but she won't believe it. She thinks I just want her."

"Well, what are you going to do to change her thinking?"

"I'm working on it. I intend to see as much of her as I can before the end of the summer and football season begins. I hope to make her Mrs. Cornell Robertson as soon as possible."

"Right is right." He drew the words out. "Me and Barb'll

help all we can."

"I'm hoping my children will help, too."

"If you get their help, their mother should be a piece of cake. Right?"

"Not hardly. I've got some breaking through to do with that lady, but I'll take all the help I can get. I've got to hurry if I want to spend some time with my lady."

"I thought you weren't seeing her until later."

"I am, but there are some things I want to arrange for Thursday."

"What things?"

Cornell slapped his friend on the back. "That's my secret, my man."

When she saw him walk through the front door, Tracey's mouth went dry. Cornell wasn't dressed in his usual T-shirt and jeans. He had on expertly tailored gray slacks that accented his narrow hips, muscular thighs and calves. His short-sleeved gray, white and blue plaid shirt exposed his bulging biceps. Without a doubt, he had to be the sexiest male on the planet.

"You ready to make your escape, pretty woman?"

"Give me a few minutes."

Cornell watched the woman he loved as she headed down the hall. It was amazing what her curvy body did for a simple sleeveless white blouse and plain navy blue skirt.

"She won't be long," Barb said as she walked up. "You look good enough to eat."

"Shame on you, Barb," Cornell teased, wagging his finger. "What do you think Bubba would say if he heard you?"

"He can appreciate that I admire good looking men as long as he knows that I consider him to be number one."

He grinned. "You're really crazy about the big ox, aren't you?"

"Yeah."

"You going to put him out of his misery?" he asked.

"You mean make an honest man out of him?" She smiled. "I hope to."

"He's crazy about you too, Barb."

"I knew there was a reason why I liked you so much. You're great for a woman's vanity."

"I just hope I can do the same thing for a certain lady."

"If I'm this certain lady," a smile trembled on Tracey's lips, "what do you hope, Cornell?"

"Trace." His face split into a wide grin. "Barb and I were just talking."

Tracey folded her arms and glanced at her friend. "Knowing my best friend, I have to ask what you were talking about."

"It wasn't anything bad, Tracey," Barb answered arching her brows conspiratorially at Cornell.

"Bubba should be here in another thirty minutes, Barb." Cornell glanced at Tracey. "You ready?"

"Yes. See you tomorrow, Barb."

"If you have somewhere special you want to take me, Cornell, maybe I should go home and change," Tracey said as they left the restaurant.

"You look fine just the way you are. And amen to that."

His comment made Tracey feel good. "Where are we going?"

"I made a reservation at the Embers. Is that all right with you?"

"That's fine." It brought back memories of what had happened after they'd gone there. Just the thought of his lovemaking aroused her.

Cornell glanced at Tracey. Had she been remembering their lovemaking after he'd taken her home? He certainly couldn't get it off his mind.

After they were shown to their table and had ordered their food, Cornell took Tracey's hand in his and rubbed his thumb over the back and gazed into her eyes.

Tracey could see the desire smoldering there. The heat and intensity of it frightened her a little.

Given the wary look in her eyes, Cornell let her hand go. They needed to talk about their situation.

"Why didn't you have the abortion?" he asked straight out.

"I couldn't do it, Cornell. I was raised to prize life, I could never destroy it. My baby was part of me, part of you and our love."

"I loved you too, Trace."

"When you suggested that I—I couldn't help wondering if you really loved me."

"I was a fool, Trace. I made a mistake. I want to make it up to you. What have you told London and Lincoln about me?"

"That you had another life that kept you busy and away from them."

"They accepted that?" He brows arched in disbelief.

"Since they had my father, they weren't overly

concerned that you weren't around." Tracey saw the pained expression on his face. "It was the truth as far as it went. Your not being there wasn't exactly your fault since you didn't even know they existed."

"If I hadn't come to town would you have ever told me about them, Trace?"

"I don't know." She lowered her eye concentrating on her hands. "It's a moot point now."

He sighed. "You're right. I want to get to know them and let them come to know me. Have you told them anything yet?"

"No. I'm trying to think of the best way to lead into it. I haven't thought of one yet."

"You could feel them out on the subject of fathers. They don't think of Brice Carter as their father, do they?"

"No. To them he's Uncle Brice."

"If you hadn't told me that I was their father would you have let him adopt them?"

"I don't know."

"That's something I guess." He glanced at the couples on the floor. "Care to dance?"

"All right."

When the song changed, they got up. It was a song by Anita Baker, "Fairy-tales". It was a thought provoking piece about a woman who waited all her life for Prince Charming and found that he was a frog. Would Cornell end up being a prince or a frog?

Cornell held Tracey tight, closing his eyes, wishing that he could do so for the rest of their lives. He wanted his children, but he wanted their mother in his life even more.

He wondered if he would he get both of his wishes?

When he held her like this, Tracey wanted to believe that Cornell was her Prince Charming.

Their dinner arrived as they made their way back to the table.

"I've planned a special afternoon for London and Lincoln. I'm definitely going to need your help with them."

"You have it." She smiled gently.

Relief washed over him. "I'm glad to hear you say that."

"Tell me," she asked curiously, "what do you have planned?"

"It's a surprise. I'm so excited about being a father." A tender expression lighted his face. "I want to be a good father to London and Lincoln. Never doubt that."

"I don't."

Tracey watched the twins eat their cereal the next morning, wondering how to bring up the subject of their father. Lincoln gave her an opening.

"Mama, you gonna marry Uncle Brice? If you do will that make him our father?"

"He'll still be your Uncle Brice whether I marry him or not."

"What about our real father, Mama?" London asked. "Will he ever come see us?"

"I've talked to him."

"You have!" Lincoln stopped eating his cereal. "When?"

"Yesterday. He wants to come see you."

"He does?" London's eyes lit up.

"Yes, he does. You're going to spend Thursday afternoon with him."

"You're coming too?"

"Yes, I'm coming too."

"All right!" Lincoln exclaimed, digging into his cereal with gusto.

Tracey studied her daughter's reaction to the news. London was more reserved than her brother. In that way she was like her father. He'd always managed to hold back a piece of himself from her.

"Aren't you happy about it, London?" Tracey asked.

"He's never been here before. Do you think he'll like us and want to see us from now on?"

"I'm sure he'll like you." She smiled softly. "And yes, I think he'll be coming to see you on a regular basis from now on."

"Well, I guess I'm happy, then."

Tracey hadn't realized how much her children had missed not having a father. Her own father had temporarily filled the void. Now that they were older they needed and wanted more. She hoped that Cornell wouldn't let them down the way he'd let her down.

She had to stop thinking about the past and erase the disillusionment and the pain. She couldn't let her feelings cast a shadow over her children's lives now that their father had entered it. She had to let them make up their own minds about him.

Tracey decided to go in to the restaurant later than usual. She wanted to take her children shopping for new outfits so they would look nice for their father.

By the time they finished Tracey was wiped out and called her father to tell him she wouldn't be in after all. Being the boss's daughter had its advantages.

The night was warm and Tracey sat out on the porch after putting the children to bed. Her mother came out and joined her.

"You nervous about tomorrow?"

"A little. It'll be the first time my children will be facing Cornell as their father and not a stranger they just met. I can't help worrying about how it's going to turn out."

"London and Lincoln are real charmers. Their father can't help but love them."

"I hope you're right, Mama. I don't know what I'd do if he hurt them the way—"

"He's hurt you? I don't believe he will."

"He never wanted them in the first place, Mama."

"As the old saying goes, he was young and dumb. Time has probably matured him. There are so many things that you don't know about Cornell Robertson the man."

"I thought I knew the Cornell Robertson of six years ago. I was proven wrong."

"I don't think that you will be this time, Tracey. Give the man a chance." She yawned. "I'm getting sleepy. Your father is probably waiting for me to come to bed."

"You and daddy are as much in love now as you were when you first met, aren't you?"

"I think we love each other even more. We've shared over thirty years of loving. We produced a wonderful daughter and have equally wonderful grandchildren. I want the same kind of loving and sharing for you, Tracey."

"If I could have half of what you and daddy have I'd settle for that."

"You're not a woman who settles, or are you?"

"You're talking about Brice now, aren't you?"

"I guess I am."

"You think I'd be settling if I marry him, don't you?"

"That's something only you can know. I'd better be going in."

"I think I'll stay out here a while longer."

Tracey had to admit just how anxious she was about tomorrow when she saw Brice's car turn into his driveway. She hadn't seen or talked to him since Sunday night. Knowing him, he was giving her time and space. He was a good man.

He saw her and waved, but didn't start up a conversation. It was as though he were trying to distance himself and that hurt. They'd been friends all their lives. Could they remain so given the circumstances? He'd said that he wouldn't settle for being second best and she respected him for that.

"Can't you sleep, man," Bubba grumbled sleepily.

"I'm sorry if the light woke you up. I'm too excited and anxious to sleep."

"It'll be all right."

"I wish I felt as confident as you sound."

"Relax, you'll do fine. Kids are pretty honest with their emotions. If they don't like you, they'll tell you. They seemed, well, Lincoln seemed to take to you Sunday."

"That's because I'm one of his favorite football stars.

What will he think of me as his father? And London was so quiet. I have no idea what her opinion might be."

"You'll never get any sleep if you don't stop worrying. And neither will I." He yawned.

Cornell turned off the light and lay on his bed trying to relax. It was no good. He hadn't talked to Tracey today. He realized that he needed to hear her voice. He reached for the phone then changed his mind. It was too late to call. They were probably all asleep.

He conjured up a mental picture of Tracey lying naked and enticing on her bed. He hardened at the thought of sliding his body over hers and plunging deep inside her. God help him, he wanted her so much.

He realized just how vulnerable he was where his children and the woman he loved were concerned. It had to work out for them. It just had to.

Chapter 13

"Lincoln, find your sister's shoes this instant!" Tracey called out to her son. "Honestly, Mama." She threw up her hands. "I don't know what I'm going to do with that boy."

Her mother smiled. "Just keep right on loving him, Tracey. You're certainly what the old slang refers to as 'uptight' today."

"I know. I'm past nervous about this afternoon." She laughed. "Look at me running around like a chicken with its head cut off."

Lincoln ran into the kitchen and glanced sheepishly at his mother. "I found her dumb old shoes."

"Lincoln!"

He ambled over to the refrigerator. "I'm hungry, Mama," he groused, studying the inside.

"He's turning into a junior Refrigerator Perry lately."

"He's just growing, Tracey. Little boys are like that, they open the refrigerator and just stand there surveying its contents, making future plans to come back and raid it later."

"It must be a boy thing. London certainly doesn't do that."

Tracey glanced at the doorway. "Where is she? London!" she called out.

"I'm coming, Mama."

"Are you feeling all right?" Tracey asked when her daughter entered the kitchen.

"Uh-huh," she answered, dropping down in her chair and reaching for a box of cereal.

Lincoln noticed how quiet his sister was and walked over to her. "I'm sorry about hiding your shoes. If it's gonna make you sad I won't do it no more."

"I'm not sad." She slipped off her chair and stepped over to the refrigerator and took out a carton of milk and brought it back to the table without uttering another word to her brother.

Lincoln looked at his mother, tears threatening. "I don't want her to be mad at me, Mama." He plopped down in his chair.

"I'm sure she's not mad at you, Lincoln." Tracey glanced at her mother then at London. Her daughter was certainly in a subdued mood this morning.

"It was pointless for you to come to this morning's practice, Robertson," the coach grumbled. "I hope your game is better tomorrow. You need to get your personal life together before the season starts."

"I know and I will." Cornell watched as the man looked at him and then walked away shaking his head. The coach was right. He'd been less than worthless this morning. The thought of spending the day with his children was stressing him out. He started swiftly across the field.

"Wait up, Cornell." Bubba sprinted to catch up with him.

"I don't want to be late," he said impatiently.

"You've got plenty of time, man. Chill. You're pulled tighter than a spring strained to the limit."

"I can't help it," he said in a voice hectic with anticipation and numb with awe. "Today is one of the most important days of my life."

"I never thought I'd see the day when you weren't confident about your ability to handle any situation that came your way. Yet two little people less than four feet tall have you feeling as insecure as hell. It'll be all right, man, trust me." He squeezed Cornell's shoulder.

Cornell managed a weak smile. "Thanks for the pep talk."

When Tracey saw Cornell's silver Lexus pull up in front of the house, her heart began to race and her palms turned sweaty. She called her children and inspected them to make sure they looked all right. She'd put London's hair in two braided ponytails that hung down her back. She looked adorable in her sleeveless pink blouse and matching shorts. Tracey had bought Lincoln a pair of jean-shorts and a denim short-sleeve shirt.

The sight of Cornell as he strode up the walk took her breath away. He was wearing jean-shorts similar to Lincoln's. He had such sexy muscular legs. His white knit shirt brought out the deep golden tones of his skin. God, he was handsome.

When Cornell reached the porch, he slid a look of appreciation over Tracey's body then shifted his attention to

London and Lincoln.

London frowned. “Mama, you said we were gonna spend the day with our father.”

“I am your father, London,” Cornell answered.

“You are?” Lincoln smiled, obviously awed by the concept.

Cornell returned the smile. “Yes, I am.” He observed both their reactions.

“All right!” Lincoln exclaimed, beaming up at him worshipfully.

London studied him, but remained quiet.

“We’re all ready to go,” Tracey said brightly, pulling the strap of her canvas bag over her shoulder.

“How are you, Trace?”

Her breath caught at the tender look he gave her. “I’m fine.”

“Amen to that.” He grinned.

London took her mother’s hand while Lincoln grabbed his father’s, and they all headed down the walk.

Tracey could tell that Cornell was nervous and insecure in his new role. She tried engaging him in conversation to get him to relax. After a few minutes she realized where he was taking them when he turned down Abraham Lincoln Blvd. Minutes later he swung the car into the Abraham Lincoln Museum parking lot.

Lincoln recognized his name over the front door of the building and pointed to it. “Mama, that’s my name, isn’t it?”

“Yes, it is. It also belonged to a great American president named Abraham Lincoln.”

“You mean I was named for a president?”

She'd actually borrowed the name from a character named Lincoln Hayes on the old TV series" Mod Squad", but she didn't tell him that. If her son wanted to believe he'd been named after a president, she'd let him.

"This is the Abraham Lincoln Museum, Linc," Cornell explained. "He lived in Springfield from 1837 until he became president in 1861."

"You mean he lived in Springfield just like me?" Lincoln asked proudly, even though he knew nothing about the man.

"Yes, like you, Linc." Cornell smiled fondly at his son. His son. He couldn't get over it. "The guided tour starts in ten minutes, we'd better go inside."

Forty-five minutes later they walked out of the museum with souvenirs and copies of the Gettysburg Address and the Proclamation of Amnesty and Reconstruction.

"I admit they may be a little young right now to appreciate these, but they will later," Cornell said to Tracey. "Now for my next surprise."

"What is it?" Lincoln trilled excitedly. "Can I call you Daddy?"

"It would make me very proud if you did." Cornell glanced at London.

"You can call him that too, London," Lincoln instructed his sister.

London shrugged, but didn't answer.

Tracey wondered at her daughter's brooding silence. How was she really taking this?

Cornell covered his disappointment with a smile. His daughter reminded him of himself at that age. He'd been a private person, too. He didn't know what it would take to win her over, but he would be patient and find out. Patient. There was that word again. He had to acquire patience. He knew he would need it if he wanted his family together. He wanted that and their love more than anything.

"Did you enjoy the museum, London?" he asked.

"It was all right."

Cornell looked to Tracey. She hunched her shoulders.

Lincoln grinned. "Where are we going next, Daddy?"

"It's a surprise."

"What kind of surprise?"

Tracey smiled. "Lincoln, just wait and see."

"Aw, Ma."

London glanced at her father and then her mother, but didn't comment or show any eagerness to find out what the surprise was.

Cornell drove out to Lake Springfield where he took the picnic basket he'd had especially prepared out of the trunk.

"We're having a picnic, Daddy! Proper! Huh, London?"

London didn't answer.

Tracey tried to cover the awkwardness of the moment by making a fuss about finding the right spot to spread out a blanket. When she found one, she had Cornell help her unpack the basket.

He looked around. "You can see the rolling plains in the distance."

"Yes, we're just a small Central Lowland plains town."

"Are you trying to say you're just a country girl," Cornell teased.

"If you'll admit to being a city dude." She laughed.

"Touché. This chicken looks good."

"I'll say," Lincoln remarked, eyeing the chicken with relish then shifting his gaze to the rest of the picnic fare.

Tracey fixed plates for everybody, while London just looked on silently.

Tracey watched Lincoln make a pig of himself while London only picked at her food. When they'd finished, she said, "If you two want to do a little exploring you can, just don't get too close to the water's edge and be careful around those rocks."

"All right, Mama," the twins answered in unison.

Cornell laughed. "Advice given like a true mother hen."

Tracey glanced at Cornell as she started cleaning up. "Where did you get this basket?"

"Barb made up the picnic lunch for me."

"I thought the basket looked familiar."

Cornell turned a serious gaze on Tracey. "How do you think things are going?"

"Lincoln seems to have taken to you, but I don't know about London."

"Do you think she just plain doesn't like me?"

"No. London is a pretty reserved person, always has been. I was nothing like that at her age. I was more like Lincoln, I think. London takes her time getting to know people so don't feel too bad." She touched his arm. "What made you decide on a picnic?"

"We'd had several at the football camps I've given and at the boys' club I sponsor. I thought it would be fun for London and Lincoln and me, too, I guess."

"What's on the agenda after this?"

"I want to take them by the football field and let them see

what my work place looks like. Then I want to take them to Dimples and turn them loose."

"London likes Dimples and so does Lincoln for an entirely different reason. He likes video games and London likes playing skirball. I'd say you've planned this day to perfection, Mr. Robertson."

"Thank you, Ms. Hamilton. I think I'll take a walk down to the lake and watch my children at play while you—"

"Finish the clean up?" she grumbled.

"Woman's work."

"Why you chauvinist . . ." Tracey threw a stack of paper plates at him. "I'll show you woman's work!"

Cornell tackled her and silenced her lips with a kiss. "You'll show me what?" he murmured against her mouth.

"Ah, never mind," she whispered.

"Trace."

She cleared her throat and eased out of his hold. "You'd better check on the kids."

"Yeah." Cornell rose and headed down to the shore.

He had almost gotten down there when he saw London teetering on a high rock. He wasn't dubbed the football league's fastest running back for nothing. His heart in his throat, he rushed to pluck her from the rock, catching her in his arms before she could hit the ground.

"Are you all right, sweetheart?"

"I-I'm fine now, Daddy," she said in a shaky voice and circled her small arms around his neck.

Cornell closed his eyes and held his daughter's soft, trembling body close. He loved her so much.

Lincoln ran up. "London almost fell, huh, Daddy? But

you saved her like the super-heroes save people on TV."

When Tracey saw Cornell walking back carrying London in his arms, her heart leaped into her throat. "What happened?"

"London almost fell off this big rock, but it's all right 'cause Daddy saved her," Lincoln said matter-of-factly.

It seemed that Cornell had won his daughter over. Tracey could understand how London might have succumbed so fast. Being held in Cornell's big strong arms had a way of making a girl feel cherished and protected.

When they went to the football field, London stayed close to her father and only let him go long enough to toss a few footballs with her brother. Later at Dimples he played video games with Lincoln and skirball with London. Tracey watched him with their children and wished they could make a life together. Maybe it wasn't too late after all.

After leaving Dimples, Cornell took them to Carl's Jr. for burgers.

"You're making a mess, Lincoln," Tracey scolded, dabbing at the blob of ketchup soaking into his shirt front.

"They say if it doesn't get all over the place it doesn't belong in your face," Cornell quipped.

"They don't have to clean his clothes."

"Lighten up, Trace."

She smiled. "Oh, all right."

On the way home the twins fell asleep in the back seat.

"I think we've tired them out."

"It was a very special day for me, Trace. I never dreamed that being a father could be so fulfilling."

"Then you plan to be around for them?"

"You'd better believe it. I have so much to make up to them. And you too, Trace."

"I told you that you—"

"I know it's not a package deal, but maybe I want to include you in it. Do you want to be included?"

"Cornell, I just don't know."

"You have every reason to be leery of me."

"How do you feel about me, Cornell? I know you want me, but do you really care for me, beyond my being the mother of your children?"

"I more than care for you, Trace."

Was simply caring enough? she wondered. What about love? Could what he felt grow into that precious commodity?

Cornell wanted to tell Tracey that he loved her, but he was afraid she wouldn't believe him. She'd come to know that, in time. Time. Would a lifetime be long enough? He was learning patience, learning to wait. Tracey was worth waiting for.

Tracey watched, following close behind as Cornell carried both children into the house, one draped over each broad shoulder. She marveled at the by-play of muscles when he moved. Cornell couldn't describe the emotions working through him at the sight of the woman he loved preparing their children for bed. To think he'd denied himself this joy all these years."They're out for the count, aren't they?"

Tracey looked up at him and smiled. "Yes, they are."

She finished tucking them in and started for the door.

"Mama," London called out sleepily.

"Yes, baby?"

"Can daddy kiss me good night?"

Tracey gazed at Cornell. "Of course he can."

Cornell stepped over to the bed and bent to kiss his daughter's forehead. She wrapped her arms around his neck.

"Night."

"Good night, London," he said softly.

Tracey's eyes misted. It could have been that way all along if only—"If only," had to be the most overused phrase in the universe.

She noticed that Cornell's eyes were suspiciously moist when he looked at her.

"London is so beautiful, Trace—just like her mother."

"You want a cup of coffee or a glass of lemonade?"

"Just your company will do me fine."

Tracey led him out of the twins' bedroom, through the living room to the front porch.

"There are some things I want to talk to you about concerning London and Lincoln's futures." Cornell sat down next to her on the porch couch. "I'm having a trust fund set up for their education. And you'll receive support money dating back to their birth." When he saw her prepare to object, he said, "Now don't argue with me on this, Trace."

"It's not necessary for you to pay me back support. I took care of their needs then. If you want to start sending support money now, that's fine."

"You're independent to the bone, aren't you?"

"I've had to be. It was my decision to have the twins."

"That's true, but I want to be a part of their lives and that means taking care of them physically as well as emotionally."

"You have changed, Cornell."

"Do you like the changes, Trace?"

"What I've seen of them."

Cornell slid his arm across the back of the couch. "Is there anything else you'd like to find out about me?"

Her breath caught in her chest when his unique male scent drifted up her nostrils. "You have a lot of admirable qualities."

"Such as?"

Tracey let out a little nervous laugh. "You don't have a modest bone in your body, do you?"

"No evasions, I want details, woman," he said pulling her into his arms."

"Details?"

Cornell moved his mouth over hers, devouring her lips with the hunger of his passion. All pretence of game playing vanished.

He slowly released her mouth. "Oh, Trace," he whispered, in a voice suddenly gone ragged with desire.

She buried her face against his neck and circled her arms around his waist.

His fingers roved the silky-softness of her hair. "It feels so good holding you like this."

"Believe me, having you hold me is no hardship, Cornell."

"I've never felt for anyone what I feel for you, girl." He kissed her again and again, her eyes, her nose, her throat.

He eased her back against the pillow of the couch and moved his hand under her shirt and caressed her breasts through the sheer fabric of her bra.

Tracey gasped when the friction of his fingers abraded her nipples. A moan left her lips when he rubbed his thumb in circular motions across her aroused flesh. The lava of desire began to slowly pour through her, pooling in her feminine core.

Cornell heard her little moan and kissed her. He moved his hand down her ribs to her hip. Lifting the hem of her skirt, he stroked her bare thigh.

"Oh, Cornell."

"I want you so damn bad, baby."

"I want you, too."

The flash of headlights as a car turned into the driveway made them jerk apart guiltily.

Tracey cleared her throat, adjusted her blouse and lowered her skirt. "It's my parents coming back from church," she said in a husky voice.

"After all these years to be caught in the act like teenagers discovered getting it on in the back seat of a car."

"I know what you mean." Tracey stood up.

Cornell wanted to wait until the evidence of his passion had subsided, but he took a chance that it wouldn't be noticed and stood up beside Tracey.

He knew that the Hamiltons had guessed what had been going on when he saw the expression on their faces.

"How did your day with London and Lincoln go?" Ruby Hamilton asked Cornell to break the silence.

"I think they like me. I more than like them. I'm awed to

know that I have two such wonderful children." He eyed her parents warily. "I know you probably have mixed feelings about me right now."

"We're suspending judgement about you, Robertson," James said. "If London and Lincoln accept you, there's no reason why we can't do the same."

"I appreciate your honesty, sir."

"I don't know any other way to be," James replied. "We'll leave you two now."

"I like your father, Trace," Cornell said after her parents have gone inside. "He's something else. I think your mother likes me, though."

"Oh, she does." Tracey laughed lightly. "We've had a few conversations about you."

"Whatever you told her, it must have made quite an impression."

"My mother is a liberal-minded compassionate person. She tends to be more forgiving and accepting than my father."

"Well, I don't want them to ever have any more negative impressions about me. I'm here to stay. Look, it's getting late. I'd better be going."

"You have practice in the morning?"

"Sure do."

He pulled Tracey into his arms and kissed her. His lips parted hers in a scorching kiss.

Uttering a reluctant groan, he put her away from him, then taking her hand, eased her off the porch and guided her down the walk to the gate. "I'll drop by the restaurant tomorrow afternoon. You *are* going to be there?"

"Yes, I'll be in at one."

"See you then, girlfriend." He kissed her again.

"Good night, Cornell."

Tracey literally floated back into the house. If all her encounters with this man would end this way, she sighed dreamily. Her body remembered the lovemaking he had started before her parents drove up. It yearned for fulfillment, and oh, how she ached to make love with Cornell again. But she wanted him to make love to her for the right reason—because he loved her, not just because he wanted her.

Tracey was watering the flowers in her front yard the next morning when she saw Brice come out of his house and signal her over to the fence.

"I guess you've made up your mind," he said tightly. "I saw you and Robertson on the porch last night."

"Brice, I—"

"You don't have to say anything, Tracey. You want the man. It's that simple. But when you find out that what you feel is only lust and that I'm the one for you, I'll be waiting. As I told you before, I won't settle for being second best."

"Brice, I don't know what to tell you. What I feel for Cornell—"

"I can see that you think it's love. Only time will prove or disapprove that. Take care, Tracey. If the children want to come over and see me they can any time."

He walked away leaving Tracey feeling strangely bereft. It was as though a part of her had been torn away. Something of what she was feeling must have remained on her face when she walked into the kitchen.

"Are you all right, Tracey?" her mother asked.

"I just talked with Brice."

She stopped washing the dishes. "He broke off your relationship?"

"Not exactly. He said that he'd be waiting for me to come to my senses after my infatuation with Cornell passes."

"So he believes it's just an infatuation?"

"He thinks that what I feel for Cornell is lust stirred to life because of our past relationship."

"I see." Her mother returned to the task of washing the breakfast dishes. "How does he feel about the twins?"

"He said they could still come visit him if they wanted to. He sounded so confident, Mama. He's so sure I'll see the error of my ways and come crawling back to him."

"Like most men he has his pride to assuage. Since the children are gone to play school, what are you going to do with yourself this morning?"

"I had thought of going to work early, but—"

"You still thinking about moving?"

Tracey smiled. "You know me so well. Yes, I am. There are several nice apartments for rent just a few blocks from here. I thought I'd go take a look this morning. You want to come with me?"

"No. You know your young man might decide that he wants you and his children to live in a house."

"I hadn't thought about that."

"Maybe you should. I'm sure he'll want the best for his children. He seems like a man who is used to getting his own way."

"He is." How well she remembered that about him. She had never been able to deny him anything back then and still couldn't. She wanted to give herself to him body and soul.

Chapter 14

Cornell had been waiting over an hour at the restaurant for Tracey when she finally swept through the door.

"I'm sorry I'm late. Have you had lunch?"

"No, I was waiting for you. Where were you?"

"I had some errands to run."

"What kind of errands?"

"Cornell!"

"I'm sorry, I didn't mean it to sound like an interrogation."

"I was looking at apartments if you must know."

"Apartments?" He stared at her, baffled.

"I'm thinking about moving into my own place."

"You should have said something to me last night. I'll buy you and the twins a house or anything else you need."

"Cornell, I—"

"I know you're an independent woman, Trace, but I can afford to give my children the best that money can buy. They need a house with plenty of space and a yard, not some little cramped apartment. London needs her own room."

"I don't think we should be discussing it here," she said,

glancing around her at the interested faces that had suddenly homed in on their conversation.

"You're right. It's just that I want to do as much as I can for you and the twins."

"I know." She put a hand on his arm.

A passionate look came into his eyes when she touched him, reminding Tracey of what Brice had said.

Cornell ordered lunch and watched while Tracey spread her magical warmth over the place. Everyone smiled when she came to their table to ask if everything was all right. His Tracey was quite a woman.

Just then Bubba entered the restaurant, and spotting his friend, strode over to his table. He glanced around.

"I see my girl hasn't come in yet." He grinned shaking his head. "She's late as usual. So what's up?"

"Tracey and I are going house hunting together."

"Does that mean that you two are—"

"No. But one day I'll get her to admit that she wants a life with me. I know she's still attracted to me, but I don't want her to come to me because it would be the best thing for our children."

"I heard that. Guess where I've been for the last hour."

"Beats me." Cornell shrugged.

Bubba pulled a small square box out of his pocket and opened it up.

Cornell grinned and then slapped his friend on the back. "I'm happy for you, man."

"I knew you would be. You think Barb'll like it?"

"She'd be insane if she doesn't. And Barb doesn't strike me as being in the least bit crazy. When did you decide that you couldn't live your life without her?" He studied him for a moment. "You sure it isn't another one of your summer flings?"

"I'm serious this time, Cornell. Barb hooked me from the start with that sexy smile and body of hers. But that's not all. She has such an alive, bubbly personality. She's funny, too."

"From the sound and look of you, I'd definitely say you're in love. So when are you thinking of getting married?"

"I don't know. One thing at a time, man. I haven't even popped the question."

"I hope that one day Tracey and I will be making an announcement of our own."

"It shouldn't take you too long."

Cornell stared at his friend. It was easy for him to say, he didn't know the reasons Tracey had for her reluctance to marry him. Even though they were best friends, there were quite a few things Bubba didn't know about him, extremely personal things he couldn't talk about with him or anyone else.

On Saturday Cornell picked up Tracey and the twins to go house hunting. London and Lincoln were excited about the prospect of choosing their own home. When the real estate agent found out who Cornell was, he was more than happy to show them the best and most expensive houses in town.

"Don't sweat it, Trace," Cornell said, when Tracey commented on the prices. "I can afford whatever he has to offer."

"I read somewhere that you have several houses."

"I bought one for my mother, and the other," he said uneasily, "I gave to my ex-wife as part of the divorce settlement. I have a condo in the suburbs of Chicago."

Tracey was curious, seeing the change on his face, and asked, "How do you feel about her? Your ex, I mean."

"We had what could be described as a friendly divorce."

"In other words she'd gladly try for a reconciliation."

"I don't want to talk about that. Keysha is a part of my past."

Tracey wondered if that were really true.

It was the third house they came to that seemed to catch everyone's attention. Tracey turned London and Lincoln loose and minutes later she heard, "Mama, there's a humongous backyard. Come and see," London chirped excitedly, practically dragging her mother in that direction.

Cornell followed. He found his son perched on the low hanging branch of a large oak tree. He was probably imagining where he wanted to put a tree house or maybe a tire swing. Or maybe that was one of Cornell's own childhood fantasies. Only there had been no tree in his backyard to attach a swing to.

Tracey thought the house was beautiful. There were plenty of windows and closets, the bedrooms were large and it had a kitchen to die for. It seemed like the perfect family home.

Cornell could picture them living there as a family—Tracey whipping up one of her culinary masterpieces, himself eating one of her out-of-this-world sweet potato pies that melted in your mouth. He got angry when he thought about all he could have had if not for his obsession.

"So what do you think, Trace?" he asked eagerly.

"It's wonderful, but it's got to cost the earth."

"Don't worry about the expense. Do you like it?"

"Yes, but—"

He looked down at his children. "What do you think kids?"

"It's tight, Daddy," Lincoln answered.

Cornell glanced at London. "What do you think, sweetheart?"

"I like it very much. My room—I mean the pink bedroom is big enough to put a doll house in." She looked up at her mother, her eyes pools of appeal. "You know the one we saw in the doll house catalog, Mama."

Tracey gazed fondly at her daughter. "Yes, I remember."

Cornell made a mental note to see that his daughter got that doll house. "It's settled then. I'll talk to the real estate agent."

"Cornell," Tracey said struggling with uncertainty, "I don't know—"

"You like the house. Don't give me a hard time, woman."

She smiled. "Mama said you'd be like this."

"Remind me to kiss your mother."

"Are we gonna move in here, Daddy?" Lincoln asked.

"If you, your sister and your mother agree."

Tracey saw the wistful look in her children's eyes. "All right, I give in. I know when I'm outnumbered."

Cornell's expression turned serious. "Do you really want the house, Trace?"

She smiled. "Yeah."

"If it's all right with you, I'd like to take you and the twins to Chicago so they can meet their other grandmother. And I want to take them sight-seeing and to visit museums and landmarks. I also want them to see the place where their father grew up."

"I think it's a wonderful idea. You're really into education, aren't you?"

"Oh, yes, I am." He gazed away broodingly for a few moments and then smiled. "I'll be by to pick you up at the crack of dawn so you'd better be up and at 'em."

Tracey saluted him. "Yes, sir. We'd best get these two home."

After Tracey had put the twins to bed, she caught her parents up with the day's news.

"I knew there was more to that young man than met the eye," James said with a knowing smile. "I think it's a good move. You and the children need your own place, not that I haven't enjoyed having you live with us."

"I can hardly wait to help you decorate it," her mother put in enthusiastically.

"Cornell wants me to start right away. It's going to be pretty hectic, so I won't be at the restaurant very much."

"That's all right. Yours and my grandchildren's welfare come first," he said emphatically.

"You need to take a break anyway," Ruby added. "You haven't had your vacation this year."

"I'm going to miss this," she said looking around the room. It was here her mother taught her to cook and appreciate the closeness of family.

Her mother smiled, divining her daughter's thoughts. "We're going to miss you, too, but it's best for the kids. Who knows, there may be a wedding to go with the new house."

"Mama, I—it's time I went to bed. Cornell will be here early in the morning to take us to Chicago to meet his family."

Her mother ignored her attempt at evasion. "That man cares for you, Tracey. I'm sure he'll want to do the right thing this time."

"You're such a romantic, Ruby," James said. "He'd better or I'll want to know the reason why."

Tracey laughed. "Oh, Daddy, you're a rare treasure."

"And don't you forget it," he said, his mouth spreading into a wide grin.

That night as she lay in bed, Tracey thought about all that had happened that day. She and her children were going to have a home of their own. Cornell had set up a trust fund and had given her a check for their care. He had contacted the best furniture store in town and set up an appointment to choose whatever furniture they wanted in the house. He certainly was generous with his money.

Although she was going to miss living with her parents, she was looking forward to the move. Her parents needed some privacy. Cornell had mentioned sending them on a cruise as a thank-you gesture for their having taken such good care of her and the twins. She had agreed that it would be a nice thing to do for them.

Tracey wondered what it would be like having Cornell

living at the house with her and their children. To have him make love to her every night—her body burned for him. Just the thought of that one time they'd made love in this very bed aroused her. She had to know if there was a possiblilty that her dreams might be fulfilled. The dream seemed so close she could touch it and yet so far away she couldn't quite reach it.

"You just getting out of the shower at this time of night, man?" Bubba asked Cornell as he came into their hotel room and found him towelling himself dry.

"It was a cold shower if you must know, Bubba." Cornell answered wryly.

"Oh, one of those." A mischievous grin quivered on his lips. "So you were hot and bothered, huh? I know the feeling well. Hopefully I won't ever have to worry about that again."

"You and Barb?"

"Yeah." He grinned. "She has agreed to put me out of my misery."

"Congratulations, Bubba."

"You're next."

"I hope I am. I'm doing everything I can to make it happen. We went house shopping today."

"And did the two of you decide on anything?"

"Yeah. But, I think she did it to please the kids more than anything else." He frowned, a twinge of disappointment tingeing his voice. "Not great, but it's a start."

Bubba gave him a sidelong glance. "You really love the

woman, don't you?"

"Yeah, I do. And I think she cares for me too. As to whether she loves me, I just don't know."

"You'll work it out."

"Things are going so well I'm almost afraid to breathe too hard for fear it'll all come tumbling down around my ears."

"Happiness is precious and also elusive. I think everybody is afraid of losing it once they've found it."

"I could have had it six years ago, but I was too stupid to recognize it," he said in a voice filled with regret.

"We all grow up, man. We learn from our mistakes and get on with our lives."

Cornell smiled. "I'm lucky to have you for a friend."

"I know." Bubba grinned and ducked when Cornell threw a pillow at his head.

The next morning Cornell drove Tracey and the twins to Chicago. The landscape changed dramatically from gentle rolling plains to a panorama of green forests and then gradually to a more industrialized atmosphere over the almost two-hundred mile trip.

As Cornell drove through the southern most part of Chicago, to the old neighborhood of Morgan Park where he grew up, Tracey noticed the bittersweet look that came into his eyes as he pointed out his old high school to the twins. She sensed that the memories weren't particularly good ones. The expression on his face made her wonder what his childhood had been like.

Cornell stopped in Jackson Park so the kids could visit the Science and Industry Museum, then headed up Lake

Shore Drive past Burnham Park to the Buckingham Fountain. Cornell was sorry that it wasn't dark, so the twins could see it all lit up.

"Daddy, you can see the water from here!" London exclaimed excitedly when they entered Lincoln Park Zoo.

Lincoln grinned. "I must really be something."

"What makes you think that, son?" Cornell asked.

"Even the zoo is named after me."

"Your modesty is awesome." Tracey laughed.

"What is modesty, Daddy?" Lincoln asked.

"It's nothing you have to worry that you don't have enough of, Linc."

As they left the zoo Tracey turned to Cornell and asked, "Where are we going now?"

"To visit my mother. I bought her a house in Oak Park three years ago."

Tracey couldn't help wondering what his mother would be like.

"Don't look so worried, my mother won't bite you, I promise."

"You mentioned that you have two brothers and two sisters, didn't you?"

"There's Kevin, who's four years younger than me, then Malcolm my youngest brother, who's sixteen and still lives at home. My sister Glynell is a year younger than Kevin and lives in Detroit with her husband and three kids. And my other sister, LaTonya, who is twenty-one and attends Northwestern University, also lives at home. She's studying to be a doctor."

"That's very impressive. I always wished that I'd had

brothers and sisters."

"They can be a pain sometimes, I can tell you."

"Since you're the oldest brother, were you cruel and overbearing to your siblings like I've heard that most older brothers are?"

"To hear my sisters tell it I was." He grinned devilishly.

"It must be where Lincoln gets his mischief-making tendencies."

"I'll have to give him a few pointers."

Tracey punched him in the arm.

"Are you and daddy having a fight?" London asked.

Tracey laughed. "Not yet."

"I don't ever want you to fight." She turned to Cornell. "Or for you to go away, Daddy," London said seriously.

Cornell and Tracey looked at each other.

"Sweetheart, I'll have to be away to do my job."

"But you're always gonna come back, though, aren't you?"

"Yes, I'll always come back to see you, your brother and your mother."

Lincoln frowned thoughtfully. "Does that mean that you're gonna marry Mama, Daddy?"

"Well, that's up to her." He gazed hopefully at Tracey. "I definitely want her to think about it."

"Will you think about it, Mama?"

"Yes, Lincoln. I'll think about it. Isn't that the turn off to Oak Park."

There was an awkward silence until they reached Cornell's mother's house. Tracey was impressed with the elegant two-story red-brick house with it's half circular drive and well-kept lawn and garden area.

Tracey's throat suddenly felt dry. What would his mother think of her and the grandchildren she hadn't known that she had? Would she be able to talk to the woman and explain why she hadn't told Cornell that he had children?

A large collie came loping out to the fence to greet them.

"Hey there, Lion." Cornell petted the dog and ruffled his shaggy brown and white coat and then opened the fence. "Come on in, Lion won't bite you as long as you're with me. He glanced at London and Lincoln. "He likes kids so don't be afraid to pet him."

They were wary at first, but kids being kids, they instantly made friends with the dog.

The front door opened and a petite woman with greying hair, dressed in an elegant African-design caftan stepped out onto the porch to meet them.

"You must be Tracey." She smiled. "I'm Lillian Robertson, Cornell's mother. You can call me Lillie if you like." She gazed past Tracey to London and Lincoln. "Oh, my goodness if this boy isn't the image of Malcolm at that age." She eyed her eldest son. "And you, too." "Come over here and let your grandmother get a good look at you," she called out to her grandchildren.

Lincoln smiled and without hesitation walked over to the woman, but London hung back studying her grandmother.

Lillie observed the two and looked at London. "She's reserved just like you were and still are, Cornell. She'll come to me when she's ready."

Lillie Robertson was a very easy person to like. In some ways she reminded Tracey of her own mother. Cornell never spoke of his father and she couldn't help wondering about him.

"Come on in. I sent Malcolm out to get some ice cream for the children."

Lillie guided them into her living room. It was a delightful room done in mellow hues ranging from pale pinks to soft browns. A huge beige and gold-veined marble fireplace took up one wall. Dusty rose floral drapes hung at the windows.

Lillie smiled at her grandchildren and asked them if they wanted to go and play with Lion and they immediately scampered outside.

"Sit down, Tracey. Would you like some lemonade?"

"That would be wonderful."

"You go and get it for her, Cornell," Lillie ordered with a smile that said he should take his time. "That'll give us a chance to get acquainted."

Cornell squeezed Tracey's shoulder. "I'll be back in a few."

As soon as Cornell had gone his mother began. "You know my son never got over you, Tracey. I thought he'd be happy when he married Keysha, but—"

"He talked about me?"

"Oh, yes." She silently assessed her. "You're a very pretty girl and nice with it, too. As you can see, my son has bought me this grand house." She waved her hands. "It's a far cry from the one he grew up in. He told me just before he started at Chicago University that he would get me out of the South Side." She smiled at the memory. "Even before he bought this house he moved us out of the old neighborhood into a better one."

"He never talked much about his home life."

"He has his reasons, Tracey. My boy seems happy with you and his children. It's all I've ever wanted for him."

The front door opened and Malcolm Robertson strode into the living room.

"I'm Malcolm. You must be Tracey."

Tracey smiled. "Yes, I am. I can see that you bought just the right thing for a very warm summer afternoon."

"I bought both vanilla and strawberry. Where are my niece and nephew?"

"Didn't you see them out front?" Lillie asked.

"No. I didn't see Lion either, but the side gate was open which probably means that they're playing in the backyard. I'll go and check on them. Pleased to meet you, Tracey."

"Why did you keep the children a secret from, Cornell?" Lillie asked when Malcolm had left the room.

"There were reasons. One was that he wanted me to have an abortion when I told him I was pregnant."

Lillie looked stunned. "He didn't tell me any of this. As much as he loves children it's hard for me to believe that he would suggest something like that to you."

"There is something very intense inside Cornell that I don't understand, a kind of barrier he won't let anyone penetrate." She gazed hopefully at Lillie for enlightenment.

"I know what you mean. He's always been a private person like his little daughter." Lillie's brows arched with concern. "Have you ever tried to get him to open up to you?"

"Oh, yes." She sighed. "He has always managed to keep

that reserve. There were rare moments years ago when I thought I was breaking through."

"Well, maybe one day you'll get him to tell you."

Cornell returned with the lemonade and handed it to Tracey. "I hope Mama hasn't been grilling you too much."

Lillie slanted a probing glance at her son. "We were having an interesting conversation."

Cornell anxiously looked from one to the other, then asked, "Where is LaTonya?"

"At the library."

"On Sunday?"

"Your sister would study in her sleep if she could. She's determined to graduate at the top of her class."

"She sounds as determined as her older brother," Tracey remarked glancing at Cornell.

"It runs in the family, I'm afraid." Lillie laughed.

After several hours Cornell and Tracey pulled the twins away from Lion.

"We've got to go, Mama," Cornell said. "I'll be bringing them back before football season starts."

"I sure hope so.

Tracey saw the proud twinkle in Lillie's eyes when she looked at her grandchildren. She would make sure he did. "Give your grandmother a hug," Tracey said to the twins.

Lincoln didn't hesitate. "Goodbye, grandma."

London glanced up at her father. He nodded. With a shy smile she walked slowly over to her grandmother and wrapped her arms around her neck.

Tears stung Tracey's eyes at the poignant exchange. Her breath caught at the look of tenderness in Cornell's eyes.

Chapter 15

"So what do you think of my mother?" Cornell sneaked a quick glance at Tracey, trying to gage her reaction.

"I like her. She doesn't back off from speaking her mind."

"No." He laughed softly. "She never has."

Tracey looked out the window into the darkening night then turned to check on the kids. She smiled because they had barely reached the outskirts of Chicago and London and Lincoln were already asleep.

"I'm glad London finally warmed up to Mama."

"Once she gets to know your mother things'll be better."

"I can tell that Mama really liked you."

"What makes you think so?"

"She took you to see her quilt room. She only shows it to people she likes."

"Your mother makes beautiful quilts."

"When things were at their lowest ebb, she made and sold a lot of them when I was growing up. She refused to let circumstance force us onto the welfare rolls," he said proudly.

"What about your father?" Tracey asked.

Cornell stiffened. "What about him? He walked out

when Malcolm was two weeks old," he said in a hard tight voice. "I really don't want to talk about him, all right?"

"All right." Tracey decided to back off for the time being.

"I didn't mean to snap at you like that, but my father is not a subject I ever discuss."

"Why?"

"Trust me, it's a question better left unanswered."

He had bluntly closed the subject. Tracey couldn't help wondering why he was so hostile when it came to his father.

"Did you have a good time today?" Cornell asked Tracey when they arrived at the Hamilton house.

"Yes, I did and so did London and Lincoln."

He glanced back at his sleeping children. "I hate to wake them up."

"They're so tired I doubt that you can."

He hefted a sleeping child over each shoulder. Tracey went ahead of him, to open the door. As soon as the twins were put to bed, Tracey followed Cornell into the living room.

"You think you'll feel up to doing any furniture shopping tomorrow? The coach switched the morning practice to a general afternoon one."

"I guess so," Tracey said absently.

Cornell frowned. "Aren't you happy about the house, Trace?"

"Of course, I am. Who wouldn't be."

"Then what is it?" His brows arched in concern.

"I'm worried that London will assume too much."

"I don't understand."

"It's just another indication that you and I . . ."

"I see. Is that so bad, Trace? I want us to be a real family as much as she does."

"I want that, too, but—"

"But you're not sure about your feelings for me."

"More like yours for me."

He pulled her into his arms. "You know how much I want you, woman."

"I know you want me, but—do you . . ."

A yearning look came into his eyes. "I care very deeply for you, Trace."

"How deeply?" Her eyes held his.

He lifted her face and kissed her lips. "More than I have ever cared for any woman."

Tracey wondered if she would ever hear him say he loved her. What he said came close and for him it was a start, but had he said it because of his feelings for her or for his children?

"I want to marry you, Tracey."

The touch of his tongue on her lips sent shivers of desire racing through her. And when she opened to him, he explored the inside. When he deepened the kiss, it sent sweet sensations to every part of her body. His lips moved to her ear and nipped gently until she was thoroughly aroused.

"I want to kiss you in the morning and make sweet love to you all night, every night," he whispered against her ear.

"Oh, Cornell," she moaned softly. "I want you too."

"So will you marry me?"

"I want to."

"But?"

"I have to be sure it's for the right reasons."

"All right, Trace. I'll give you time, but not too much time."

"It seems like I've heard those words before."

Cornell nodded. "I spoke them before I knew there was a London and Lincoln. I'm for real, Trace. Give us another chance." He fondly grazed her cheek with his knuckles. "I'd better be going." He bent to kiss her again before he left.

She knew she wanted to marry Cornell. Why was she stalling? *Because he's hurt you in the past.* An inner voice whispered.

Yes I know, but he's changed.

But can you trust him? Are you ready to trust him?

I'll have to risk it if I say yes.

You have some deep soul-searching to do, girlfriend.

Tracey thought they looked like the perfect family when she, Cornell and the twins left the next morning to go furniture shopping. Cornell had talked to the real estate agent, who assured him they could move into the house right away.

She could see the joy in Cornell's eyes when he helped their son choose his bedroom furniture. It definitely had a sports flavor about it. Cornell made sure Lincoln had plenty of study space and a place for books. His attitude about education almost bordered on obsession. And not for the first time she wondered why.

Shopping for London's bedroom furniture was a delight for Tracey. Her daughter's choice was totally feminine, with ivory and gold French Provincial furniture, complete with canopy bed. Here also her father insisted that she have a wide study area and a bookcase.

When it came to the living and dining room furniture, Cornell watched and offered his opinion as they strolled through the showroom. They went through carpet and drapery swatches, color schemes and charts. The kitchen he left strictly to Tracey, since she knew what she wanted in that room.

Tracey came to a bedroom suite that she just had to have. It was semi-modern, done in light mahogany wood with brass and glass trimming. She was glad her bedroom had a lot of windows to pick up the airy comfortable color scheme she had in mind.

Her bedroom.

She stared thoughtfully at the bed and around her. If she decided to marry Cornell, it would be their bedroom. The thought of sharing a bed with him both excited and frightened her. But why should she feel afraid? They had already created two children together.

"Trace, are you all right?" Concern crinkled Cornell's forehead.

"I'm fine." She looked up at him. "Just indulging in a little daydreaming."

"I hope I'm a major participant."

"Oh, you are most definitely." Her mouth curved into a half wick smile.

Was the look he saw in her eyes a promise? Did he dare hope that she was planning to include him in her life permanently?

When they came to sample bathrooms, Tracey chose a sunken aqua and gold-veined marble tub that would easily accomodate two. She saw that the same thought had occurred to Cornell, and she felt her face heat up at that moment of shared intimacy.

"You're really happy about this, aren't you?" Tracey asked Cornell as they all left the furniture store.

"I'd be even happier if you agreed to be my wife, Trace."

"Cornell, you promised not to pressure me."

"I know I did, baby." He shoved his hands in his pockets. "But I can't seem to help myself."

"Are you going to marry daddy?" London asked worriedly.

Tracey looked down at her daughter, wanting to reassure her yet knowing that she couldn't. "I'm still thinking about it, London."

"As long as you do it, everything'll be all right."

"London, I—"

Cornell stopped and hunkered down to his daughter. "We can't rush your mother. She has to come to that decision in her own time. Okay?"

"Okay, but, Daddy, I hope she doesn't take too long," she said, wrapping her arms around her father's neck.

As Tracey stood holding Lincoln's hand, guilt at her indecision churned in her stomach. Marrying Cornell was what she wanted and what her children wanted. But was it really what she needed?

"You do want us to be a family, don't you, Mama?" Lincoln asked.

"We'll always be a family whether I decide to marry your

father or not," she answered.

Her son didn't look convinced and neither did her daughter.

Later when Tracey went in to work, she was greeted by an excited Barb who flashed her engagement ring under her nose.

"Since you were so busy this weekend I didn't get to touch base with you until now. I'm still not sure my feet are touching the ground. I been walking on cloud nine all weekend."

"I take this to mean that you're happy." Tracey laughed.

"I'm more than that, Tracey." A dreamy smile framed Barb's face.

"Well at least he's rich enough to keep you in clothes. You did warn him that you're a shopaholic."

"He knows and it doesn't bother him."

"I hope he knows what he's getting into making a statement like that around you."

"He knows, Tracey. He's so—I don't know how to say it."

"Just say you love the guy and everything about him."

Barb laughed. "Something like that."

"So when's the big day?"

"We haven't decided yet, but I think he's considering the week before Thanksgiving. I don't care. We could do it tomorrow if it was left up to me."

"It's a little impractical during his training season."

"Yeah, I know. There are only a couple of weeks left of that."

Tracey hadn't considered that. She realized how unfair it

was of her to make Cornell wait for an answer. He'd be gone in a matter of days. If she was going to say yes, would it be better to get married before he got well into the season so they could spend some time together?

"Do you have something you need to tell me?" Barb asked.

"Cornell has insisted on buying a house for us."

"Us meaning him, too?"

"Barb, I think I'd better get to work."

"Still avoiding making that big D, aren't you? I can understand why after all you've been through, but, Tracey, you have to get over it and get on with living your life. I mean really living it, taking chances, trusting. There's a special something between you and Cornell. That something is definitely missing when you're with Brice, the nerd."

"Barb!"

"It's the truth, Tracey."

Tracey lowered her gaze. "Brice isn't in the picture anymore."

"So it's the thought of being completely involved with Cornell that bothers you. I have to admit that he seems like an all or nothing type of man."

"He's that all right. He'd want everything a woman had to give."

"You love him, don't you?"

"Of course I love him. Why do you think it's so hard for me to make a decision?"

Barb gave her friend a look of tender sympathy. "You'll make the right one when the time is right. I have confidence in you, girlfriend."

Tracey heard a knock at her office door. "Yes."

"It's your poor old father. Can I come in?"

"Come on in, Daddy. You're no longer poor and you're definitely not old."

"Tell these aching bones that when I wake up in the morning." He laughed and turned on the light. "You still seeking escape these days?"

"Not escape really, Daddy."

"That young man is what you need in your life, Tracey. For the last few years you haven't been completely happy. When he comes into a room your eyes light up. Your mother agrees that you seem happier when you're with him. Don't let fear or insecurity rob you of a second chance at love."

"Thank you for saying that, Daddy."

"But will you follow your old daddy's advice?" He laughed again and added before she could answer. "End of lecture 101. You about ready to go home, daughter?"

Chapter 16

Tracey drove over to the new house. It was only a mile and a half away from her parents' home. The promise of a happy new life stood before her if she chose to take it.

When she walked into the house, she realized that a light was on in London's bedroom. She found Cornell sitting on the window seat with a gift wrapped package on his lap.

"What's in the box?" she asked him.

He looked up at her and smiled. "It's a surprise for London."

Tracey put her hands on her hips. "Is that all you're going to tell me?"

"Yes, it is." He flashed her a devilish grin. "If you want to know what's in here, you'll have to wait until London opens it."

"You're a cruel man, Cornell Robertson. By the way where's your car? I didn't see it when I drove up."

"I had Bubba drop me off. I took my car in for servicing this morning. I was going to walk over to your parents' house when I left here and bum a ride home."

He set the package on the window seat and walked toward her.

Her heart jolted and her pulse throbbed as they always had a way of doing around him.

"I bought one for Lincoln, too. I was going to give them their presents when we came here tomorrow." Cornell took her hand and guided her to the master bedroom. "I have something for you, too, Trace." He opened the closet door. On the top shelf was a box. "You want to open it now?"

"What's in it?"

His mouth twitched with amusement. "Open it and find out."

She ripped the wrapping off the box and lifted out a beautiful terra cotta statuette of a young black woman sitting in a rocking chair with an open book draped across her lap. The face of the woman looked remarkably like Tracey's. Delicately written in gold letters across the pages were the words 'Our love is a love to cherish.'

"Do you like it?"

A soft loving smile touched her lips. "Oh, Cornell, it's beautiful."

"When I saw it, it reminded me of you. I had to get it."

"I'm glad you did." Something released inside her. Her heart suddenly felt as free as an eagle. He'd opened a door on tender as well as volatile emotions that had remained locked away for the last six years. Even though he hadn't said that he loved her, he had done everything he could to show her that he cared.

"The answer is yes," she whispered softly, "I'll marry you."

He took the statuette from her fingers and set it down on the floor then he drew her into his arms and held her close, exulting in the feel of her soft body and the peachy fragrance of her hair. He groaned, closing his eyes letting the rapture take him. "Baby, I want you so damned much."

"And I want you."

He moved to turn out the light.

The darkness had always been Tracey's escape, now it was a form of enlightenment. There was no need for escape. She no longer wanted to escape. She wanted this man with every fiber of her being and the children had nothing to do with it. She wanted Cornell for herself.

Tracey sensed that whatever it was that made him hurt her before had nothing to do with what he had felt for her. His reasons were complicated and deeply entrenched in his mind and it was going to take careful excavation to bring them to the surface and help him deal with them. She would do it, but not tonight. Tonight belonged to them.

The darkness was not complete, a splash of moonlight shone through the window shade throwing the inside of the room into a soft light. His shadowed figure moved toward her. Cornell stopped in front of her and took her face in his hands and lowered his lips to hers.

Pleasure radiated between them. Every nerve ending came alive as Cornell changed the kiss from gently arousing to tenderly demanding.

Tracey opened her mouth to receive the bliss she knew he would give her. The caress of his tongue stroking against the sensitive roof of her mouth left her senses whirling in an essence of sensation so profound she felt as though she were melting in it.

He eased his hands to her throat, then her shoulders. "Oh,

God, Trace," he moaned, nuzzling his cheek against her throat kissing the tender flesh behind her ear. He felt her body quiver.

His sensual message surged through Tracey like electricity through a power line, short-circuiting what little control she possessed.

"You have always belonged to me, Trace." The last time they'd made love she'd held something back from him. He didn't want her to ever hold back anything again.

"I know that now." She rested her head against his shoulder. "For years I've tried to pretend that the bond between us didn't exist. When you came back, I resisted you because I knew you had the power to destroy me. I was afraid to take a chance. Then when we were alone at the lake that first time, I found myself succumbing to you despite everything. I couldn't deny to myself that I still wanted you."

"And tonight?"

She raised her head and gazed into his eyes. "And tonight I want you with everything that's inside me, Cornell. Please, my darling man, make love to me."

"You don't have to beg me to do that, Trace," he whispered hoarsely. "I'll give you all that's in me to give. You're the best thing that ever happened to me, girl. I was just too blind to see it."

Her eyes glowed with the love she felt for him. She whispered against his mouth. "Love me, Cornell."

As he started unbuttoning Tracey's blouse, his hands brushed her skin and made her gasp. He slipped the straps of her bra down and kissed her shoulders. Mere seconds later he freed her breasts and cupped them in his hands, teasing the nipples with his thumbs. A jerky moan escaped her lips as his caress had her breasts growing heavy, throbbing with desire. His mouth seemed to heat as he closed it over her nipple and circled it with his tongue again and again until her heart threatened to leap out of her chest.

He held her up and moved her against the wall as he continued to undress her until her clothes pooled at her feet. As he rubbed his body against hers, his soft T-shirt brushed against her breasts in contrast to the roughness of his jeans that abraded her thighs, the sensual friction making her groan in his ear.

Cornell shuddered at the feel of her warm breath across his face. Groaning desperately he slid his fingers inside the waist of her panties and stroked her stomach before easing his hands around to cup her firm soft buttocks.

"Your skin is so unbelievably soft, Trace," he murmured tenderly as he caught her sighs of pleasure in his mouth.

"You have too many clothes on," she whispered huskily.

"I need you to help me out of them."

"Leave the entire job to me." The shower-fresh scent of his body made her moan, and she closed her eyes with the pleasure of it. Sliding her fingers up under his T-shirt to caress his nipples, she traced her fingers across the tips, smiling when she felt him jerk.

Tracey lifted the shirt over his head and let it fall to the floor. Then as her eyes held his, she unsnapped his jeans, and hooking her fingers into the waistband, pulled him down to the carpet.

The next moment they were on their knees facing each

other. She rubbed her breasts against his, taking pleasure in the way the tiny whorls of chest hair brushed the tips of her breasts. She closed her eyes as he lowered her to the floor and stroked his fingers down her belly to the juncture of her thighs, opening for him as he delved between the protective folds of her femininity. She arched up against his fingers, quivering as he fondled and teased that special place until he felt her quiver.

"I can't stand it, Cornell. I—"

"This is for you, baby," he whispered, continuing to move his fingers back and forth across her throbbing flesh until he felt her explode. While her body still pulsed, he shed the rest of his clothes.

"I wanted to undress you," She pouted.

He grinned. "There's one item left. Do you want to do the honors?"

"Oh, yes." She moved her fingers across the front of his briefs. The feel of his erection through the soft cotton caused the level of desire in her blood to rise again. She rubbed her fingers across the growing swell of his manhood. When a tortured groan left his lips, she pulled his briefs down and pressed her lips against his arousal.

"I can't take any more, Trace!" He moaned. "Let me love you now, girl!"

She straddled his hips and sheathed him deep inside her, the triumphant female enveloping the male.

He cried out arching upward, gripping her hips so that he could delve into the very heart of her. As he began to move against her, she quickly picked up his rhythm and they moved in unison. Her breasts dangled enticingly over his face and he lifted his head to capture her nipple in his mouth. Her wild, wanton cry heated his own desire even further.

When he reversed their positions, bringing her legs up around his hips, he drove himself into her to the hilt. Her body shuddered violently as he pulled almost all the way out then thrust forward hard again and again. He moved deeper, harder, faster. Suddenly she was liquid fire, scorching him into oblivion, as her feminine muscles convulsed around him.

"Yes, yes! Oh, baby, yes!" he shouted, as he let himself go completely.

Tracey continued to ride out every last quiver of sensation until she lay still for a long time. They lay entwined, their breathing gradually returning to a normal range.

"I think you just blew my mind to pieces, Tracey Hamilton," he groaned. "And I thought football was better than this? I should have had my head examined. Only you can make me feel this way, woman."

"I'm glad you're no longer that man."

"So am I."

She began to kiss him again and move her body against his in strong circular motions.

"Oooh, baby, baby." He swallowed hard, his breathing becoming ragged as he began to swell and harden again. He placed his hands on her hips, moving them forward, pushing himself back onto his knees. Her thighs over his, he thrust hard and deep, hard and deep.

"Oh, what are you doing to me?" Tracey cried.

"I'm loving you with all I am and all I will ever be." He stilled and gazed lovingly into her eyes. "With my mind I adore you, my body I possess you, but my soul belongs with yours until the end of time."

"I love you, Cornell."

"And I love you. As it said on the statuette, our love is is a love to cherish. I don't intend to ever let it go. You're mine forever, Trace." He touched her face. "And I do mean forever. Do you understand what I'm saying?"

"Oh, yes, Cornell."

He began to move then, even more vigorously than before, building the levels of ecstasy higher and higher. Then he thrust one last time and together they shattered into a million tiny particles of rapture.

"I'd say we gave this house one hell of a christening, don't you?" Cornell said, once he could speak again.

"The only thing missing is the champagne."

"Were going shopping for an engagement ring tomorrow and then I'm going to take you out and celebrate with a magnum of champagne."

"I'm so happy," she said snuggling against him.

"Hearing you say the words, 'I'll marry you' is almost as good as hearing you tell me you love me."

She rubbed her fingers across his chest. "Are there any other words you want to hear me say?"

"Don't tempt me, woman. I won't be worth a fig at practice tomorrow as it is."

"Oh, all right." She smiled. "Besides, I have to give this bum a ride home."

"I'll get you for that," he threatened.

"You promise?" She moved against him teasingly.

"You can take that to the bank.

"Would it make me a rich woman?"

"Beyond your wildest fantasies."

When Tracey got back to her parents' house, they were in the kitchen drinking coffee. She was bursting over with the need to tell them their good news.

James smiled when he saw the sparkle in his daughter's eyes. "What date have you two chosen for the wedding?"

"The soonest date we can arrange, sir," Cornell answered.

"I'm so happy, Daddy."

"I can see that. And, Cornell, call me James."

Tracey walked over to her mother. "You were right."

"That's a mother's job." Ruby gazed at Cornell. "You'd better make my baby happy, young man."

"I intend to, Mrs. Hamilton," he vowed.

"Please call me Ruby."

"Things are the way they should have always been." James nodded. "Sometimes a man has to lose what is most precious to him and experience life without it before he realizes what he had."

"I'm going to take care of my second chance at happiness, sir—James," Cornell said, then shifted his gaze to Tracey's smiling face. He wanted to see that happiness on it always. He was determined to do everything in his power to make sure she never regretted her decision to marry him.

"We're not needed in here, Ruby," James said. "Let's go to bed and leave these young people alone." He put his arm around his wife's shoulders and guided her out of the kitchen.

"Your parents seem so happy together," Cornell said in a voice filled with wonder.

"They are."

"I can't help—never mind."

"What were you going to say?"

"It's not important. I've got to be getting back to the hotel. You still going to give this bum a ride?"

"Cornell, I—yes, I am." She couldn't help wondering if what he said that wasn't important was more important than he wanted her to believe. Cornell would have to start being more open with her. This man she loved was a complex individual. One day she would come to fully understand him even if she had to make it her life's work.

Cornell glanced at Tracey from the corner of his eye as she drove him to the hotel. He knew she was more than he deserved after the way he had hurt her. She'd borne his children, loved and cared for them without any help from him. What he owed her could never be measured in dollars and cents or any other earthly system of exchange. He owed her the complete truth, but his sterility was a truth he had a hard time dealing with. How was he going to go about telling her.

When Tracey stopped the car, he leaned across the seat and brushed her lips with his. "I'll drop by the restaurant after practice. Always remember how much I care about you."

With a puzzled look on her face, she answered, "I'll remember." As she watched him walk into the lobby, she wondered at his last words. Was there some deeper meaning that she didn't catch?

As she showered later that night, Tracey remembered in vivid detail every phase of their lovemaking. Her breasts were tender from his worship of them and her whole body tingled. She smiled. Cornell was all the sexual stimulation she'd ever want or need.

She could hardly wait until they were married and moved into their new home. She'd make it a home he would be eager to come back to. As she prepared for bed, she couldn't help wishing he were sharing it with her now. But in just a few short weeks they would be the family she and her children wanted them to be.

Morning found Tracey joyfully busy fixing everyone's favorite breakfast.

"I like seeing my only child like this. Remind me to tell Robertson to keep up the good work." James' eyes twinkled. "It's not everyday a man gets his favorite grits, sausage and eggs."

"Yeah right, Daddy. You own a soul food restaurant and can get it any day of the week."

"But not so lovingly prepared by my daughter, I can't."

"Oh, Daddy. I need to talk to you later about taking time off from the restaurant."

"Do you two plan on going away for a honeymoon?" her mother asked.

"I don't know, Mama."

"Keep spoiling us like this and we might not let you get away," James said digging into his breakfast with relish.

"I love you both."

"And we love you, Tracey," Ruby answered softly.

"Is that pancakes I smell?" Lincoln asked, hurrying into the kitchen.

"Sure is." She glanced past him to his sister. "And I made bacon waffles for you, London."

A curious smile on her face, she said, "You look so happy this morning, Mama."

"I am, baby. You're going to get your fondest wish."

"You gonna marry my daddy?" Her eyes rounded.

"Yes, I sure am."

London rushed to Tracey's side and wrapped her arms around her mother's waist. "Oh, Mama, I'm so happy."

"Me, too," Lincoln added, not to be undone, joined them and looked up at her, a big wide grin spread across his face which reminded Tracey of his father's.

❧

"What fairy godfather has been visiting you lately, Robertson?" the coached kidded Cornell after practice. "Whoever he is I'd like to sign him to a contract."

"No fairy godfather. Just the love of a good woman."

"I might have known. The all-American fairy tale of happily ever after. Are congratulations in order?"

Cornell grinned. "Yes, the lady in question has finally consented to take on the job of being my wife."

"I'm happy for you, Robertson." The coach slapped him on the back. "Now maybe, just maybe we'll get a record-breaking football season out of you."

Bubba walked up. "You were a changed man out on that playing field today."

"I can't believe my luck, man. She loves me as much as

I love her. It's more than I ever dared hope for. I'm so close to having it all." He tossed his helmet up in the air. "I have to keep pinching myself to remind myself just what a lucky son-of-a-gun I really am."

"You deserve to be happy, buddy. We'll have to have a bachelor party to top all bachelor parties. It isn't every day the top two studs of the football league sign such exclusive contracts."

"You're crazy, Bubba."

"No," Bubba laughed. "Just crazy in love." Although his friend seemed happy, Bubba could tell by the look in Cornell's eyes that there was something still haunting him. He sure wished he would talk it out with someone.

"Can't we come, Daddy?" Lincoln pleaded the following afternoon.

"Not this time, my man," Cornell answered. "This is something your mother and I want to do alone."

"But why?" he whined.

"It's something special, dummy," London told him.

"I'm not a dummy."

"He certainly isn't a dummy, London," Tracey chided. "I'm surprised at you."

"Everybody knows that people pick out wedding rings by themselves."

"I think we'd better go before World War Three breaks out," Tracey said.

Once inside the car and on their way to the jewelry store, Cornell said, "London and Lincoln sure are excited about the wedding, aren't they?"

"Yeah. They aren't the only ones."

"Are you really happy, Trace?"

"Happier than I ever dared to dream."

"I want you to always be as happy as you are today."

"As long as I have you I will be."

He grew silent, hoping that when he told what he had to, she would still feel that way.

Seated on a velvet cushioned chair at the jewelers, Tracey began to feel nervous when the clerk brought over another tray of rings.

Cornell looked them over and none of them caught his eye. "Don't you have anything else?" he asked the clerk.

"Well we do, but—they're more expensive."

"Get them."

He cleared his throat. "Right away, sir."

"Now these are more like it. What do you think, Trace?"

"I don't know, Cornell." She bit her lip.

"Cornell?" The clerk's eyes widened. "You're Cornell Robertson the football star?"

"I'm Cornell Robertson."

"In that case let me show you some very special rings that we have in the vault."

Minutes later he returned with a tray of two and a half karat or larger engagement rings along with matching wedding bands.

Cornell saw the one perfect ring for his lady. It was a diamond solitaire with seven rubies surrounding it. He picked it up and pushed it on her finger. It was a perfect fit.

"Oh, I love it." Tracey gasped.

He examined the matching wedding band. “We’ll take the complete set.”

The jeweler measured Cornell’s finger for his ring.

“We’ll have it ready for you in a few days, sir,” the jeweler promised.

Tracey sat marveling at the beauty of her engagement ring as Cornell drove. The approaching wedding seemed more real to her now.

After Tracey’s parents and the twins had seen the ring, Cornell insisted that she go get dressed up.

“Where are we going?” Tracey asked.

“Out to celebrate, of course. I promised you a magnum of champagne. One of my teammates recommended The Dreamland Club.”

Lincoln looked pleadingly at his father.

“Not this evening. Your mother and I—”

The boy stuck out his bottom lip ready to stalk from the room, but Cornell stopped him. “We’ll do something tomorrow just the two of us and leave your sister and mother do something together. Okay?”

His faced brightened. “Okay.”

Tracey watched Cornell hug his son, marveling at the rapport between them.

Cornell returned for Tracey, looking handsome in a beige summer suit. The look of appreciation in his eyes said that she looked good in her aquamarine sundress.

At the Dreamland Club Cornell informed the hostess that they were celebrating their engagement and no sooner than they were seated a ballad singer started to sing ‘We’re in this Love Together’.

Tracey sensed that this night, her special night was turning into the fantasy that every woman dreamed about. The Dreamland Club's four rooms, the Western, Modern Nineties, Cinderella and the Moonlit Tropical Night were set up in dream sequences, each having a different romantic theme.

Tracey and Cornell agreed that the Moonlit Tropical Night room was the most romantic of all. Each table was bathed in artificial moonlight. The ceiling had twinkling stars, the walls were painted to look like the Pacific Ocean at night and the sound of the waves lapping against the shore added to the ambiance. Even the menus were printed on giant palm tree fronds.

"This is all so wonderful, Cornell," Tracey whispered as they danced after their meal, "but—"

"But what?" He brushed the top of her head with his chin.

"I want to be alone with you." Her hands slid up his chest. "Could we go to our house?"

"I'm easy," Cornell said as he guided her off the dance floor. "We can do anything you want to do, Trace."

"I thought you looked beautiful in that dress," Cornell murmured, "but seeing you without it—"

"What?" she said flicking a finger over his nipple.

He lifted her into his arms. "I want to do this." Lowering his mouth, he closed it over her nipple.

Tracey moaned as her senses spun away, an aching rush of desire spilled into her core. "I need you inside me,

Cornell." Her whisper was urgent.

He eased them down on the carpet in the master bedroom and covered her body with his own. She moaned, crying out her pleasure when he thrust into her.

"If this isn't heaven I don't know what is," he groaned.

As she arched her body into his, he moved rhythmically against hers and together they found exquiste harmony.

Their passion swiftly soared to an awesome crescendo, shattering like the clash of symbols and eventually ebbing in murmured vibes of fulfillment.

Cornell watched as Tracey dozed. She was his life, his love, his woman, his everything. For the first time ever he felt completely happy.

Cornell put a rush on the delivery dates of their purchases for the house so that it would soon be ready for them to move into. He and Tracey had decided to get married the first week of September and take a two week honeymoon before football season started.

Tracey and the twins visited the house daily, arranging and rearranging the pieces of furniture as they arrived. Cornell spent the afternoons with Lincoln and London. They went to the pet store and got a collie puppy like Lion and named him Lion Two. He helped them build a dog house for their pet and got the materials to construct a doll house for London, which he decided to build himself.

To see the people in her life so happy and content was a dream Tracey had never thought would come true. A little sadly she thought of Brice. She caught glimpses of him from time to time. She wanted to share her happiness with him, but knew it wasn't possible. Maybe later when he accepted the fact that she and Cornell were meant to be together, they could be friends again.

Tracey prepared their first meal in the new house. It was wonderful cooking in such a well equipped kitchen, but the real pleasure was seeing the smiles on her children's faces and the love in their father's eyes when they all sat down to eat dinner together. Life couldn't get any better than this.

She invited Bubba and Barb over to the house to celebrate their respective engagements.

While Bubba and Cornell talked in the living room, Tracey and Barb went into the kitchen to finish preparing dinner.

"I would think that after all the cooking and hostessing you do at the restaurant the last place you would want to spend your free time would be in the kitchen," Barb said.

"This is different, Barb." Her eyes sparkled with happiness. "This is for me, the man I love and my children. We're a family, something I thought we'd never be. Do you know how much that means to me?"

"I have a vague idea," Barb said wryly. "I told Bubba not to expect to chain me to the stove."

"I'm sure you'll make up for your lack of interest in cooking in, shall we say, other ways." Tracey arched her brows wickedly.

Barb answered softly. "Oh, he already has an alternative plan. He wants us to start having a family as soon as possible."

"What do you think about that?" She gazed curiously at her friend.

"I like the idea actually. If I can have children like yours

I don't think I'll mind."

"I've definitely been blessed there." She smiled, thinking about it. "I'm almost afraid to breathe too hard these days for fear that it will all disappear.

"What could go wrong now? I know you love him and he obviously loves you. Look around you." Barb waved her arms expansively. "He's spent a fortune on you and his children."

Tracey laughed. "You *would* put things on that basis."

"I didn't mean it to sound—"

"I know that. You were trying to make a point. Believe me, it was well taken. I'm just being paranoid, I guess. It's just a little bit frightening being this happy after—"

Cornell poked his head around the door. "Are you two going to stay out here gossiping all evening?"

"I'll have you know we were not gossiping." She lifted her chin in mock indignation. "We were having a discussion about a certain pair of hunks in the living room."

"If I could only be a fly on the wall," he kidded.

Tracey walked over to him and kissed him. "You'd get an earful that's for sure."

Later they toasted their "up and coming marriages" with champagne.

Bubba raised his glass. "May we all be as happy for the rest of our lives as we are tonight."

"I second that." Cornell raised his glass. "And I want to add one of my own. To the two most beautiful women in mine and Bubba's universe."

They clinked glasses.

Tracey put on some soft music. Everything was so fresh

and new. Thoughts of the past were just that—past. They were all at the threshold of a whole new life.

"So when are you and the twins going to officially move in here, Tracey?" Barb asked.

"We'll be moving in in a matter of days. The big guy doesn't get to move in until I put that ring through his nose."

Cornell came after her and tackled her to the floor. "What was that remark you made, woman?"

"I meant on his finger." She giggled.

"I'll just bet you did."

Bubba cheered. "That's the best tackle I've seen you execute in a long time, Cornell."

"All I needed was the right incentive. And besides, she has the kind of body I love to land on."

"Why you—"

Cornell stopped Tracey's words with his lips on hers.

"I think it's time we went home to finish our celebration," Bubba whispered loudly to Barb.

"Just watching them gives me ideas."

After Bubba and Barb left, Cornell and Tracey expanded on those ideas and added a few variations of their own.

When they were finally ready to leave, Tracey took one last look in her daughter's bedroom. She gazed lovingly at the half finished doll house in the corner. London was really into dolls, especially baby dolls.

Cornell walked up behind her and kissed the back of her neck. "What are you thinking?"

"I was just wondering if we'll have any more children. London has mentioned on more than one occasion how much she is looking forward to having a baby brother or sister." Tracey felt him stiffen. "Don't you want any more children, Cornell?"

"I think London and Lincoln are enough for me right now. If you're thinking about managing your own restaurant chain, it could be a tricky thing to juggle with energetic children and a demanding husband." He pulled back against his body. "Believe me, I intend to be very demanding."

"Oh, you do, do you? You'll be on the road a lot during the season."

"But there is always the off season." He cupped her breasts.

"I've heard that that's when the players produce the most offspring."

"An interesting theory." He moved his hands down her midriff to her hips. "I'm sure practice of another kind is involved. I always say practice makes perfect."

Her voice turned husky. "I don't think I'll mind being your practice partner."

"I know," he moved his hips against her buttocks, "I won't mind you being mine."

"You still up, man!" Bubba said as he walked through the door of the hotel room and found his friend sitting in front of the TV.

"I can't sleep." He jumped up from the bed and started pacing. "I guess it's all the excitement."

"You sure that's all it is?"

Cornell switched off the television. “What do you mean?”

“I know you, Cornell. There’s something bugging you, man. Can’t you tell me what it is? Maybe I can help you.”

A brooding look came into his eyes. “Nobody can help me with this.”

“You’re supposed to share the good and the bad with the woman you love. Whatever it is I’m sure Tracey will understand.”

He hunched his shoulder. “I know you’re right, it’s just that—it’s hard for me.”

Bubba walked over to his friend and put his hand on Cornell’s shoulder. “I know it is, but you’ve got to do it anyway. If you start keeping things from her now, it’ll wreck your marriage down the road. You’ll have betrayed her trust. I’m sure you don’t want to risk losing Tracey again. She loves you, but if you—”

Cornell sighed heavily. “You’re right. I have to be completely honest with her.”

He felt drained when he finally got into bed. He hoped after he told her the truth she’d still want to marry him.

Chapter 17

Cornell and Bubba had just finished their lunch at the Heaven the next afternoon when Trace came in carrying a box.

Bubba glanced at his watch. You can set your watch by her. I can't say the same for my lady." Bubba shook his head. "Barb'll probably be late to our wedding."

"You'll have to tell her a different hour than planned that's all."

"That's an idea." Bubba laughed jovially.

"I have a surprise for you, love of my life," Tracey announced when she made it to their table.

"What kind of surprise?" Cornell asked, curiously eyeing the box.

"If I told you it wouldn't be a surprise."

"Can't you give me a hint?" he wheedled.

"I could, but I'm not. You'll just have to wait," she said with a mysterious smile and headed in the direction of her office.

Cornell smiled as he watched her. "I love that woman, man," he said, then glanced back at his friend. The expression on Bubba's face made him follow his line of vision. Suddenly his cheerful mood disappeared.

There in the entryway stood his ex-wife, Keysha Barrette, her eyes roving the room. He assumed that the coach had told her where she would likely find him. He wondered what else he could have told her?

"What is she doing here?" Bubba asked, his voice strained. "With Keysha only she and God knows." Cornell knew it was only a matter of time before she spotted him. It was like waiting for red-hot lava to roll down the side of a volcano and cover you. What did she want? His life was finally going in the direction he wanted it to. Why did she have to show up now? He was close, so damned close.

The next moment Barb came sweeping through the door past Keysha to the hostess stand and put her things away. When she turned around the expression on her face said that she recognized who the woman was.

"May I show you to a table?" she offered politely.

"No." Keysha smiled. "I see the person I'm looking for."

Heads turned as the elegant statuesque model glided through the restaurant toward Cornell's table.

He had to admit that she was one of the most beautiful women he'd ever seen, but she didn't come close to firing his blood the way Tracey could. They'd tried to make a go of their marriage, but in the end nothing had worked. He'd never gotten over Tracey for one thing and there were other problems besides.

He noticed that she was dressed in a short, close-fitting white dress that clung to every curve of her nearly six-foot slender frame. Her skin was the color of burnished gold and she wore her long cinnamon-brown hair loosely around her shoulders. Her most arresting feature was her large hazel eyes.

"I'd forgotten what a fox Keysha was," Bubba murmured.

"She's that all right."

"The coach told me I'd find you here, since they served the best food in town." She gazed at Bubba. "How goes it, Bubba? It's been a long time."

"It sure has. Everything is fine with me. How about yourself?"

"Great," she answered absently, immediately focusing her attention back on Cornell. "And I hope a lot better for me and you. How's the training going, babe?"

Cornell finally found his voice. "What are you doing here, Keysha?"

"As greetings go that rated a zero on a scale of one to ten. You could have said, how are you Keysha? How's life been treating you? Or something to that affect."

"Keysha—"

"Oh, I'm not offended. May I join you?"

As she made to sit down Bubba got up from his chair. "You can take my chair. I'll leave you two to talk. It was nice seeing you again, Keysha."

As she watched Bubba leave, she said to Cornell, "I always liked him. He knows when to make himself scarce. The hostess his new love interest?"

"Look, Keysha. I thought we said everything there was to say the last time we were together. I was more than generous with the divorce settlement."

"I'm not here to bash you about that. We were married

for three years, Cornell. I thought that maybe—"

"What we had is over."

She crossed her long legs. "You still haven't come to grips with your problem, have you?"

"Since we're no longer married, it's my business, not yours."

"I have to take exception to that. It was a problem that destroyed our marriage. I have a better insight into what you were feeling then. I want us to have another chance, that's why I'm here."

A waitress came to the table.

"The lady won't be staying," Cornell said sharply and the woman walked away.

Keysha hooked her arm around his. "Where can we go to talk?"

"Haven't you been listening to me. We have nothing to talk about." As he tried to extricate his arm, he saw Tracey. When Curry called to her from the kitchen before she could head in his direction, he breathed a sigh of relief. "All right, Keysha, I'll take you somewhere more private." He rose from his chair, and pulling Keysha to her feet, hustled her toward the door.

"Cornell, what—"

"Pay for the lunch, Bubba, I'll straighten you up later." Without waiting for an answer, Cornell rushed Keysha out the front door.

"Where are we going?" Keysha demanded.

"To my hotel room," he snapped.

Keysha smiled lazily. "That's about as intimate as you can get."

"Intimacy isn't quite what I had in mind. We won't be disturbed there."

"You're different."

"Time changes all of us."

Minutes later Cornell ushered Keysha inside his hotel room.

"Have a seat."

"The bed would be much more comfortable," she said, circling her arms around his neck. Before he could say anything she took his mouth in a devouring kiss. When he tried to pull away, she deepened it, savoring every moment.

Cornell removed her arms from around his neck and pulled her away from him. "I brought you here so we could have it all out, not to make love to you, Keysha."

"You have the most kissable mouth I've ever seen, did you know that? We can talk later, baby."

When she moved to kiss him again, he turned away from her. "I said we're going to talk, and I meant it, Keysha."

"The only kind of talking I want to do with you is body language. You know how good I am at that. I want us to get remarried as soon as possible."

"I don't."

"Why?" Her eyes narrowed. "Have you found somebody else?"

"Yes, I have."

"And you want to marry this woman? Have you told her everything?"

"Whatever I've told her is none of your business, Keysha."

"You haven't told her then." She crossed her arms over

her chest and walked over to the window. "You'll have to tell her the truth sometime, you know."

"Keysha, the only problem I have at the moment is you."

She walked back over to him. "I never was the problem. I'm the only woman who truly understands you, Cornell."

"It's over, Keysha."

"Is it?" She gazed thoughtfully at him. "I wonder. Things would have worked out between us."

"No, they wouldn't have. At first I tried to convince myself that they would. The problem was that I've always loved Tracey. That was the reason our marriage really never stood a chance."

She put her hands on her hips. "You may think that was the reason, but I know you loved me when you asked me to be your wife. We were always so good in bed."

"Making love and being in love are two different things. I did love you, in a way, but—

"But not in the same way you love this Tracey?" She raised her brows inquiringly.

"It's hard to explain," he muttered uneasily.

Keysha smiled and slid her arms around his neck and snuggled up against him. "I can still make you want me." She rubbed her hand across the front of his jeans.

"It's no good, Keysha. What Tracey and I have is special."

"It can be special between us," she whispered, touching him again.

"It can never be that way between us. I love Tracey and she loves me."

Her eyes narrowed. "If she knew the truth I wonder how

long this relationship would last."

"I don't think it'll change how she feels about me."

"You think!" She twisted her lips in a cynical smile. "You can't run away from your problem forever. You'll only carry it into this new relationship, don't you see that? I wonder if you really love this woman. Or is it—"

His eyes bore into hers. "All you need to know is that it's over between us."

"All right," she said, eyes flashing. "You go ahead and marry this woman. Mark my words, you'll come to realize what a big mistake you're making." She grabbed up her purse and left.

What Keysha said worried Cornell. She was right about one thing he had to tell Tracey the truth.

Tracey looked around for Cornell after leaving the kitchen. She walked over to where Barb and Bubba were sitting.

"Where's Cornell?" she asked.

"He—ah—had to leave," Barb faltered.

Tracey frowned looking from one to the other. "There's nothing wrong, is there?"

"Nothing he can't handle," Bubba said strongly.

"Well, is he coming back?"

"I don't know. He didn't say, but knowing him, he'll be here by the time you get off."

"He'd better be or else he won't get his present." She laughed and walked away.

"I hope you're right about him handling things," Barb sighed. "Because Keysha Barrette doesn't look like the kind of woman who'll be easily handled, or one who gives up anything she wants."

"She didn't use to be," Bubba admitted. "I doubt if she's changed. She saw Cornell and decided that she wanted him and that was that."

"What do you think will happen?" Barb asked, her voice worried.

"I don't know, Barb. I wish I did."

Cornell came back at closing time as Bubba had predicted.

"Did you take care of that urgent business?" Tracey asked him.

"Yeah," he answered too quickly then hastened to cover it. "Now no more stalling. I want to see my surprise."

Tracey frowned, throwing a glance at him. "Is anything wrong? You don't seem like yourself."

"Everything is right." He smiled, "because I'm here with you."

Not completely convinced, she gave him a half smile. "I'll drive my car home, you can follow me, then you can take me to the house." Her smile brightened several watts. "I can't believe that the twins and I will be moving in tomorrow."

Caught up in the happiness she exuded, he drew her into his arms. "You're the most important thing in my life, Trace. No matter what happens in the future I want you to remember that."

"Nothing is going to spoil our happiness this time. I won't let it, so stop talking like the voice of doom. I love you, Cornell Robertson." She kissed him hungrily. "If we don't stop this, I'll never get home."

"And I won't get my present."

"Everything is so perfect, Cornell," Tracey said when they arrived at their new house. "Lincoln can't stop raving about the dog house you helped him build. And the doll house you made London is precious. I never knew you were so good with your hands."

"Oh, you didn't, huh." He moved his fingers across her breasts. "Maybe I've neglected to properly demonstrate my expertise." He placed his hands on her hips and pulled her against him, splaying his hands over the soft padding of her buttocks.

"I'm beginning to see how clever your hands are." She pulled away from him and picked up the box. "First your present before you get carried away."

He gave her a quick kiss. "Before who gets carried away?" He moved the gift up and down. "It's heavy."

"Stop trying to guess what's in it and open it up."

Cornell ripped off the wrapping and opened the box. Inside was a plaque with two pairs of bronzed baby shoes welded to the base. Behind each pair were baby pictures of London and Lincoln with the date they were born inscribed.

"Oh, Trace. They were so beautiful. Damn it, I've missed so much."

"They were nine months old when those pictures were taken. You won't ever have to wonder about what you've missed any more. There's something else in the box."

He lifted out the plaque and beneath it was a photo album. He opened it and there on the first page were pictures taken right after the twins were born. As he looked through the book there were pictures of London and

Lincoln at every stage of their development. His eyes misted with emotion.

"I love you so much, Cornell."

"And I love you, Trace." He put the photo album on the coffee table, moved to where Tracey stood and cupping her face in his hands, sealed his avowal of love with a kiss so touchingly tender it took her breath. He raised his mouth from hers and gazed into her eyes. "I love you," he whispered.

"I don't think I'll ever get tired of hearing you say those words."

He skimmed his hands up her thighs to her slender hips. "I want to touch all of you, Trace. You have on way too many clothes, woman."

"So do you."

"Let's do something to remedy the situation," he groaned.

As she moved to unbutton her blouse, he took over the task and as he uncovered her, he kissed every inch of skin he exposed. By the time she was naked from neck to waist, her skin was tingling. Her nipples had stiffened to pebble-like hardness and she moaned when he took one into his mouth and circled it with his tongue. The roughness of his tongue drove her crazy and she felt the damp readiness between her thighs.

He removed her skirt and panties and then his fingers found the pulsing center of her desire, stroking it again and again until she cried out, arching against them.

"Oh, Cornell, I have to touch you. I have to. Let me love you," came her urgent plea. Without waiting for his help, she pulled his T-shirt off and ran her tongue over his nipples.

To him it felt as though tongues of fire were flicking him. The touch of his jeans against his hardened sex was almost painful. He let her remove the rest of his clothes, crying out at the abrasion of fabric against his aroused flesh.

"Ssh, I'll kiss and make it better," Tracey whispered.

He jerked against the touch of her lips. "Oh, Trace, what are you doing to me?"

"I want to touch every part of you." She stroked him again.

Cornell managed to ease back from her and gain a measure of control. "We'll never make it to the bed otherwise, and I'm looking forward to christening it properly."

He lifted her in his arms and headed for the bedroom.

They made wild, sweet love the first time. The second loving was tender, almost reverent, a physical celebration of their love, renewing the promises they'd made.

Later, as they lay entwined, he kissed the top of her head then her forehead.

"There's something I have to—"

"Not tonight, Cornell. The night belongs to us. Tomorrow is soon enough. I just want to keep you all to myself for a few more minutes before we have to leave."

"All right, but tomorrow we talk. There are things that-"

She stopped his words with a kiss as her fingers slid around his manhood. In moments they were again caught up in passion, embracing esctasy, exploding in glorious abandonment.

"So today's the big day," James said, sipping his morning coffee. "Where are the twins by the way?"

"They're so excited about the move." Ruby said with a smile. "They were having a discussion about what box to put what toy in."

"You sure you don't need any help moving, Tracey?" her father asked.

"No, thanks, Daddy. Cornell is going to take care of the big boxes."

"That young man has really come a long way in my estimation. I'd say he was as eager as London and Lincoln for you all to get moved in."

"It's hard to believe that he ever suggested . . ." Her mother looked at Tracey. "You know what I—"

"I know what you mean, Mama. I still haven't learned why he was so adamant about that, but I will."

"Has Keysha left town?" Bubba asked Cornell as they rode down on the elevator to the hotel dining room to eat breakfast. "I don't know. She should have after our 'discussion' yesterday."

The hostess led them to a table.

"You laid it all out for her, then?"

"Yeah," Cornell muttered.

"She didn't take it too well if your expression is any indication."

"You know Keysha." He shrugged.

"She's one very determined lady. Do you think she might still cause trouble between you and Tracey?" Bubba asked.

"If she's wise she won't."

"I'd make sure she leaves town if I were you."

"You're right. I'm going to attend to that right now." Cornell had a waiter bring a phone to the table.

"Knowing Keysha's tastes, she's probably staying at the Ramada since that's the best hotel in Springfield. Cornell got the number from information and punched it in.

A smile of relief washed over Cornell's face a few minutes later. "She checked out early this morning."

"We'd better hurry up and eat so we won't be late for practice."

Chapter 18

"Lincoln, don't you and Lion Two track dirt into my kitchen!" Tracey shouted out the back door. Things were in surprising order considering the confusion of moving. She never knew she had accumulated so much stuff.

There were boxes and boxes of toys and clothes to sort through plus her crystal and books to unpack. But at least she'd gotten the living room in reasonable order.

Tracey peeked in London's room. She was unpacking doll clothes and lovingly putting them away in the wardrobe Cornell had built for that purpose. If he ever quit playing football he could make a fortune doing carpentry work. She laughed. Somehow she couldn't see the football league's MVP doing that.

She heard a car pull up in front of the house and started for the door. Had Cornell played hooky from practice to be with them? Her smile changed from one of anticipation to a frown of confusion when she saw a tall woman climb out of a taxi and head up the walk. By the time she reached the porch, Tracey recognized her from the pictures she'd seen on the covers of the top fashion magazines. It was Keysha Barrette, Cornell's ex-wife!

Tracey opened the door. "May I help you?" she asked.

"You must be Tracey Hamilton." Keysha smiled, extending her hand. "I'm Keysha Robertson. May I come in?"

Tracey was in a state of shock. What was this woman doing here? "Yes, do come in."

Keysha's mouth twitched with amusement when Tracey didn't shake her hand. "Such warm hospitality."

"We don't know each other. Why are you here?" Tracey demanded. "I presume it's about Cornell since he's the only thing we have in common."

Keysha looked Tracey up and down. "I wanted to see the woman he's so determined to marry."

It may have been what she said, but Tracey was sure that the reason the woman really came there was to size up the competition.

Keysha wandered around the room. "He bought you this house, I take it."

"That's really none of your business, Ms. Barrette," she said tightly.

"The name is still Robertson, Ms. Hamilton."

"Let's not play games, all right? What did you come here for?"

"As I said before I wanted to see the woman who thinks she can just take what belongs to someone else and not expect a fight."

"I'm not taking anything from anyone else. You and Cornell are divorced. I'd say that leaves him free to marry whomever he pleases."

"He still cares about me."

"That may very well be true, but I'm the one he's marrying. Now if you would—"

"Mama, tell Lincoln to leave my things alone. He has one of my doll's dresses and he's waving it in front of Lion Two."

Lincoln came running in after her. "I didn't hurt her dumb old doll dress. Me and Lion Two just want to have some fun."

"Where are your manners?" Tracey said more sharply than she intended. "We have a guest."

"I'm sorry."

"We're sorry."

They said in unison.

"I want both of you to say hello to Ms. Barrette and then go play in your room or outside until I call you."

"Hello, Ms. Barrette," they chorused.

"I'm Lincoln and this is my sister London," Lincoln introduced. "Pleased to meet you."

Keysha sat down on the couch and studied the two children for a moment then she smiled. "I'm pleased to meet you, too."

The twins gazed curiously at this tall pretty lady.

"She's not one of our cousins, is she, Mama?" Lincoln innocently asked.

"No, she's not related to us, she's—"

"A friend of your father's," Keysha finished.

"You know our Daddy? He's a great football star, you know," Lincoln spouted importantly.

"Yes, I certainly do." She smiled knowingly at Tracey. "And I know him very well as a matter of fact."

Tracey cleared her throat. "Ms. Barrette and I need to talk. You two go play *now.*"

They picked up on the edge in their mother's voice and obediently said their good byes and left the room.

"I found out you had children, but I had no idea they were *his* children. It explains a lot."

"What do you mean?"

"You must have been one of his college flings that resulted in, shall we say, 'little consequences.'"

"Listen, Ms. Barrette—"

"The name is Keysha Robertson. You lucked out, didn't you, Ms. Hamilton? Cornell went on to become a very rich super star. You think you have all the cards stacked in your favor. I must say they look just like him, at least his son does."

"So why are you here? What's the point of all this?"

"The point is, *honey*, that Cornell still loves me. You can produce a hundred bas—children and that fact won't change."

"If he loves you so much then why aren't you still together?" She countered.

"There were problems." A triumphant light shone in her eyes. "But now that you've solved the biggest one, we can eventually get back together."

"What are you talking about?"

She rose from the couch, towering over Tracey. "Cornell likes children. Don't you find it a little strange that he doesn't have any others?"

"A lot of couples choose not to have a family. Maybe he didn't want children at the time you were married to him."

"Maybe, but that's not the reason we didn't have any together."

"Well, what is the reason? I can see that you're dying to tell me what it is."

"He's the reason we didn't have any children."

Suddenly Tracey recalled his statement that London and Lincoln were enough children for him. She knew that he liked children. And he said he loved her. None of this was making any sense to her.

"I see he hasn't told you."

"Told me what!" She exclaimed in frustration as she jumped to her feet.

"I guess to find out that he has children must have made him think he'd hit the lottery."

"What hasn't Cornell told me?" Tracey practically shouted.

"A year after we were married he was in a motorcycle accident and almost died," Keysha said smuggly. "I can see that you didn't know about that either."

Tracey shot her a belligerent look. "Get to the point, Ms. Barrette."

"The accident changed him. He withdrew into himself, shutting out everything and everybody. For a while we weren't sure he'd return to playing football. Cornell is a very private person."

"I know that."

"Do you really?" She studied Tracey intently for a moment. "You don't know just how private, but you will. It was two years later that we decided to end the marriage."

"What has all this got to do with—"

"I tried to convince him that we could work things out if he just gave it time."

"And you think enough time has passed, am I right?" Tracey bit the inside of her cheek. "Is that why you came looking for him? Too much time has passed, Ms. Barrette. You're too late."

"I thought so, too, when I found out he was getting married."

"How did you find out?"

"He told me," she revealed with obvious pleasure.

Tracey's eyes widened in shock. "You've seen him!"

"I came to your restaurant yesterday after finding out from the coach where Cornell usually ate his meals and spent his time."

"You mean you were in my—he never—"

"Oh, I'm not surprised," she said condescendingly. "He was never very good at that. It always took someone close to him to—"

Tracey nodded her head. "I get it, Ms. Barrette. And you think you're that someone close. Right?"

"You're smarter than I gave you credit for."

"Now wait a minute, you can't—"

"Save it, Tracey. I didn't come here to insult you."

"Then why in the hell did you come here?" she demanded.

"To thank you actually."

"Thank me!" She eyed her suspicously. "For what?"

"You did something for him that neither I nor any other woman will ever be able to do—give him children."

"I don't understand."

"Cornell is sterile, Tracey dear."

"I don't believe you!" She whirled away from her then swiftly swung around. "That's impossible, he—"

"Has children? That's right. Children you gave him years ago. The motorcycle accident I mentioned left him unable to father a child. I tried to get him to consider adoption, but he wouldn't. Because he couldn't give me a baby is what led to the break-up of our marriage. So now do you see why your children are so important to him, to us?"

"Oh, God!" Tracey closed her eyes. Could that be the real reason he was marrying her? No, it couldn't be true, her tortured mind cried out. Cornell loved her.

"Now that he has children, he'll come to realize that his future is with me unless, of course, you make waves."

"Make waves?" she echoed the words numbly.

"You know, insist that he marry you. You really shouldn't make it a condition that he marry you so he can be a father to his children."

Tracey's eyes blazed. "You don't know a damn thing about his relationship with his children or with me."

"I know one thing. He'll do anything to get his children. Think about it, Tracey. He's a wealthy man. After you marry him, he'll find a way to get his children and come back to me."

"I think you'd better get the hell out of my house, Ms. Barrette, before I rip your face off."

Keysha laughed. "Before I go, I want you to remember one thing."

"And what's that?" She replied with mounting rage.

"He really loves me," Keysha said confidently. "I came

here to tell him that we could work something out. I'm glad to see he's worked things out for himself. You're the only obstacle in the way of complete happiness for us. If you love him let him go, Tracey. Let him be with the woman he truly loves."

Keysha walked to the front door. "I love Cornell. I'm willing to accept another woman's children if it'll make him happy. What sacrifice are you willing to make to that end?"

Tracey collapsed on the couch, so numb and disoriented with shock she barely heard the cab drive away.

Cornell was sterile! Was he marrying her just to get her children? No! That couldn't be true! She refused to believe that.

Tracey laughed, her voice rising, her mind teetering on the point of hysteria. Six years ago he couldn't suggest fast enough that she get an abortion and now— She bit her bottom lip in anguish as tears scalded down her face. Now he wanted the children he had once urged her to get rid of! And in order to get them he was willing to marry her!

She groped desperately inside her mind for some plausible explanation. He wanted her before he'd known about the twins. They made love with such wild sweet abandon. He said that he loved her. If that were true then why hadn't he confided in her about his condition?

Keysha Barrette—Robertson had to be lying.

Did she? Why didn't he tell you she had come to the restaurant?

Bubba and Barb had been there yesterday. They had to have seen her, she realized. That explained why they seemed so edgy and evasive. Had that look in Bubba's eyes been one of sympathy? God forbid, pity! She shook her head to dispell that awful notion.

"Is it all right to come in now, Mama?" Lincoln asked from the doorway. "Did that lady leave?"

London ran over to her mother. "Mama, why are you crying? What's wrong? Did that lady say something to hurt your feelings?"

"I'm all right." Tracey wiped the tears away. "I just got something in my eye."

"Are you sure you're all right?" London asked suspiciously.

Tracey knew she had to pull herself together. London was a very perceptive child and picked up on everything. Tracey smiled. "Yes, I'm sure. Lincoln, you didn't track up the kitchen floor, did you?"

"No, Mama." He grinned sheepishly. "At least not much. I left Lion Two outside."

"I want you two to wash up for lunch. And don't give me an argument, young man."

Tracey noticed that London was observing her very carefully. "You, too, young lady."

London hesitated for a moment then turned to do as she'd been told.

Tracey sighed. What was she going to do? Her children had gotten to know their father and expected their mother to marry him.

Acting on automatic pilot, she went out to the kitchen to prepare lunch. The pain of betrayal twisted inside her. It hurt even more this time around. How could he have kept something this important to himself? Love meant sharing.

She had thought they were doing that. He'd been more open than he had in the past. Why hadn't he told her the truth?

He'd confided so many of his hopes and dreams in her. Why couldn't he have trusted her with this unless what Keysha had said was true and he really *did* love her more.

Tracey heard a truck drive up. It had to be the furniture people bringing the last of the furniture she ordered. After they'd gone, she remembered that Cornell would be there in less than an hour to eat lunch with her and the twins.

She couldn't see him now! She had to have time.

Time to do what, Tracey?

Tracey reached for the kitchen extension and punched in her mother's phone number. "Has Daddy left for the restaurant yet? Can you get him to bring you over right now? Nothing's wrong—I just need to run an errand."

Four hours later, Tracey turned her car into the driveway. She saw the silver Lexus parked in front of the house and knew she would have to face Cornell. With a weary sigh she got out of the car.

The twins ran ahead of their father to meet her.

"You've been gone so long, Mama!" Lincoln exclaimed.

"I'm sorry I'm so late," she said, forcing her lips into a happy smile. "There were—things I had to take care of."

"I'm glad you're back." London gave her mother an extra hug. "Daddy's been keeping us. We took Nana home. He said, if it was all right with you, he'd treat us to pizza tonight."

"That sounds good, huh, Mama?" Lincoln angled for her agreement.

Tracey half smiled. "Sounds wonderful, baby."

Cornell could see the enthusiasm wasn't there and wondered what could be bothering Tracey.

At the pizza place he saw how she just picked at her food. And on the way home how she only spoke when someone asked her a question.

After the twins were bathed and put to bed, Cornell followed Tracey into the living room. As he pulled her into his arms, he felt her stiffen and he frowned. "What's the matter, Trace?"

"Where did you disappear to the other day?"

He looked away guiltily. "I, ah, had something to take care of."

Her chin lifted. "The same thing I had to take care of this afternoon?"

"You're not making any sense."

"The something we had to take care was your ex-wife, Keysha Barrette Robertson."

Cornell's heart dropped to his shoes. "You know that Keysha was at the Heaven?"

"Oh yes. The lady in question came to see me today and took great pleasure in telling me that."

His hands fell from her shoulders and his jaws tightened. "What did she tell you?"

"Does it really matter." Tracey glared daggers at him. "She told me something you should have."

"Trace, I—"

"When were you planning on telling me the truth?" she said, fighting the stinging tears that threatend to fall from her eyes. "Next week? Next year? Never?"

"I—" He turned away from her.

She walked around in front of him. "I think I had every right to know about something that affects our future together, Cornell," she cried, stabbing her finger into his chest. "When I mentioned having other children, you should have told me then. Why didn't you?"

He cast her a pain-filled look. "I don't know."

"Did you ask me to marry you because you thought that was the only way you could get close to your children? I told you that we didn't have to be a package deal."

"Trace, no, damn it." He raked his fingers over his head. "I love you, I told you that. I love my children, but—"

"But you wouldn't think of marrying their mother just to get them? Right?" she said, fury almost choking her.

"No." He reached for her. "You've got to believe that."

She moved a step back. "Do I? Your ex said that because you couldn't have children it led to the break up of your marriage. Is that true?" she demanded.

"Yes, it is, but—"

"Then what she said was all true?"

"Trace, listen to me. I love London and Lincoln, but I would never use you to get them."

"That's funny, isn't it." She smiled without humor. "You once thought I'd use a pregnancy to force you to marry me."

"That was then. Things are different this time."

"Apparently not that different. You've been keeping secrets."

"Keeping secrets? He laughed bitterly. "You mean the way you kept London and Lincoln a secret from me all these years? And you *dare* to talk about keeping secrets?"

"You never wanted them, Cornell," she grated out.

"Tracey." He reached his hand out to her again. "You don't know how much I regretted what I told you that day."

"So you say *now*. I want to know why you didn't tell me Keysha was in town?"

"I thought I could convince her to leave without causing any problems. Evidently I was wrong." His jaw twitched and tightened in suppressed anger, and he turned away from her.

"Were you trying to convince her to leave or just to bide her time until you could get London and Lincoln away from me?"

He swung around violently. "To do what?" he demanded.

"You'd have the children you want. And if she waited until after you divorced me, you could marry her and have it all."

"That's crazy. I want to be with you, you know I do." He grabbed her and pulled her toward him, bending his head to take her mouth. He only meant to show her that she had no business questioning his feelings for her, but the moment he tasted her sweet mouth he lost control.

Tracey struggled against him at first, but his passion ignited hers like a match touched to a piece of paper.

Within moments they were tearing each other's clothes off, and they came together in wild savage possession on the living room carpet.

When it was over, Tracey wound her arms around his neck and cried.

"I'm sorry, Trace, I never meant to hurt you."

She sniffed, pulling back. "I think you'd better go."

"Tracey, we have to talk about this. Surely you don't

believe everything Keysha said?"

She tilted her chin up, wiping at her eyes. "I don't know what to believe."

"If I wanted Keysha, do you think I could make love to you like I just did?" he asked as he pulled his clothes back on.

"We all know a man doesn't have to be—"

"Don't say it, Tracey!" His eyes blazed with fury. "You're right. I had better go."

After he left, Tracey gathered her clothes and stumbled down the hall to her room. Why did she have to love this man so much? Nothing seemed to stop her from loving him, not pride, not self-respect, nor years of separation. But no matter how much she loved him, she knew she couldn't trust him.

Chapter 19

Cornell was heading for the elevator when the hotel clerk called to him to tell him there was someone in the lounge waiting for him. He saw Keysha the moment he entered and stormed over to her table.

"Why did you do it, Keysha?" he spat.

"Sit down and we'll talk about it." She smiled.

Cornell noticed the curious onlookers staring at him and sat down. He said in a voice only she could hear. "I could break your damned neck for what you've done."

"I just told the woman the truth," she said matter-of-factly.

He glowered at her. "What truth? You lied through your teeth and you know it."

"Calm down, baby," she uttered gently. "We both know you didn't mean what you said to me yesterday."

"Do we?" He grabbed her arm and said through clenched teeth. "Do you know what you did, damn you?"

"I stopped you from making the biggest mistake of your life, that's what. Tracey Hamilton is all wrong for you. Just because she had your children doesn't mean you have to sacrifice your whole future. There are ways for a father to gain custody of his children, you know."

"You refuse to see the real truth. I happen to love Tracey

and it's not because of the children the way you seem to think." He curled his hands into fists, trying to keep control of his temper. "I would never, never try to take them away from their mother. Besides, you don't know the circumstances."

Keysha put her hand on his and gazing into his eyes, she said in a low sultry whisper. "Explain them to me, baby."

"No." He pulled his hand away. "That's between me and Tracey, no one else. Keysha, I don't love you any more."

"You don't mean that," she said with a you-must-be-joking look on her face. "You're just fascinated by this woman because she's the mother of your children. It'll wear off."

"It'll never wear off," he said emphatically.

"You care about me." She flashed him a confident smile. "I know that."

"I'll always care about you, but, Keysha, caring is not loving. Maybe I'm saying this badly, but I've never really loved anyone but Tracey. It's the main reason our marriage failed. Her ghost was always there haunting my mind and soul."

"Then why didn't you marry her?"

"There are reasons that I won't go into with you."

"You know what your problem really is?"

He sighed. "I'm sure you're going to tell me."

"You're a much too private person. I told Tracey that we understood each other." She laughed. "That was a joke. I wouldn't have even found out the doctors' findings if I hadn't overheard them discussing your case. You don't share any of yourself with anybody."

"I would have with Tracey if you'd stayed out of it. I love her, Keysha."

She sat back in her chair hard and sighed. "I'm finally

starting to believe you. I really thought we could—"

"There's someone out there for you." He put his hand on hers. "I'm just not that man."

Keysha cleared her throat. "What are you going to do?"

"I don't know."

"I really messed things up, didn't I?"

"I can't put all the blame on you. I should have been honest with Tracey from the jump. Now I have my work cut out for me."

"I said and did what I did because I love you. You know me when I want something."

"You have a one-tracked mind. Bubba reminded me about that. I should have known when you walked away what you might do."

She drew invisible circles with her finger on the tablecloth then looked up at him. "It's really over, isn't it?"

"Yeah, it is." He rose from his chair. "Take care." He lifted his hand in a farewell gesture and walked away.

Tracey called her father to tell him she wouldn't be in to work.

"Are you sick? You didn't hurt yourself moving?"

"No, Daddy, it's nothing like that."

"What's the matter? And don't tell me nothing because I won't believe you."

"The marriage is off," she said dully.

"What happened? You two seemed so happy the other day."

"I don't want to get into it over the phone, Daddy."

"It's one of those times when a parent is completely helpless to help his child, isn't it?"

"I'm afraid so. This is something I have to work out for myself."

"Take as much time as you need to sort through it, all right?"

Tracey dropped the twins off at the Play School Center and drove out to Lake Springfield where they'd had their picnic. She didn't want to go back to the empty house. There was plenty of work to do, but she just couldn't gear herself up to do it.

Thoughts from the night before flooded her mind. After what she'd found out how could she have let him make love to her. She should hate his guts for not telling her the truth, but she didn't, she couldn't. She may not trust him, but she still loved him.

Trust was a basic part of love and without it— Tears started to fall from her eyes. She reached inside her purse for a tissue and encountered her package of birth control pills. She realized that she'd forgotten to take them the last two days.

Since Cornell was sterile, she thought ironically, there was no need to bother so she tossed them into a nearby trash container, then focused her thoughts on her children. She was sure that London had guessed that something was wrong. How was she going to tell her children that she wasn't going to marry their daddy? How was she going to handle it with them?

Most importantly, how was she going to handle her own emotions? All she had to do was look at Cornell and she melted. It was an impossible situation. She would just have to stay away from him.

And what about his feelings for his ex-wife? Could she really believe him when he said he didn't love Keysha?

He said that he loved *me* not Keysha. I want to believe

him. God only knows how much. I know Cornell wants me as I want him.

If he really wanted to be with Keysha he would be with her, wouldn't he? Keysha had been his wife after all.

She was so confused. She didn't know what to believe, how to feel.

You love him, Tracey.

Yes, she loved him, she admitted. She'd loved him six years ago, too. He'd hurt her then and he'd hurt her now with his inability to discuss his problems and hang-ups. She needed to share not only his dreams and his bed, but his problems, his anxieties— everything.

What it boiled down to was trust, and since it was lacking on both their parts, their relationship was doomed. How were they ever going to make their way back to each other, if they ever did make it back to each other?

"You've been down ever since last night. What happened?" Bubba asked Cornell.

"Keysha paid a visit to Tracey."

"And?"

Cornell hesitated for a moment. "I never told you this, but you remember when I had that motorcycle accident?"

"Yeah?"

"It was more serious than I led you to believe." Cornell walked over to their hotel room window and looked out. "There was internal damage."

"What kind of internal damage? Bubba asked, his voice filled with concern for his friend. "Where?"

"In the groin area." He turned and looked at Bubba, his eyes were sad. "They thought that I would heal, but—"

"You mean you're sterile!"

"Yeah," he said bleakly. "After the doctor gave us the go ahead, Keysha and I tried for two years, but nothing happened. I was tested six months ago and my condition hadn't changed. I'm sterile."

"It could happen, though?"

"Anything's possible, but in my case it's not very likely. It's been three years and no change."

"I'm sorry, man."

"Me, too. More than anything I wanted to have more children with Tracey. Every time I hear my daughter talk about having a baby brother or sister it tears me up inside."

"At least you have London and Lincoln. What about Tracey?" he asked. "How did she take what Keysha told her?"

"She's angry of course, but most of all she's very hurt."

"She has every right to feel that way under the circumstances. You should have confided in her, man."

"Don't you think I know that? But I was afraid she'd think that I only wanted to marry her because of the twins. Don't get me wrong. I love them, but I love Tracey more. But she doesn't believe me and she certainly doesn't trust me."

"What are you going to do?"

"Damned if I know. Keysha tried to make Tracey think I was just using her to get my children and I would go back to her once I'd done that. I could have strangled Keysha when she told me what she'd said. But the damage was already done."

"After Tracey's had time to think about it she'll come around."

"There's a lot that you still don't know. In the past I've given her reason to despise me. I thought I'd gotten past that, but this thing with Keysha and my own inability to..."

"Was what you did so bad?"

"Yeah. It's something I can't bear to talk about with anyone. I want to, but—"

"You're going to have to open up to Tracey, man, or you can forget getting back with her." Bubba put his hand on Cornell's shoulder. "Give her a little time and then go for it."

Tracey knew she couldn't stay away from her job forever. When she went in to work the next day, she found Barb who just happened to pick that day to come to work on time.

"Moving must have really wiped you out," Barb said.

"It has a way of doing that, Barb."

"What is it, Tracey? " Barb frowned. "I thought everything was going great between you and the hunk."

"I'll tell you about it later."

"Uh-oh, there's trouble in paradise. A certain serpent named Keysha Barrette wouldn't have anything to do with it, would she?"

When Tracey didn't answer she said, "I'm right, aren't I? I knew there would be trouble the minute I saw her. What did she say?"

"Barb, why didn't you and Bubba warn me she was in town?"

"I wanted to, but Bubba said I should stay out of it."

She sighed. "I guess it wouldn't have made any difference if you had, the result would have been the same. She revealed a few home truths."

"Her truth no doubt." Barb folded her arms.

"I can't marry Cornell," Tracey said in a low tormented voice.

Barb's eyes widened in shock. "What?"

"How can I trust a man who keeps the kind of secrets he's kept and is probably still keeping from me?"

"You kept a pretty big one from him yourself."

"Cornell has already reminded me about that." Her chin went up defensively. "I had my reasons for not telling him about London and Lincoln."

"Maybe he has his own reasons for not telling you certain things."

It irked Tracey that Barb seemed to be so understanding about those certain things without even knowing what they were. Maybe she was overreacting. But then maybe she wasn't. Maybe Cornell's first thought had been the children. She always came back to that one burning question. Did he love her for herself or because of the children? Was he confusing gratitude and responsibility with love? Would she ever learn the truth about that? There was no way she could ever marry him if he was lying to her about that.

"You look like one tortured sister," Barb said.

"Oh, Barb, I am."

"Tracey, I—"

"Just leave me alone, okay?" Tracey rushed back to her office and shut the door.

"Is Daddy coming to see us today, Mama?" London asked that evening.

"I don't know, London."

She came and sat down beside Tracey on the living room couch. "Why are you so sad, Mama?"

"I'm not sad, baby. I'd better start dinner. Tracey smiled and made to get up.

"Did you and Daddy have a fight?"

"Why would you ask that?"

"You did, didn't you?" She got off the couch. "You're not gonna get married, are you?"

"London, baby, I—"

Tears slipped down her cheeks. "I want us to be a family, Mama."

"We're still a family, London. Just because—"

"No, we're not." She ran from the room.

"London, wait!" Tracey heard the door to her daughter's room slam.

Lincoln came running into the living room a few minutes later. "Why's London crying, Mama? I didn't do anything to make her mad, I swear it."

"I know you didn't, baby."

"Then why's she crying?"

"I had to tell her that your father and I aren't getting married after all."

"Not getting married? But I thought we we're gonna be a real family. Daddy told us . . . Why, Mama?"

"I can't explain—it just isn't going to work out, that's all."

He sniffed and looked sadly into his mother's eyes before slowly ambling out of the living room with his head down.

Tracey's heart was breaking. She hated doing this to them. They'd been so excited and happy about the marriage. Damn you, Cornell.

She went into her bedroom, walked over to the dresser and picked up the statuette Cornell had given her. As she hugged it to her breast, the tears began to fall, and when she dropped down on the bed they changed to wracking sobs. Minutes later she felt a hand on her shoulder. She looked up and it was London.

"Don't cry, Mama. Please don't cry."

"I can't help it, baby."

London hugged her mother and cried along with her.

Cornell parked his car in front of the house. He dreaded going inside. What could he say to Tracey now? As he got out of the car, Lincoln came out of the house, Lion Two following close behind him.

"Mama's crying, Daddy. Can't you do something to make her stop? She said you and her ain't gonna get married."

Cornell's heart sank. He'd hoped that Tracey— "No, I'm afraid I can't do anything to make her stop crying. I'm the one who caused it though I didn't mean to."

"Why can't you do something to fix it?"

"She won't listen to me right now, son."

Lincoln's shoulders slumped. "I've never seen her cry like this before." He looked accusingly at his father.

Cornell felt his insides rip apart at the sadness in his son's voice.

London came outside. "Mama don't wanna see you, Daddy, and I don't either."

"London, I—"

"Why did you make her cry? I hate you. I don't ever wanna see you again," she cried and ran back inside the house.

Cornell turned away, tears stinging his eyes. London didn't give her affection easily. Now, whatever ground he had gained was lost. How was he going to deal with this?

"I still love you, Daddy."

Cornell picked his son up and hugged him tight. "Thank you, Linc. I love you, too."

"Do you love London and Mama?"

"Yes, very much."

"Can't you talk to Mama and fix it?"

"I don't know, son. I hope I can." He put Lincoln down. "I'd better go."

"Ain't you gonna stay."

"I don't think that's a good idea. I'll talk to your mother another day when she's not so upset. Now I want you to take good care of her and your sister. You'll be the man around the house when I'm not here."

"I'll take care of 'em, Daddy," the boy said proudly.

"I know I can count on you, Linc."

Tracey felt as though she were one of the walking wounded and for the next few days she worked tirelessly to get the house into shape.

London brooded around the house, but Lincoln was the complete opposite, attempting to cheer everyone up.

Tracey had decided to use the time off to pull herself together. She was in the kitchen baking when she got an unexpected visitor.

"Uncle Brice is here, Mama," Lincoln called in to her.

All she needed, she groaned inwardly. Once Brice knew the situation he would have that I-told-you-so look in his eyes. Tracey washed her hands and took off her apron. She closed her eyes steeling herself to deal with the man who had almost been her husband.

When she walked into the living room, she had a cheerful expression on her face. "Brice, it's good to see you. What do you have there?"

His mouth eased into an easy smile. "It's just a housewarming present."

"Thank you," she said taking the gift.

"Aren't you going to open it?"

"Sure. Have a seat." She indicated the loveseat while she seated herself on the couch and began taking the wrapping paper off the box. She gasped. "It's beautiful, Brice," she said running her fingers over the crystal punch bowl that she'd admired when she was considering marrying Brice.

"I know how much you like crystal." He frowned. "Tracey?"

She lowered her head. She must have a face like the crystal sitting on her lap. Could everyone see through her?

"If that bastard's hurt you, I'll—"

"*I* called off the marriage, Brice."

"But why? You were so high on marrying the guy. He loved you, you said."

"Go ahead and say I-told-you-so, Brice."

He moved over to the couch and took the crystal from her cold fingers and set it down on the coffee table. "Want to tell me what happened?" he said gently. "You're obviously upset." He glanced worriedly at her. "You've lost weight."

She bent her head and sat wringing her hands in her lap.

"Tell me, Tracey."

"It just isn't going to work out between us that's all."

He put an arm around her shoulders. "Are you going to be all right?"

Tracey gave him a weak smile. "I'll survive."

"How are the children taking this sudden change in plans?"

"They're not happy. They don't understand and I can't find the right words to explain."

"Now," he said hopefully, "that you've discovered the truth—"

"You have nothing to do with my decision, Brice. I'm sorry. You've always told me you wouldn't be second best. That's the only place you or any other man can ever have. I still love Cornell and I always will."

"If you love the man then why—"

Tracey lowered her eyes. "I can't tell you, Brice."

He sighed. "My offer of friendship is still good, Tracey. I don't want to lose that."

She looked up. "Neither do I."

"Isn't there anything you can do to—"

Tracey shot him a look of surprise. "I don't believe I'm hearing this."

"I may not like Robertson, but I thought that you and he— I want you to be happy, Tracey. If not with me—"

"After the way I've treated you, you still—Oh, Brice."

He drew her into his embrace. As he did so, Lincoln led Cornell into the house.

"Mama, Daddy's here."

Cornell stood frozen in the doorway, taking in the scene between Tracey and Brice.

Brice cleared his throat then he let Tracey go and stood up. "Robertson."

"Carter," Cornell gritted out, a muscle twitching in his jaw.

Brice turned to Tracey. "Remember what I said." He kissed her forehead before heading to the door.

Cornell moved aside to let him pass even though he wanted to grab him and break him in two.

"Lincoln, your daddy and I need to talk, why don't you go play with Lion Two. Okay?"

Lincoln shifted his gaze from one parent to the other, his expression hopeful.

Cornell smiled at his son. "Go ahead, Linc."

When he'd left, Tracey stood up. "Why did you come here, Cornell?"

"To see you, but evidently you—"

"Say what you have to say and then leave."

"Obviously nothing I have to say is going to cut it with you, is it?"

"Did you come by to make arrangements to see London and Lincoln? You could have called. I won't try to stop you from seeing them."

"Trace, you can't just—"

"Can't do what?" she said defiantly.

"What Keysha told you isn't true. You and my children are what's most important to me. I made a committtment to you and to them."

"But for what reasons? Why couldn't you have been honest with me? You've always held something back, Cornell. Is it me?" She splayed her hands over her chest. "Am I not woman enough for you to trust me with your innermost feelings?"

"You know you are. I was going to tell you the truth that day, but Keysha beat me to it. And no, there's nothing wrong with you. Remember when we made love the night before?"

She remembered that, but she also remembered the wild frenzied lovemaking the day she found out he'd kept his sterility a secret from her.

"All I know is that I had to hear it from your ex-wife. Do you have any idea how that made me feel? In a way it was like being rejected then betrayed again."

"Trace, I never meant to hurt you." He put his hand over his forehead and moved it around uneasily. "Sterility isn't an easy subject for a man to discuss with a woman."

"Even the woman he supposedly loves?"

He hauled her into his arms. "I don't 'supposedly' love you. I *do* love you."

"Do you really?" She pulled out of his hold and walked

away from him. "Or are you confusing it with a different emotion?"

His eyes narrowed. "What different emotion are you talking about?"

"Are London and Lincoln the real ties binding you to me?"

"I've told you they're not, but you refuse to believe that."

"What Keysha said made sense."

"Only because you don't trust me. I made a mistake six years ago. Are you going to make me pay for it the rest of my life?"

"I didn't call off the wedding because of the past."

"I think it's part of the reason, whether you'll admit it or not. You're afraid to take a chance on me because of what I did back then. I don't know what I can say or do to make you trust me."

She crossed her arms over her chest. "A little honesty would help."

"I am honest in my feelings for you."

"Where the twins are concerned maybe, but I don't believe you can separate what you feel for them from what you feel for me. I think you feel guilty about not wanting them, and then finding out you couldn't father any more children."

"I admit feeling guilty about what I did. And I won't deny that I'm ecstatic about London and Lincoln. I feel grateful to you for having them, but it doesn't mean that I can't love you too."

"Don't you see that we can't build a happy marriage on gratitude and guilt?"

"If it was what I felt for you," he sighed patiently, "But it isn't, Trace. You're not convinced of that, though, are you?"

Tracey didn't answer.

He gritted his teeth. "Then there's nothing more I can say."

"No, I guess there isn't."

"I want to talk to my daughter before I go."

"London is in her room, but she isn't in any mood to—"

"I know how she feels," he interrupted. "She told me in no uncertain terms the last time I was here, but I've got to try to reach her, Trace."

"I'll help you all I can, Cornell. This has hit her very hard, she so sensitive."

"Maybe you'd better stay here and let me see her alone. Please, Trace."

She nodded her head. "All right."

Tracey saw the look of anguish on Cornell's face as he left the room. She wanted to reach out and offer comfort, to say everything was going to be all right, but she couldn't promise that it would be. If there was no trust, there was nothing to build a life on.

Cornell found London playing with her dolls in her bedroom. He stood shaking his head in awe. She was so like Tracey in looks, so much like him personality-wise. Dolls were her escape, as football was his, both something you could care about and give to without fear of being hurt.

"London." He winced when he saw the closed expression that slid over her face. "Sweetheart, let me talk to you."

She ignored him and continued to dress one of her dolls.

He walked over to the doll house he'd built for his daughter and hunkered down to where she sat on the floor. "I didn't mean to make your mother unhappy or you either, honest," he pleaded. "Sometimes grown-ups do and say things to hurt each other and the people around them without really meaning to. And sometimes, sweetheart, it's hard to fix it or make it better.

"I'm pretty new at being a father so I don't always know the right thing to do or say. Do you think you can help me?"

London gazed at him with a puzzled look on her face. "How can I help you?"

"You're doing it right now by just talking to me. You're my little girl and because I love you very much, London, I don't want you to hate me."

London put her doll down and threw her arms around his neck. "I don't really hate you, Daddy. I love you, too."

"I didn't think you really hated me. When we're hurt we say things we don't mean and are sorry about it later."

"Is that what happened between you and mama?"

"In a way. You see I didn't tell your mother something I should have."

"And now you're sorry?"

He nodded.

"If you're sorry, then why can't you kiss and make it better?"

Cornell smiled gently. "I wish things could be that easy. It's up to your mother to decide whether she wants to marry me. We can't pressure her into it because we want it so much."

"What are you gonna do, Daddy?"

"There's nothing I can do right now, sweetheart."

"You aren't gonna go away, so we'll never see you again?"

"No, I'm not, don't worry. I'll be there when you need me. I may be away playing football, but I don't ever want you to think that I won't come and see you. I want you to help your mother. She's going to need you and Lincoln while I'm away."

"Does mama still love you, Daddy?"

"I'm sure she does, but I've hurt her and she's having a hard time dealing with it." He stood up. "I'd better be going."

"Do you have to go?"

"I'm afraid so. You know when you hurt yourself it takes time for it to heal, right?"

"Uh-huh."

"It's the same when someone hurts your feelings."

"You think it'll take a long time for mama to heal?"

"Yeah." She might never heal, he added silently. He'd destroyed Tracey's trust years ago, the hurt never really healed properly, and now he'd reopened the wound.

Tracey looked up when Cornell came back into the room. A feeling of relief washed over her when she saw London in his arms.

"I'll call you about coming over to see the twins."

"Can't you stay a little bit longer, Daddy?" Lincoln pleaded from the doorway.

He put London down. "No, I'm sorry I can't, Linc." He glanced at Tracey and then walked to the front door.

London walked over to her mother. "Daddy told me you were hurting real bad and you had to heal and that me and Lincoln should try to help you."

"He's right."

"When will you get well, Mama?" Lincoln asked.

"I don't know, baby. I just don't know." She had to admit that Cornell was turning out to be a wonderful father. She'd been worried about London's reaction to the break up. If she could only come to terms with these contradictory feelings and doubts, not just about him, but about herself as well.

Chapter 20

In a few more days Cornell would be gone. A feeling of despair descended on Tracey. She'd tried to convince herself that she was relieved, but she knew deep down she was lying to herself. He continued to come by, spending every spare moment he could with London and Lincoln. Tracey found herself envying the time they spent with him.

This hanging in limbo was driving her crazy. Why couldn't she decide what to do? Why couldn't her feelings be easy to sort out?

When she looked around her at the house he'd bought for them, she wanted to cry. They'd all been so happy about moving in, especially after she decided to marry Cornell. Now the house seemed so empty. She wanted to change her mind about not marrying him, but she couldn't. Something inside her just wouldn't let her do it.

She had the house to herself while the kids were at play school. Without them around the walls seemed to close in on her, the memories swamp her. When Cornell said they'd christened the house, he hadn't lied. When she was in bed at night, the memory of how she spent her first time in it came back to haunt her. When she gazed at the statuette, she recalled vividly the night he'd given it to her and what happened afterward. Her body heated up at that desire-arousing recollection.

The thought of his lovemaking made her ache for him. She threw herself across the bed and cried. "Oh, Cornell, I miss you so much."

Cornell stood packing the rest of his things. Training camp was over. He had hoped to be taking his belongings to the house he'd bought for his woman and his children. They were to have been married in just a few days. Now all his hopes and dreams for the future were ashes. He held no illusions about Tracey forgiving and coming to trust him anytime soon, if she ever did.

"You have everything?" Bubba asked.

"I think so."

"Still no go?"

"She needs time, Bubba."

"Maybe, but I wonder if you're not being too—"

He looked up at him. "Too what?"

"I don't know—maybe you need to be more aggressive."

"I've thought of that, but it's not the way to go."
All those years ago, I damaged her trust. She's managed to survive, but the scars are deep. Now she's clinging to the role that's safe—herself as a mother. He shook his head. "I never meant to hurt her like that, Bubba."

"She's got to be feeling pretty fragile and insecure right now," Bubba said thoughtfully.

"I know what you're getting at, but I won't use her vulnerability to seduce her into marrying me. I'm sure she already feels pressured to do that for the children's sake." He picked up the plaque Tracey had given him and lovingly stroked the two pairs of tiny, bronzed baby shoes.

"You really understand her, don't you?"

"Yes, I do. And I love her so I'll wait."

"I hope not too long."

His lips curved into a tender smile as he gently lowered the plaque into his travel bag. "So do I."

❧

Tracey saw Cornell get out of his car and head up the walk. Before he reached the porch, Lincoln and Lion Two came from around the side of the house to greet him.

"You're almost as big as your namesake, Lion Two," Cornell said, ruffling the dog's deep shaggy coat.

"You gonna take us to Dimples today, Daddy?" Lincoln asked.

"Not today, Linc."

Tracey's heart lurched at his attempt to keep the sadness out of his voice. It had to be hard for him to put on a calm face for the children, considering that today was his last in Springfield.

London walked up beside her mother and seeing her father, rushed out on the porch. "I'm so glad to see you, Daddy."

He opened his arms and she went into them. "I'm glad to see you, too, sweetheart. I thought we might have one last picnic. Aunt Barb fixed a special lunch for us."

"Is mama gonna come, too?" Lincoln asked.

"I hope she will." Cornell looked to Tracey for confirmation.

"I'll come," she said softly.

"Thanks, Trace, we want you with us."

Tracey found her daughter watching them and wondered what was going through her mind. It was hard to tell with

London, and Tracey was reminded again of how much like her father she was.

⁂

They set up the picnic on a different side of Lake Springfield this time. The late August day was humid and sultry. London and Lincoln had on swimming suits under their clothes and could barely wait to get out of them and into the water. Lion Two raced ahead of them.

A look of concern crossed Cornell's face.

"Don't worry, they're water babies. I taught them to swim when they were six months old. They took to water like ducks." She laughed as she watched her children frolicking in the water.

"I wish I'd been there to see it." He cleared his throat. "You have the numbers where you can reach me and my pager number?"

"Yes. And I have your family's too."

"Trace, I—"

"Please don't—"

"Is there nothing I can say to restore your faith in me?"

"Don't you think I want to?" she said, her voice as bleak as her expression. "I just can't."

He sighed. "All right, Tracey. Let me help you with the food."

"You don't have to. It's your last day with the kids, go ahead and join them. We can eat later."

"Won't you come into the water with us?"

"All right, I'll be down in a minute."

Tracey couldn't help admiring his beautiful body as he took off his clothes. His black swimming trunks outlined his narrow hips. He wasn't overly muscled, but his body exuded health and vitality. It was enough to turn any woman's mind to mush.

Watching the way his muscles rippled made her weak in the knees. He'd always had that effect on her and she was sure he always would. Oh, God, she loved him so much. She was afraid to trust him, yet she didn't want to live without him. What in the world was she going to do?

Cornell saw the anguished look on her face and it wrenched his guts. He'd done that to her. It shook him up to see the brave front she put on for the kids' sake. A feeling of frustration sliced through him. He had to face the fact that there was nothing he could do but wait.

They all dug into the potato salad and barbecued ribs like hungry termites into dry wood. There was hardly anything left. Barb's special oatmeal raisin cookies disappeared as if by magic. Tracey was amazed by the amount of food her son consummed and said so.

"I used to be like that myself according to my mother," Cornell laughed. "My father used to call me the bottomless pit." A distressed look suddenly flashed across his face and then was gone as though it had never been.

There was something deep inside Cornell that was haunting him, Tracey thought. There was so much he needed to talk out, but he'd never share with her. She had tried to get him to years ago and it hadn't worked. She wondered if he would ever confide in anyone. He hadn't to his mother. She doubted if he even confided whatever it was in Bubba, and they were as close as brothers.

As they headed home, Tracey found herself dreading the days to come without him, but she couldn't bring herself to put a stop to it.

That night Cornell took pleasure in putting his children to bed, listening to their prayers. London's was almost more than he could bear. She prayed that he and her mother would get back together. He saw Tracey blink away the tears and knew how hard it was for her.

She led him into the living room.

"If I want an early start, I'd better—"

"Cornell—"

"Tracey?"

Suddenly they were in each other's arms.

Tracey could no longer fight the desire raging through her. Her love for this man was her undoing. Whether she could trust him or not, she wanted him to make love to her.

Cornell's reaction to having her in his arms was swift and violent. Giant eruptions of love and desire burst over him. His mouth claimed hers in a soul-burning kiss.

"I want you, Trace," he said raggedly. "Oh, God, how I want you, girl."

"We shouldn't—"

Cornell dammed the flow of her words his lips.

Tracey found herself sinking in the quicksand of desire with nothing to hold onto except this man. There was no one to save her. But then did she really want to be saved?

Cornell swept her up in his arms and headed for the bedroom. She knew what would happen if she didn't stop him, but she couldn't say the words. It was the last time they would be making love unless she could override her feelings of betrayal.

How can you trust him with your body and not your mind?

Tracey knew her feelings for him had nothing to do with reason. She didn't want to think about anything but being with him.

A series of wild, marauding kisses completely decimated any remaining resistance she may have had. Her emotions whirled and skidded. There was no right or wrong now, only her desperate need to be loved by this man.

He quickly undressed her because taking it slow was an impossibility. When he had her naked, he worshipped her body with more kisses and caresses. He took her nipple into his mouth and sucked, glorying in her moans of pleasure as she collapsed against him.

When his fingers delved inside her femininity, he felt her quiver. Her little sighs of ecstasy echoed in his head.

Cornell laid her on the bed, kneeling in front of her, parted her thighs and moved his mouth over her, caressing her, tasting her. He stroked her with his tongue, rejoicing as he felt her throb in climax against his mouth.

Shedding his clothes, he covered her with his body and slipped inside her. She was still pulsing from her climax when he began moving deeply, rhythmically within her.

She cried out and he felt the flames of her passion begin to to rise again, matching his own fire. He couldn't wait any longer and squeezed her buttocks, drawing her even closer. He was inside her to the hilt, but he couldn't seem to get close enough. He thrust one more time and shouting out in triumph, poured himself into her.

Tracey joined him, crying out her joy and her love. Slowly their bodies cooled and their breathing returned to normal. She sighed drowsily, blissfully lethargic from his lovemaking. As she closed her eyes in sleep, she heard him utter softly that he loved her.

Just before dawn Cornell awoke to the feel of Tracey's warm, soft body snuggled against him. He eased up on an elbow and gazed into her lovely face. It was hell knowing this could very well be the last time he made love to her.

He had to leave before she woke up. He moved his arm from across her waist, eased from the bed, then gathering his clothing, quietly dressed. Taking one more look at the woman he loved, he slipped out of the room.

After almost three hours of driving Cornell pulled his car into the driveway behind his mother's Mercedes. He imagined that Tracey was awake by now. He wondered if she missed him as much as he missed being there with her. He let himself into the house and headed out to the kitchen to make a pot of coffee.

He was just finishing his second cup when his mother came into the kitchen.

"Cornell! I thought it was Malcolm out here messing up my kitchen. What are you doing here? I thought that you were with Tracey."

"Tracey called off the wedding," he said in a flat voice.

"But why? I know that girl loves you."

"She may love me, but she can't forgive me, and she sure doesn't trust me, Mama."

"I was sure she'd forgiven you about what happened when you two were in college."

"So was I. Evidently she still—I don't know, Mama. Can a woman really forgive a man for asking her to do something that despicable? Maybe the betrayal is too deep. Besides that, I wasn't the one to tell her about my inability to give her another child. Keysha did and you can imagine what else she added in the telling."

"Yes, I can. I knew she wanted you back."

"You did?"

"Yes, she came to see me."

"Why didn't you tell me?"

"I didn't feel there was a need. I told her it was up to you whether the two of you ever got back together, and I didn't think she should get her hopes up. But you know Keysha. She made trouble between you and Tracey, didn't she?" she continued.

"Big-time. I think I managed to convince Tracey that it was all over between me and Keysha, but because of her feelings of insecurity, she feels that I asked her to marry me for all the wrong reasons."

"Well, didn't you tell her that you love her?"

"Yes, Mama, over and over again, but after what Keysha said she has doubts about me. What can I do?"

"All you can do is leave it up to her."

"How do I cope in the meantime?" He slammed the cup down. "I'm going crazy, Mama."

Lillie walked over to her son and took him in her arms.

"I don't know what to tell you, son," she said sadly. "Maybe in time—"

He moved out of her embrace and started pacing. "I keep telling myself the same thing, but it's hell trying to make myself be patient and wait, Mama." He stopped suddenly. "I've got to get away for a while before the season starts, to get myself together. If Tracey should call or need anything—"

"We'll be here for her." She put a hand on his arm. "Where will you go?"

"I don't know. I'll call you in a week or so." He headed for the door.

Lillie followed him. "Surely you don't mean to leave now. You just got here."

"I can't stay, Mama. I'm too restless."

"Be careful, Cornell."

After he'd gone, Lillie noticed that he had left his pager on the kitchen counter.

Warm fingers of early morning sunlight reached inside the room and touched her face, waking Tracey to the calm feeling of contentment. That contentment vanished when she realized she was alone. Cornell's musky male scent mingled with the scent of their lovemaking permeated the sheets and lingered on her body, but he was gone.

No! Her mind cried out. He can't be gone!

The doubts began to seep in. She had thought that what they had shared was unique, their separation seemed to have intensified the feelings they had for each other. At least she had thought that it had. Evidently Cornell hadn't felt that way.

She forced herself to get up and shower. And minutes later as she headed for the kitchen, she took in her surroundings. This house and everything in it had been carefully and lovingly chosen by her, Cornell, and their children with a thought to the future happiness they would share in it.

Her heart ached. Had her relationship with Cornell been so flimsy, so fragile that when dashed with doubt it could be so easily destroyed? Surely their relationship had not been reduced to just physical gratification? No! She wouldn't believe that. There was more to it than that.

How will you ever be sure unless you take a chance? You love the man, Tracey. Take that chance.

She felt torn apart, her mind at war with her heart. Her body ached and burned for his. Her soul craved its mate.

"Is daddy really gone, Mama?"

Tracey jumped at the sound of her daughter's voice. "Yes, he is."

"He promised that he would come back and see us."

"And I'm sure he intends to keep that promise."

"He looked so sad last night."

What could she say? She couldn't tell her daughter that she could have done something to take that sadness away and hadn't.

Lincoln came in a few minutes later rubbing his eyes and flopped listlessly into a chair.

"How about some pancakes?"

"Okay."

Tracey frowned at his uncharacteristically dull reply. Later after the twins had gone to their room to get dressed, she stared at her son's barely touched breakfast. It wasn't like him not to eat everything on his plate and ask for more. She wondered if he was coming down with something or just depressed about his father leaving Springfield.

If it was the latter, he wasn't the only one feeling down about that. She shifted her gaze to her daughter. London certainly wasn't happy.

And neither was she.

Tracey called Barb after she had cleaned up the kitchen.

"What's up, Tracey? You sound depressed."

"Maybe a little lonely."

"Cornell's gone, huh?"

"Yes, he is."

"You know what'll bring him back. Nobody's perfect, Tracey. We all make mistakes. Maybe it was wrong of Cornell to keep things from you the way he did, but we're all allowed to make mistakes, even you."

"What are trying to say, Barb?"

"If he's allowed to make mistakes, you're allowed to forgive and forget them. Love heals all wounds, haven't you heard? If pride is keeping you from being with your man, you're going to have to get rid of it."

"Pride? What does pride have to do with this?"

"It means that if you want Cornell, you're going to have

to go to him. It's up to you to find out what has really kept him from confiding in you. You're a woman—be creative."

Tracey laughed. "Thanks, Barb. Tell Bubba he has a treasure in you."

Tracey thought about what her friend had said and she agreed.

When she was a little girl and didn't want to face things she'd always sought escape in the dark and put off dealing with it. After college when things were more than she could handle and the wounds so deep there was no medicine to heal them, she sought refuge in her parents' love, then later in the security of a relationship with Brice.

She now realized that by keeping his children's existence from Cornell she had insured that she would have a part of him without him being a part of her life, thus allowing herself to stay in her cocoon and build up her walls.

She had been confused when he'd shown that he could be a good father to his children. And when he'd been so tender and loving with her, she agreed to marry him. But when she realized that he hadn't shared something as important as his sterility with her, she had allowed her insecurities to shake her confidence in herself as a woman.

Suddenly she understood that by refusing to marry him she was in essence punishing him.

She couldn't keep punishing him for the past, and for whatever it was that he couldn't bring himself to talk about.

If that was true that meant he was hurting just as badly as she.

Oh, God. What had she done to him? To herself? To their children? To their future together?

Tracey reached for the phone and rang his condo. There was no answer. She felt a stab of disappointment as she hung up. But then she picked up the phone again and began punching in the next number on the list he'd left for her.

Chapter 21

"Lillie, it's Tracey. Do you know where I can find Cornell?"

"He was here earlier, but—"

"You don't know where he's gone?"

"No, I don't. He said he had to get away."

"I really need to talk to him, Lillie. I've got to get him to open up to me."

"If anyone can do it, you can, Tracey."

"I tried his pager but he hasn't called."

"He left it here. By the time I found it he was gone and I couldn't catch him."

"When you hear from him, you'll let me know?"

"You know I will."

A deluge of frustration swamped her, but there was nothing she could do but wait, and she knew it was going to be hell. She understood now how he'd felt since she'd called off the wedding. She felt desperate to see him, to feel his arms around her, to experience the ecstasy of his lovemaking.

Several days later when Lincoln hadn't come to breakfast, Tracey went into his room to get him up.

"Get up, lazy bones." Her smile faded when she saw that he was still in bed. He hadn't been himself since Cornell had left Springfield. He'd hardly eaten anything in the last couple of days. She walked over to him and sat down on the bed. "Baby, what's the matter? Do you feel sick?" When he didn't answer, she touched her hand to his forehead and found that he was very warm.

"I hurt all over, Mama," he said in a hoarse whisper.

Tracey went to get something for his fever. It was probably a summer cold. London came in and Lion Two loped in behind her. He jumped on the bed and crawled up the length of Lincoln's body to lick his face. Lincoln listlessly patted the dog's head then let his hand drop back down on the bed.

"Is he all right, Mama?" London asked worriedly.

"He doesn't feel good right now. I gave him some medicine; he should start to feel better in a little while. I think we should let him rest now."

"I wish daddy was here."

"Me too, baby, me too."

"Can't you call him or something?"

"He's gone on a little private holiday, but he should be back in a few days. Then we can call him."

At two o'clock in the morning Tracey rushed her son to the hospital. His fever had risen several degrees instead of going down.

"Ms Hamilton, your son is a very sick little boy," the doctor said grimly.

"What's the matter with him?"

"We can't find a reason as yet, but we're running tests.

He keeps calling for his father. Is he out of town? I suggest you get him here as soon as you can."

"How serious is it?"

"We're doing everything we can to get his fever down. If it continues to rise—"

"Can I see him?"

"Follow me."

Hospitals always made Tracey nervous. She remembered when her father's mother passed away. They had her hooked up to so many different machines it had frightened her. None of them were able to keep her alive in the end.

She had to stop thinking about death; her son wasn't going to die. "Oh, Cornell, I need you," she whispered.

Tracey stayed by her son's bedside. He looked so small and helpless, she thought.

"Mama, where's daddy?" he rasped out through fever-cracked lips.

"I don't know, Lincoln, but I'll find him for you."

A smile touched his lips before he closed his eyes.

Tracey glanced at her son and knew instinctively he was pining for his father. She'd read somewhere that small children often reacted this way to the absence of a parent. She had to get Cornell here as soon as possible. She'd also read that brain damage could result if a high fever continued over a long period of time.

And she had to get back to London before she end up with two critically ill children.

"Tracey, you're not going to drive to Chicago, are you?" Ruby asked worriedly.

"No, Mama. Bubba is going to take me."

"Can't I come too, Mama?" London pleaded.

"I think it would be better if I went by myself. We don't know where your father is, and we'll have to search for him.

Besides, I need you to help Paupau and Nana when they go see your brother."

"I hope you find Daddy quick."

"We will." Tracey kissed her daughter. "I'll be back before you know it."

"I wish I could think where he might be," Bubba said as he drove. "Lillie and Malcolm haven't come up with anything?"

Tracey sighed. "No. I wonder if Keysha Barrette knows where he is?"

"I doubt it. He really doesn't love her, you know."

"If I had only—"

"Stop beating yourself up. It was something you had to work out for yourself. Decisions would be easy if feelings didn't get in the way. But since they do we have to work them out in our own way."

"I guess you're right." She bit her lip. "But Lincoln is so sick, Bubba." Tears trickled down her cheeks. "If I had made up my minder sooner he might—"

"Don't worry, we'll find Cornell."

"But suppose we don't find him—" Her shaky words faltered abruptly.

"We will, Tracey. Think positive, girlfriend."

"Why couldn't I have fallen in love with you?"

"Because Barb would have killed you if you had." He laughed.

Tracey smiled a watery smile, grateful for his friendship.

Tracey paced back and forth before the fireplace in Lillie's living room, trying to remember whether Cornell had ever mentioned any particular place he might go to, but none came to mind.

The Vincennes Boys' Club. She suddenly remembered. He spent time helping the boys learn to play football. She remembered hearing him say that he was their major sponsor.

"Bubba, is there a place close to the Vincennes Boy's Club where Cornell might be staying?"

"The boys' club!" He smacked his forehead. "Why didn't I think of that?"

"Our old house is around the corner from there," Lillie commented absently. "He bought our old house and had it fixed up. It's being rented out, but there is a garage apartment that he uses when he spends time at the boys' club."

"Come on, Bubba." Tracey grabbed his arm. "Let's go.

"His car is here. Do you want me to go up with you?"

"No thanks, Bubba. This is something I have to do alone."

"I'll wait just in case."

Tracey got out of the car, and taking a deep breath, headed over to the garage apartment. She climbed the stairs and knocked at the door. There was no answer. She knocked again and waited, but there was still no answer. She returned to the car.

"I'll drive you around to the boys' club," Bubba said.

A few minutes later Bubba braked in front of the club building and walked over to the office to talk to someone then came back to the car. "He's here."

"You can go now, Bubba."

"You sure you don't need me?"

Tracey smiled. "Yes, I'm sure." She walked around to the play yard in back and saw Cornell showing a group of boys how to aim and throw a football.

She realized that he was a natural for the job. He seemed to have a special rapport with the kids and a patience he didn't show when dealing with adults. It made her wonder why he had suggested she have an abortion when she told him she was pregnant. She was even more eager then ever to find out everything there was to know about this man that she loved.

When the boys fumbled the plays, Cornell made them repeat it again and again. Finally he called time out, and when he turned, he found Tracey watching him.

"Tracey!" He strode over to her. "What is it? Is something wrong with the kids?"

"Lincoln is sick in the hospital. Since you left your pager at your mother's there was no way to get in touch with you. I remembered you mentioning the boys' club and figured that you would come here."

"I'm glad you did. What's wrong with him, Trace?"

"The doctors don't know. He's running an extremely high fever and they're worried that—" Her voice broke and tears glistened in her eyes. "He's been asking for you."

"And you couldn't reach me. I'm sorry, Trace. I never thought anything would happen."

"It's all right. I found you. That's all that matters."

They were on the road less than thirty minutes later.

Once inside the car he asked, "What happened? Linc was fine when I left."

"That morning after—he wasn't his usual self. I think he had begun to miss you. It's all my fault."

"No, it isn't anybody's fault. I should have stayed a while longer, but I didn't want to say good bye to you again after we'd made love."

"I understand. When I woke up and found you gone, Cornell, I realized—"

"What?" His heart began to beat erratically, hope building inside him like a head of steam in an engine, as he waited for her to answer.

"I—I knew that I didn't want you to go, that my life would be so empty without you. The house was just a house, only you made it a home. I love you, Cornell."

"Oh, God, I waited so long to hear you say that. I love you with all my heart, Trace."

"There's something we have to discuss before we go any further."

"You mean about why I hadn't got around to telling you I was sterile."

She saw his hands tighten on the steering wheel. "Not just that, but also what happened in college. I have to know why you suggested that I have an abortion."

"I'm not sure if I can."

"This is important, Cornell, you have to try or else—" Her voice trailed away.

He sighed heavily and was silent so long Tracey thought he wasn't going to answer.

"After I said that to you, I tried to find you to stop you, but it was too late. You were gone. When I didn't see you around campus for a few days I figured that you had gone through with it and it tore me up. I was tortured with regret and shame for what I'd forced you to do. When you did return, you were different."

"What did you expect?" She clamped her hands together.

"When you told me you never wanted to see me again, I really felt guilty. The look in your eyes said you hated me."

"I guess I really did hate you at that time."

"Why didn't you do it?"

"I loved you and our child. If I couldn't have you then I would have your child. Even if you didn't love me I knew our baby would."

He swung his head around for a second. "But I did love you, Trace. I have since that day I ran into you on the way to football practice."

"If that was the way you felt then why would you suggest something that would wreck our relationship?"

"It wasn't my intention to wreck it. My family struggled hard after my father—after he walked out on us."

"Yes, your mother told me a little and you mentioned it when you showed the twins and me the neighborhood where you grew up."

"I didn't tell you why. I never told my mother either. In fact I've never discussed it with anyone."

Tracey waited for him to compose himself and offered an encouraging smile.

He gave her a quick-second glance before returning his eyes to the road. "Mama had just had Malcolm. My father seemed agitated. He looked like a shell-shocked soldier, walking around as though he were dazed and hurt beyond bearing. He wouldn't even talk about the new baby.

"Mama had a few complications and had to stay in the hospital a few days longer than was usual," he continued. "That night I saw him taking his things out of the dresser throwing them into a suitcase and I asked him where he was going."

Tracey watched his strained profile. She could see that whatever he had to say was tearing him apart. She put her hand on his arm.

"It was two days before my tenth birthday. He handed me a present he'd made for me. My father was good with his hands. I guess that's where I got my affinity for carpentry work. He told me once that he had wanted to be an architect. He'd met mama his last year of high school. He had a chance to go to college on scholarship, but he had to be single or married without children.

"Mama got pregnant and he had a choice—to walk away or give up his chance to go to college. Mama's parents and his own pressured him into marrying mama. When I was two he had another chance, but Mama got real sick."

"So he had to give it up?."

"Yes." Cornell sighed. "Mama had to have special treaments and they were very expensive. He worked seven days a week, five at a job as a carpenter and on the weekends he waited tables to pay the bills. And mama kept getting pregnant, first with Kevin, then Glynell and LaTonya.

"I guess when Malcolm came along it was the proverbial straw that broke the camel's back and he couldn't cope any more. That night he took me out to the garage where he kept his tools." His voice shook. "He told me not to let anything or anybody stop me from reaching my goal. He told me not to get involved with girls until after I graduated from college.

"He said that he loved mama and us kids, but he had to escape before he lost the rest of himself. I guess he felt like he was drowning in responsibility. I didn't understand what he meant then. I couldn't understand why he wanted to leave us." His hand tightened on the wheel. "He said 'whatever you do, don't give up a chance to do what you love or you'll regret it the rest of your life the way I did'."

Tracey said thoughtfully. "Your mother said you were different after your father left. She was sure that he'd said something to you to bring about the change."

Cornell's featured harshened as did his voice. "I loved my father, but I never forgave him for what he did. I vowed that I'd never be weak like him. I got a job cleaning office buildings when I was twelve. I always looked old for my age. When I got a scholarship to Chicago U, I was in seventh heaven." His face brightened "Mama was making enough money doing quilts and Kevin and Glynell had part-time jobs by then."

"Then you met me," she said, throwing a glance at him.

He smiled. "I fell in love with you, Trace. You were the prettiest girl on campus." His smile faded. "When you told me you were pregnant, history seemed to be repeating itself, and I was determined not to let that happen." He blew out a weary breath.

"I went a little crazy when I suggested that you have the abortion. All I could think of was that I wouldn't have my chance at a pro ball career. I saw a mental image of my life, bills, kids and problems piled one on top of the other until..."

"Until you were drowning in resentment and regret, hating the one person you loved for trapping you," she finished. "And you would have ended up hating me if I had insisted that you do the right thing."

"I don't know if I would have done that."

"I do." She cast a sage look his way. "Your father instilled in you what he himself felt and believed. He molded the vulnerable boy you were with his fears and resentment. He must have been a pretty miserable man. Have you seen him since?"

He stiffened and said sharply. "No. I tried to track him down, but no luck. After you walked away from me, I was more determined than ever to succeed, to be somebody and help my family. After my first season with Green Bay, I moved Mama out of the old neighborhood."

"Why did you buy your old house?"

"To keep as a reminder." His jaw tightened.

She gazed curiously at him. "A reminder of what?"

"Of where we came from and all I had suffered when I lost you in my quest to get my family out of that place. The funny thing about it was that when I succeeded and was richer than my wildest dreams, it didn't mean a damned thing without the person I loved."

"You met Keysha Barrette," she said resentfully, remembering all that woman had done to break them up.

"She was a free spirit. I guess I admired that about her. We dated for six months then decided to get married. I thought I'd found someone to help me forget about you, but it didn't work. You were there like an invisible third person in our marriage.

"Keysha was into her modeling career. I took up riding my motorcycle. I could almost forget my hangups and my feelings for you when I was on it. Almost, but not quite." His jaw tensed. "Then one day I crashed my motorcycle into a truck. I was unconscious for two weeks and they thought I wouldn't make it. I had a lot of internal damage."

"And," she swallowed hard. "It left you sterile."

"They performed reconstructive surgery and monitored my progress. They were encouraging, but when Keysha and I tried to have a family, it didn't happen.

"I decided to set her free to find someone who could give her a child of her own. She made noises about it not making any difference and we could adopt, but I knew she wanted her own child and that she would one day resent the fact that I couldn't give her one."

"Then you were traded to the Grizzlies and came to Springfield for your summer training camp. You knew I lived here. Didn't you think we would see each other?"

"I knew it was a possibility, but I figured that you had probably moved away and gotten married. And if I saw you—"

"Nothing would happen. And that what we felt for each other had died? Little knowing that was as far from the truth as the distance between Heaven and Hell."

"It was heaven when I came into Soul Food Heaven and saw you again, Trace." He glanced adoringly at her. "All the old feelings resurfaced and took over."

"It was hell for me, Cornell. I felt guilty about keeping the twins from you."

"I want you to know that I wanted to marry you, kids or not. You're a part of me, Trace. I wanted you because I love you and for no other reason. I was going to tell you about my sterility, but—"

"But Keysha beat you to it. I think she really cares for you, Cornell."

"I care for her too, but I'm not in love with her. You and my children are all that's important to me. I'm praying that Lincoln will be all right. I don't want anything to hurt us again."

Chapter 22

All the traveling and worrying caught up with Tracey and she stumbled against Cornell as they walked toward the entrance to the hospital.

"Trace, are you all right?"

"Just exhausted. As soon as I know about Lincoln, I'll be all right."

Cornell didn't like the way she looked. She looked about ready to collapse.

They reached the third floor and stopped at the nurses' station.

"Dr. Meyers is with your son now, Ms. Hamilton."

Tracey and Cornell waited outside Lincoln's room for him to come out. When she saw him, she rushed over to the door.

"How is he?"

He looked at the man who walked up beside her. "Are you Lincoln's father?"

"Yes. How is our son?"

"Not good, his temperature has gone up another degree and he's had convulsions."

Tracey's legs buckled, but Cornell kept her from falling.

"It's not uncommon in children with a temperature as high as his. If he were an adult, it would be extremely critical. We've placed him under ice blankets and have tried to make him as comfortable as we could, but I think the best medicine we can give him is seeing you," he said to Cornell.

They walked into Lincoln's room.

"Oh, Cornell, he looks so . . ."

Cornell touched his son's flushed face and emotion welled in his eyes. "Lincoln, it's your daddy. Can you hear me?"

For a moment there was no sound then, a small voice said, "Daddy?"

"Yes, son, I'm here."

"Mama said she'd find you."

"And she did."

"I'm so glad you're here," he said in a low, tired voice, barely above a whisper. Then he closed his eyes.

"Is he all right?" Cornell hoped he'd made it back in time to affect a reversal in his son's condition.

The doctor checked Lincoln's vital signs. "It's too soon to tell, but the next twelve hours should tell us something."

They waited in the visitor's room. Tracey fell asleep in Cornell's arms. He noticed the dark circles under her eyes and knew how truly wiped out she was. The waiting was killing him, too.

He moved Tracey onto the couch and covered her with his jacket and stepped over to the coffee machine when the door to his son's room opened. The doctor signaled to him to come inside.

"The ice blankets have been removed. Does that mean he's going to be all right?"

The doctor smiled. "Lincoln's fever has dropped and it shows signs of continuing in its downward trend. I think your son's out of danger, Mr. Robertson."

"Thank God and all his angels," he whispered and went out to the visitor's room to wake Tracey.

"Why did you wait to wake me up?"

"You were out on your feet, Trace." He held her close, relishing her soft feminine warmth and scent. How he loved this woman.

A few days later Tracey and Cornell took their son home. The following Sunday Cornell's family all came down for the wedding.

"You've been quiet since everyone left," Cornell said as they lay in bed after making love. "Want to tell me what's on your mind, Mrs. Robertson?"

"There's something I have to tell you." She traced a finger across his chest. "You did say that you were sterile, didn't you?"

He tensed. "Yes."

"When was the last time you saw your doctor?"

"Trace, what are you leading up to?"

"I found out Friday that I'm four weeks pregnant."

"Pregnant! But that's impossible."

"No, it's not. I'd say it was a miracle. And in all probability we'll be having another set of twins. They do run in my family."

He grinned. "I'm so happy, Trace.

"I'm glad you are. I love you, Mr. Roberston."

"As I love you, Mrs. Robertson. We're lucky to have a second chance at happiness."

"I know it." She reached up and touched her mouth to his. "How I know it."

Genesis Press titles are distributed to the trade by
Consortium Book Sales & Distribution, Inc.
1045 Westgate Drive
St. Paul, MN 55114
1•800•283•3572 phone
612•221•0124 fax

GENESIS PRESS

A leading publisher of African American books

315 3rd Avenue North
Columbus, MS 39701
Tel: (601) 329-9927
Fax: (601) 329-9399
http://www.colom.com/genesis

Production By Interlink Media Group
Advertising/Marketing Firm
www.interlinkmedia.net